Animal Lovers Praise
Kristin von Kreisler

W9-CAB-259

An Unexpected Grace

"Kristin von Kreisler is an acute observer of dogs and a fine novelist. Her novel about the healing powers of dogs is enchanting. I was captivated from page one and I learned a great deal from this heartwarming, thrilling book."
— Jeffrey Moussaieff Masson, *New York Times* bestselling author of *Dogs Never Lie About Love*

"Kristin von Kreisler weaves a modern tale that seems at first to be a relentless search to understand a workplace shooting. But wait; von Kreisler takes us deeper into the powerful connections between humans and animals who are wounded by the incomprehensible and bound together by love."
— Jacqueline Sheehan, *New York Times* bestselling author of *Picture This* and *Lost and Found*

"In *An Unexpected Grace,* Kristin von Kreisler deftly tackles the age-old question of how to make sense of tragedy. When Lila's world falls apart, she learns that hope can come from unexpected places. With vivid descriptions and true-to-life characters, von Kreisler proves it's possible to heal, trust again, and love deeper than before. A heartwarming story on the healing power of dogs."
— Susy Flory, *New York Times* bestselling author of *Thunder Dog*

"Kristin Von Kreisler understands the unique bond between survivors of trauma in this captivating novel of a woman and a dog learning to trust each other in a threatening world. You have to root for them as the damaged heroines of *An Unexpected Grace,* woman and dog, find the healing power of trust and love in each other."
— Susan Wilson, *New York Times* bestselling author of *The Dog Who Danced* and *One Good Dog*

"A sweet and charming story of the tender, patient, and forgiving nature of our canine friends, Kristin von Kreisler's *An Unexpected Grace* will warm the heart of anyone who has ever loved a dog."
—Amy Hill Hearth, *New York Times* bestselling author of *Having Our Say: The Delaney Sisters' First 100 Years* and author of *Miss Dreamsville and the Collier County Women's Literary Society*

For Bea

"[*For Bea*] kept me reading late into the night. Bea is unforgettable. Her story will touch your heart."
—Mary Tyler Moore

"We all love our pets, but there is always that 'special one' from whom we learn so much and whose influence lasts a lifetime. Bea is such a one. A lovely story."
—Betty White

"This moving and extraordinary story needed to be told. I say 'Brava!' for caring individuals like Kristin von Kreisler."
—Rue McClanahan

"The book is beautiful."
—Bea Arthur

"It's tough to look at a beagle without smiling, even though those soulful eyes often belie strong wills and independent natures. From the first to the last page of this deeply touching love story, you can't help thinking, 'What a lucky dog, what a lucky person.' "
—Jon Katz, *New York Times* bestselling author of *The Second-Chance Dog*

"With the keen eye of a journalist and compassionate heart of a dog lover, Kristin von Kreisler paints a portrait of an unassuming but unforgettable little dog. Beyond Bea's endearing ways and forgiving spirit, this book explores a larger issue: mankind's seemingly infinite capacity to hurt—then heal—the animals with whom it shares the world."
—Paul Irwin, president, Humane Society
of the United States

"[*For Bea*] is a journey beautifully captured . . . a lyrical tale of the sometimes miracle-making bond between human and beast."
—*San Francisco Chronicle*

"This is the perfect feel-good read."
—*Tribune Media Services*

"[Von Kreisler] weaves a lovely tale. As you read the book, you can feel the softness of Bea's ears, sense what is behind the soulful stare, and ache at her obvious reluctance to trust."
—*Pittsburgh Post-Gazette*

[*For Bea* is a] colorful, high-energy memoir . . . If you like happy endings with a poignant magic in the air, von Kreisler delivers."
—*The Seattle Times*

"This book is a charming, inspirational story."
—*Knight Ridder*

"I urge you to check out *For Bea* because it's more than a story of an animal rescued from a terrible life. It's also the story of the gifts that special animals like Bea bring to us, if we'll just take the time to discover them."
—*San Jose Mercury News*

"A story such as this one . . . will be heartwarming to any animal-lover."
—*AKC Gazette*

"A worthy addition to collections of true dog stories and reminiscences."
—*Library Journal*

"Compassion and love abound in this short but life-changing book. Read, weep, and share Bea with everyone you can."
—Marc Bekoff, author of *The Emotional Lives of Animals*

"A lovely, gentle heart-pleaser of a story."
—Susan Chernak McElroy, author of *Why Buffalo Dance*

"Von Kreisler has captured the rare and wonderful relationship between a dog and a person who have rescued each other, who respect each other, and who grow closer day by day. Told with wit, compassion, and intellect, the story of Bea is hard to put down."
—Joanna Burger, author of *The Parrot Who Owns Me*

Beauty in the Beasts

"If you love animals, you're going to be crazy for Kristin von Kreisler's new book, *Beauty in the Beasts*."
—*USA Today*

"This is a feel-good overview of animals' heroic deeds. Readers of all ages will eagerly welcome this charming study."
—*Publisher's Weekly*

"The stories collected for this book are heartwarming examples of animals caring for one another and for their human companions . . . This book is for any animal lover."
—*Booklist*

"Through dozens of inspiring true stories, Kristin von Kreisler makes a strong case for a 'controversial premise'—that animals demonstrate genuine acts of compassion toward others every day. This book will remove the 'controversial' from the premise!"
—Paul Irwin, president, Humane Society
of the United States

"Ms. Von Kreisler is fearless, intriguing, and compassionate. Highly recommended."
—Roger Caras, president, ASPCA

"Nobody writes about animals better than Kristin von Kreisler."
—Christopher Willcox, editor-in-chief, *Reader's Digest*

An Unexpected Grace

Also by Kristin von Kreisler

The Compassion of Animals
Beauty in the Beasts
For Bea

An Unexpected Grace

Kristin von Kreisler

KENSINGTON BOOKS
www.kensingtonbooks.com

KENSINGTON BOOKS are published by

Kensington Publishing Corp.
119 West 40th Street
New York, NY 10018

All Kensington titles, imprints, and distributed lines are available at special quantity discounts for bulk purchases for sales promotion, premiums, fundraising, and educational or institutional use.

Special book excerpts or customized printings can also be created to fit specific needs. For details, write or phone the office of the Kensington Special Sales Manager: Kensington Publishing Corp., 119 West 40th Street, New York, NY 10018. Attn. Special Sales Department. Phone: 1-800-221-2647.

Kensington and the K logo Reg. U.S. Pat. & TM Off.

ISBN-13: 978-0-7582-9194-3
ISBN-10: 0-7582-9194-9
First Kensington Trade Paperback Printing: January 2014

eISBN-13: 978-0-7582-9195-0
eISBN-10: 0-7582-9195-7
First Kensington Electronic Edition: January 2014

10 9

Printed in the United States of America

For Jimmy Wolf, the brother I've adopted,
and Debby Harrison, his wife and my dear friend

With love and thanks

Now is the time for the world to know
That every thought and action is sacred.
This is the time
For you to compute the impossibility
That there is anything
But Grace.

—Hafiz

1

Lila's father called her stubborn, but she preferred to put a positive spin on it and say she was determined. Today only a determined person would go outside and brave the storm. The sky was charcoal gray; rain was pounding down in sheets. The local NPR newsman had said that wind had toppled trees and battered boats moored in San Francisco Bay.

Waiting at the door of her apartment building, Lila braced herself for getting wet. She shouldn't go to work today, she thought. She could snuggle under her down comforter, sip Morning Sunburst tea, and listen to rain tap her windows. She could escape eight long hours at Weatherby and Associates Public Relations, the last place she'd ever expected or wanted to work.

But, mustering her resolve, Lila chased away these tempting thoughts. She could not go back to bed. Not when she was living in an apartment she called Cockroach Manor, existing on tuna and beans from the Grocery Outlet, and saving every penny for six months to be a full-time artist. Since breaking up with her ex-boyfriend, Reed, in whose house she'd lived the past five years, she had to get back on her financial feet and put together her next art exhibit. Striking out into a storm was nothing compared to picking up a brush and doing her real work. On Lila's scale of importance, getting rained on was a mouse's squeak, and painting was an elephant's trumpet.

Her best friend, Cristina, pulled up at the curb in front of the door in her Volvo station wagon. She'd insisted on driving Lila to work to keep her from riding her bike in the rain. Lila stepped outside and opened her umbrella. As wind ruffled her fleece-lined poncho and blew her hair across her face, she sloshed down the steps. By the time she reached the sidewalk, water had gotten into her size-eleven loafers and was squishing between her toes. A moving van rumbled by and left a trail of exhaust fumes. A chill from the Bay blew in her face. She shivered.

"I'm glad you made it. Nobody should be driving this morning," Lila said as she opened the door.

"Sorry I couldn't get here sooner. There was a wreck on the Golden Gate." Cristina tossed her purse in the backseat to make room for Lila.

She climbed into the car, set her backpack at her feet, and clicked on her seat belt. As she fluffed damp bangs off her forehead, she said, "I think it's time to build an ark."

Cristina's dark Italian eyes shone when she laughed. "We're late." She sped down the street. To get downtown to the Crockett Building, where she and Lila worked on different floors, she turned left onto Geary and ran a yellow light. "I've got a surprise," she said. "Look in my purse. Get the manila folder in the side pocket."

"I know what the surprise is going to be." Cristina had been springing the same one on Lila for eighteen years. With reluctance, she reached to the backseat, grabbed the folder, and set it in her lap.

"Open it," Cristina urged. "I've made a new poster."

"I don't have to see it. What do you have this time? A poodle? A Lab?" Another ambush was in the making. Cristina would badger her about adopting a dog.

"Her name is Grace. She's the best one yet. The world's most precious."

Cristina flipped on the car's interior light so Lila could see the poster better. As usual, at the top was written in three-inch block red letters, NEEDS A HOME! This time what needed a home, however, was not the world's most precious. It was the world's saddest golden retriever.

Grace's lugubrious eyes looked straight at Lila and begged for a bowl of kibble and a reassuring hug. Grace's forehead was rumpled as if she were worried, and she was so scrawny that her ribs stuck out like a corrugated roof. Cristina had obviously tied a red bandana around Grace's neck to add a cheerful, festive look, but it had failed. Anyone could tell this dog had seen hard times. Her odometer had too many miles on it. She looked as worn as a tennis ball that had lost its fuzz.

That was probably why the man next to her in the photo seemed protective. Lila couldn't read his expression because he was looking down at Grace. But his body language said he was keeping her from harm. He'd wrapped his sturdy arm around her back, pulled her close, and curled his hand across her chest. His plaid wool jacket's softness must have comforted her. She looked small, nestled against his shoulder, which seemed to say, *I'll keep you safe and warm.*

Lila asked, "Who's the man?"

"Adam Spencer. My friend from the dog park. I'm not looking for a home for him. It's Grace I'm worried about."

"No need to worry. You always find somebody for your dogs."

"Why don't you take her?"

Here we go. The inevitable question. Cristina had asked it more times than Lila wanted to remember.

"You even match. You're both strawberry blondes. People would kill for your curls," Cristina continued. "She could protect you."

"I don't need protection."

"Keep you company, then."

"How do I know she won't attack me?"

"You've got to get over what happened twenty-five years ago. You have to forgive and move on."

"Not a chance. I'm scared of dogs. I can't help how I feel."

Every time Lila saw a dog—especially a large, galumphing one—she thought only of fangs, and her heart pounded like it was trying to break out of her chest and run down the street. Her mind always flashed back to the white-and-tan mutt she'd met the summer after fourth grade as he was lounging around, as big as a moose, in front of Walmart. Then an ardent dog lover, Lila had stooped down to pet him, just as she petted every dog she found. She had expected him to give her a dopey smile and thump his tail on the sidewalk. Maybe he'd slobber on her, though she wouldn't mind.

But he'd snapped his eyes open, jumped to his feet, and stuck his face in hers. When he snarled, she'd smelled his sour breath and cringed at his yellow fangs. He'd lunged at her and sunk his teeth into the very hand she'd reached out to pet him with. Lila had the scars to prove you couldn't trust dogs. If she'd created the world, there wouldn't be a dog whisker in it.

"If Grace were a cat, I'd adopt her," Lila said. "But I can't afford a pet right now."

"You'd love a dog if you'd give her a chance. Grace would never hurt you." Cristina sighed with exasperation and passed a FedEx truck. "I'm not giving up till you get a dog. You're missing out . . ."

"Truce?" Lila patted Cristina's arm to convey *I love you, but let it go.*

"Okay, okay." Cristina stopped at a red light.

To steer her to another subject, Lila returned to the storm. "About building that ark? Where do you think we could get some wood?"

Armed with four dog posters that she had agreed to put up in restrooms, Lila rushed twenty minutes late into Weatherby's reception area. It was a brightly lit, cheerful place, where you could practically grab the urge for teamwork from the air. Nature photos on the walls suggested mountains climbed to get things done for clients, and rivers flowing toward their fame and fortune. A promise of public relations success was practically woven into the sofa's royal-blue upholstery.

Lila waved to Emily, the receptionist, who was about to retire. "At lunch I'll bring you the begonia I rooted for you," Lila said.

She stopped at the office of Madeline, the head copywriter, whose morning sickness had turned her face a pale gray-green. Lila asked, "Are you feeling better?"

Madeline smiled. "Graham crackers to the rescue."

"Good! See you later." With a full day's work ahead of her, Lila had to get going.

After a quick drink at the water fountain, she hurried to her office, a tiny cubicle with fluorescent lights and no windows or doors. The walls, covered with felt the gray of smog, barely came to her shoulders because she was a shade less than six feet tall. She had a faux-birch desk, a gray-upholstered swivel chair, and a black rug with magenta specks that made her dizzy if she stared at them too long. To remind herself of the art career she'd vowed to return to, come hell or high water, she'd propped against the wall her boldest, brightest abstract painting, with greens and golds and reds that danced across the canvas. When she got bored or claustrophobic in her cubicle, she looked at the colors for consolation. They never failed her.

Lila put on headphones and called the first person on the three-page list she'd been assigned: G. Roger Earling, features editor of the Bay Area *Herald*. As the phone rang, the smell of coffee traveled from the staff lounge. A cable car clanged its bell from the street below, as if to encourage her for a day of making cold calls.

When Mr. Earling answered, Lila roused her most chipper self. "Good morning! This is Lila Elliot at Weatherby and Associates Public Relations. I was wondering if you got our press packet about the exciting ergonomics conference at Moscone Center."

"I don't remember it," he said, as flat as Illinois.

Bad memory. The perennial excuse. Lila called up her determination. "I'll send you another packet."

"Don't bother. Waste of time."

"But it could interest you."

"Look, an ergonomics conference isn't for us." Mr. Earling sounded surly. His oatmeal must have boiled over that morning, and he'd run out of milk. Lila could tell these things after three long months of phoning hundreds of people.

Calling editors and TV and radio producers was like marching toward an enemy in armor made of lace. You were vulnerable and had nothing but your wits and grit to get the job done. For the media coverage you begged and cajoled out of people, you often got hit with apathy, impatience, or rejection. Sometimes it was hard to shrug off the bad feelings, though Lila always clenched her teeth and kept going.

"The conference is going to be fascinating. Really. Your readers will want to know about it." To keep her foot in the door of Mr. Earling's attention, Lila reeled off the products that would be displayed: potato peelers for arthritics, office chairs for people with bad backs, garden tools approved by the AARP, computer keyboards guaranteed to ward off carpal tunnel syndrome.

He muttered a stifled "aargh" that sounded like a consumptive tiger's growl. "Try calling our business section."

"Any specific person?" Lila pressed.

"I don't have time to lead you by the hand, miss."

Don't take it personally. Lila pulled his arrow from her heart. "It would really help to have the right name."

With hopes Mr. Earling might be looking for one in a directory, Lila forced herself to wait in the silence that spread between them like a field of snow. As she glanced at her painting for moral support, she heard loud voices down the hall. A man was shouting, and a woman seemed to be trying to calm him. That was odd for Weatherby. Lila got up and looked out her open doorway. Seeing no one, she sat back down.

"Okay," Mr. Earling said. "Here's somebody for you. Call Charles Saunders."

The woman's voice got louder, higher pitched. It was Emily. "Please, please." She sounded like she was begging.

The man yelled garbled words that Lila couldn't understand. Emily screamed, "No. Oh, God . . . Don't!"

Lila jumped to her feet to run to her friend. Just as Lila yanked off her headset and threw it on her desk, a blast, like a balloon exploding, only louder, came from the reception area. Then silence.

Lila blinked and tried to figure out what the noise had been—but then came more explosions, one after another, too startling to comprehend. Something horrible was going on, but she couldn't understand what it was. *Surely no one would set off firecrackers in our office.*

When shouts came from around the corner, Lila froze. What she'd heard must have been a gun. More shots crackled and pinged, as if ricocheting off metal window frames. Glass shattered. So many people were screaming at once that she couldn't make out single voices. Then somebody shouted, "Lock your doors!"

Lila shrank back from the doorless entry to her cubicle. She smelled smoke, and her stomach felt like it was grinding lead. As her knees wobbled, she grabbed the phone, but her hands shook too hard to call 911. To keep from toppling over, she leaned on her chair.

Should she dive under her desk? She wouldn't fit. Run to the supply closet? She'd be an easy target in the hall. Hide behind her chair? It was too small a shield. Her bright red turtleneck invited bullets.

More yells and shots. Thuds and slams like fighting in the hall. As heavy footsteps scuffled outside her cubicle, she steeled her will and forced her feet to take three steps to the wall adjacent to the entry. Trembling, she crouched down, folded her legs close to her chest, and tried to disappear.

A man loomed in her open doorway. Without looking up, Lila heard his crazed, ragged breaths. On the floor his shadow twitched, and his agitation traveled into her and made her tremble harder. Her heart pummeled her chest.

She hunched lower, but she felt his stare bore into her. She raised her eyes from black wing-tip shoes to a herringbone sports coat—to the contorted face of Yuri Makov, Weatherby's janitor, who just last week had collected her trash and smiled at her. "Not you!" she yelled.

Two sweaty ringlets clung to his forehead, and veins bulged at his temples. His lips were chapped, and a small, round, flesh-toned Band-Aid was on his quivering chin. With each breath, his chest heaved, and the flight bag hanging from his shoulder hit his hip. Everything about him jittered—except his eyes, which pierced her.

Screaming in Russian, he jerked back his shoulders and shoved his handgun's stubby barrel toward her. He pulled it away and slapped it against his thigh. He lifted the gun to his waist and held it in both hands, and the flesh around his eyes seemed to soften as if he were remembering something. Then with resolution in his eyes, he aimed the gun at her again and curled his finger around the trigger.

"Yuri, what are you doing? Don't *shoot!*" She stood, the better to plead.

He shouted words she didn't understand.

"Please . . . Please, don't . . . Please, oh, please."

Just as Lila lunged behind her office chair, fire seared a path through her chest. The force sent her reeling against the file cabinet. As she collapsed, her head hit metal and she bit her tongue. Her hand swept across the desk and sent the posters of Grace through the air. Lila crashed to the floor and gasped for breath.

A shot crackled in the hall.

Please, don't let me die. Her left side felt like she was being burned alive. As her eyes sagged closed, her mind fogged. She retreated to an ice floe, roiling and bobbing in a dark, distant territory.

2

When Lila woke, her world was a thick, furry gray. She couldn't tell how long she rode up and down on a seesaw of awareness, but eventually she rose toward the light and opened her eyes to slits. Her eyelids felt as if a pebble had been tied to each lash. No matter how hard she tried, she couldn't will away the grogginess.

On her back, she couldn't move because her right arm was strapped down, and a needle connected to an intravenous tube was stuck into the back of her right hand and taped to her skin. Her left arm was in a plaster cast, and something pressed on her chest. When she shifted her shoulder's position just half an inch, adhesive tape tugged her skin.

She glanced around at bare white walls and a blank TV screen. Through the mini-blinds, the fading sun shone in soft stripes across her blanket. A curtain was drawn, like a partial cocoon, around one side and the foot of her bed. She heard rubber soles squeak softly on linoleum, and she smelled bleach and bruised flower petals.

What happened? How did I get here? Suddenly, she remembered getting shot. *Shot,* for God's sake. *Shot!* One minute she'd been sitting at her desk, and the next, she was sprawled on the floor about to die in a pool of her own blood.

But she wasn't dead. She was in a hospital. She was alive.

Still, maybe she could die or be permanently disfigured.

As Lila cringed, her pain medication jumped in and bound her brain with golden cords that restrained her fear. Her world faded again to gray and furry.

Lila woke to moonlight on her blanket. A low-wattage fluorescent light had been turned on above her head. Her mind had cleared enough to stop the feeling that she was groping, blindfolded, through a forest, but shock, confusion, and medication still muddled her brain.

Her roommate's TV screen flickered and blurred on the other side of the privacy curtain as an anchorman with a deep voice described a flood in the Santa Cruz Mountains.

"There was another tragedy today," he said. "Here's our own Sasha Pinsky to tell us about a shooting at the Crockett Building on Post Street."

Desperate to hear what Sasha Pinsky would say, Lila strained to listen and searched the fuzzy TV colors on her curtain for hints of images that might tell her what had happened.

"Yes, Mike," said Sasha. "Behind me on the fifth floor is Weatherby and Associates, one of San Francisco's oldest and best-known public relations firms. This morning a man went on a rampage here. He shot and killed seven employees and wounded three others."

Lila gasped. Her lungs felt like they'd collapsed. As she worked to breathe, her teeth began to chatter.

"The three wounded are at San Francisco General," Sasha Pinsky said. "Two are in satisfactory condition. One is critical."

Am I in critical condition? Oh, God, who is dead?

As if Sasha Pinsky had read Lila's mind, she added, "So far the police haven't released any of the victims' names."

"Does anyone have an idea how this happened?" Mike asked.

"Not yet. Yuri Makov, the alleged gunman, shot and killed himself before the police arrived. They're only saying he was a Russian immigrant who'd worked as a janitor for the firm the last eight months."

Lila's body shook. Her brain roared. Tears slid from the corners of her eyes onto her hair, fanned out on the pillow.

Seven dead, three wounded. It wouldn't sink in. She couldn't grasp the magnitude of the tragedy. It was too much to take in at one time.

Till a nurse gave her a sedative that knocked her out again, Lila mentally replayed Yuri Makov aiming his gun at her and pulling the trigger. Again and again she heard the blast and smelled the smoke. She saw his contorted face, as real as if he were standing close enough for her to feel his heartbeat. And on her neck she felt the turpentiney breath of terror.

The next morning Dr. Lovell, the head of Lila's medical team, must have sensed that psychologically she was dragging a ball and chain through tar. When he pulled up a chair to her bed and studied her face, his expression hardened like he thought she'd inspired Edvard Munch's *The Scream*. He sat next to her and looked into her eyes, whose navy blue seemed black against her pale cheeks. He asked, "So how's it going? Are we feeling okay?"

"I've felt better."

"Not surprising." A strapping man with an incongruously soft mustache, like an Easter duckling's down, Dr. Lovell crossed one leg over the other so his pants' pleat protruded, as sharp and clean as a knife blade. "Well, I've got good news for you. The killer used a .38-caliber gun. He shot you at an angle so the bullet traveled through your breast and lodged in your arm."

"That's good news?"

"You bet. If he'd shot you head-on with something like a Terminator magnum, the bullet could have ripped through your heart or lung or ricocheted off a rib and landed God knows where. Somebody was watching out for you. You should thank your lucky stars."

"Oh." Lila shivered.

"All you've got is flesh wounds, a fractured humerus, and some muscle and nerve damage. We'll have to wait and see how the nerves heal."

Alarmed, Lila sat up straighter even though it hurt to move. "It's all got to heal. I have to get back to work and save money. I want to do my art."

"You will if you don't have complications."

Complications? "You think I will?"

"Let's hope not." When Dr. Lovell clasped his hands over his clipboard, his starched white coat crackled.

Hoping for no complications was far from reassuring. Lila wanted guarantees. She was about to ask what complications she should be looking for—and whether she'd go through life with half a breast—when Dr. Lovell flicked a speck of lint off his immaculate trousers and asked, "Has anybody talked with you about going for counseling?"

"No."

"I'm not an expert, but you're a candidate for post-traumatic stress. You know that, don't you? You seem edgy and depressed."

"I just got shot," she reminded him. She'd earned her edge and depression.

"Granted, but some people handle it easier than others," Dr. Lovell said. "Have you had any flashbacks?"

"I can't get what happened out of my mind."

"A psychologist could help."

Lila didn't think so, not when terror seemed embedded in her. She pressed her head deeper into her pillow. "I appreciate your suggestion, but I'd like to work things out myself."

"It's up to you." Dr. Lovell checked his watch.

Before Lila could ask questions, he got up and headed for the door.

Wait! What about the complications? And my breast? What happens next? She was too weak to call after him.

With courtesy that her mother had instilled in her, Lila said "thank you" to the back of his head.

3

Every day Cristina came to visit. When Lila's hospital room-mate left, Cristina took over the room. She set get-well cards on the windowsills and tables and dragged chairs from the hall to hold the flowers, stuffed animals, and boxes of candy that kind people had sent. She tied balloons to the doorknobs and bed rails and went to Lila's apartment for toiletries, books, and clothes, which she laid on the empty bed.

From friends in the Crockett Building, Cristina also brought news of Weatherby employees who'd died. She told Lila about the bullet that had torn through the St. Christopher medal Emily had worn around her neck, and the futile emergency C-section to save the baby of Madeline, the head copywriter. Cristina described the marks Edmond, the vice president of marketing, had clawed into Yuri's neck after jumping him from behind, and the raincoat that Max, a graphic designer, was still wearing when a bullet killed him.

Lila lay in bed and pondered these details as if she were trying to decipher the Rosetta stone. Though in her mind she could not seem to process the tragedy, she longed for information about what had happened. Since she'd cancelled her smartphone in order to save money, she couldn't surf the web. So every few minutes she flicked on the TV and searched the channels for news.

One morning she came to a broadcast of a woman reporter holding a red-and-white umbrella outside the Crockett Building. As pedestrians with coat collars turned up against the rain passed behind her, she said, "The police have just released a photo of Yuri Makov, the alleged gunman." When Yuri's picture appeared on the screen, Lila, though sore and feverish, bolted up in bed.

The very sight of him made her queasy, yet she couldn't take her eyes off him. He appeared ten years younger—perhaps in his late twenties—and his shining eyes and plump cheeks made him look almost cherubic, like Cupid after growing up and putting his archery and nudist days behind him. His hair curled at his shirt collar, and a dapper white handkerchief peeped out of his sports coat pocket. In his agreeable expression, there was not the slightest trace of a capacity for violence. What had changed him into a killer?

The reporter pushed a wayward strand of hair behind her ear and said, "I've talked to every policeman I can find this morning. They're still trying to figure out why anyone would commit such a heinous act, but so far they've come up with nothing."

An anchorman wearing an eggplant-colored tie that clashed with his auburn hair broke in: "Maria, do they have any theories?"

"Not yet. They're still questioning people, but so far no one's been willing to speculate on what could have driven him to a shooting spree."

"Maybe we can get some insight here," the anchorman said. "I've got Dr. Alan Leibowitz, a Cal psychology professor, with me in the studio. He's a stress-and-violence-prevention consultant with the U.S. Postal Service, where this kind of tragedy has occurred before. 'Going postal,' some people call it?"

"Yes." Dr. Leibowitz's eyes looked like raisins pressed into his doughy face. He fidgeted and glanced shyly at the camera.

"What causes going postal? Does anybody know?" the anchorman asked.

Like a dog, Lila pricked her ears to listen.

"One main cause can be pressure on the job. If you've got someone with emotional problems, and you make him work overtime too much, or you pass him up for promotion, or you downsize people around him so he feels insecure . . ."

"Then that can set him off?" the anchorman interrupted.

"Possibly."

Yet our office was a friendly, easy place to be, Lila thought. No overtime or downsizing, and to what job would Yuri Makov have hoped to be promoted?

"Working with a dysfunctional boss can set off someone too," Dr. Leibowitz said. "If somebody resents a my-way-or-the-highway supervisor, it can be like putting a match to gasoline. A trivial thing can make some frustrated person explode in a rage."

It crossed Lila's mind that she and Yuri had shared Agnes Spitzmeier, the office manager, as their boss. She was no gentle lamb, but she wasn't a tyrant. She couldn't have caused him to shoot people.

"So what about a PR firm? Can you imagine something going on there that could create that kind of emotional explosion?" the anchorman asked.

Lila held her breath for Dr. Leibowitz's opinion.

"I don't know any specifics about that place where all those people got shot five days ago, but the killer probably had some grievance. He must have been angry about something."

What about our anger at him? You don't just smile and forgive someone who tried to kill you. Lila turned off the TV and scrunched down in bed. With her face turned to the wall, she brooded about Yuri Makov's possible grievance till her anger tasted like Tabasco sauce.

How could something so bad happen to decent people like all of us at Weatherby? she wondered. How could she not have seen it coming? Lila was usually a reasonable judge of character, and Yuri had not seemed like a crazed and murderous fiend. How could her perception of him have been so far off?

And why had he shot everybody? *Why?* More than anything else, that's what Lila wanted to know. She needed to make sense of what had happened. Aside from the horror of the shootings, the hardest part was not understanding what had prompted Yuri's violence.

Cristina had said Lila would never understand. "Asking why is pointless. Just leave it! He was nuts. No sane person would shoot a bunch of people."

"It can't be that simple. There has to be more to it," Lila said.

With impatience, Cristina swept her hand through the air. "Forget it. He was cuckoo. That's all you need to know."

But Lila couldn't settle for such a general explanation. Yuri Makov's motive had to have specifics—*what* had made him nuts or turned him into a killer. Everything that happened had to have a reason, no matter how small.

In high school, Mr. Hamilton, Lila's physics teacher, was telling her class one day about the butterfly effect. He dangled a leg over the edge of his desk and tossed a marker pen back and forth between his hands. "Sometimes the tiniest difference at the start of something can lead to enormous differences in the end," he said. "Take some butterfly. If he's flapping his wings in Brazil when weather conditions are right, he can cause a hurricane in Florida."

At her desk Lila imagined all the desperate people in Fort Lauderdale, hammering plywood over windows, screaming at their kids to get in the car, and driving west as fast as they could go. Surely none of them would be thinking, "That beastly monarch going at it down there in a mahogany tree outside São Paolo. What a vicious little twit he was." And yet he might have been the cause of all their troubles.

That was how life worked. Sometimes just a whisper of a force could have huge consequences. Even if you couldn't see why something had happened, somehow, somewhere, there had to be an explanation.

Lila pulled the covers over her ears and told herself that after a disaster, you couldn't just sit there and spend the rest of your life traumatized. You had to go on, and you had to *do* something—and she was going to figure out why Yuri had shot everybody. If she didn't, she'd always feel like she was living in a no-man's land where everything was crazy, violence happened for no good reason, and nobody had ever heard of cause and effect. In a place like that, she'd never heal or have peace; she wouldn't be able to get herself out of bed in the mornings. Anybody terrorized by someone could understand that.

She wriggled out from under the covers and went through the TV channels again with hope for something that would help her understand Yuri Makov. But all she found were sports and soaps—and *Why?* kept nagging her. She promised herself that she'd keep up the search until she found an answer so she could get control of her life again. With her good hand, she rubbed determined circles in her forehead.

4

When Lila was a senior in college, she called her father and announced that she was dropping out of school to paint full-time. He was an investigative journalist, and he was rabid about an education and career for his only child.

"For Christ's sake!" he barked into the phone. "You can't quit school. A degree will help you get a decent job."

"All I want to do is paint."

"Umf." His shortened version of "harrumph." "Lila, goddamn it. For once will you just try not to be stubborn?"

She pictured his face, red whenever someone crossed him. His teeth would be clenched on the pipe he'd stopped filling with tobacco since his heart attack four years before. He would be shaking his head with exasperation and motioning to her mother to get on the extension phone and back him up.

Before Lila gave in and agreed to finish school, he said, "You've got to be able to take care of yourself. You have to be independent."

She'd heard that from her father since she was three and didn't understand what independence was. Her sneaker's shoelace had been slapping the floor, and she asked, "Daddy, fix this?"

A sturdy oak tree of a man, he rested his hands on his hips and looked down at her. "You're a big girl now. I'll bet that's something you can do for yourself."

Together they sat on the floor, and several times he tied and untied her shoe. "Now you try," he said. For half an hour she struggled until shoelace bows were ingrained in her for life.

As she grew up, her father drilled independence into her so she would be in control of every situation. On backpacking trips he taught her how to survive in the wild in case her plane crashed in the mountains and she had to wait for help. Before she left for college, he signed her up for a karate class so she could protect herself on campus alone at night. Later, he showed her how to change a tire and what to pack in a first-aid kit to prepare her for future cuts and burns.

However, he did not prepare Lila to get shot, or to become the newly dependent woman Cristina was pushing out the hospital's glass doors in a wheelchair, grabbing on to like a fragile vase, and helping into her car. Lila's father didn't prepare her for Cristina to reach across and fasten Lila's seat belt, either. "There you go!" Cristina said. Lila could have been her daughter, Rosie, age five.

"Thanks, Cris. You're being wonderful. I appreciate it more than I can tell you," Lila said.

"You don't have to thank me. You just have to get well."

"It's hard to be needy."

"You won't be for long."

"I felt safer in the hospital."

"Don't worry." Cristina gave Lila's shoulder a reassuring pat.

But vulnerability stung her. Her rational mind couldn't seem to tame her anxiety about being out in the world, where someone could shoot her even if she kicked and bit and smacked him with her plaster cast. Lila chewed her lower lip and scanned the block for men with guns as Cristina, with her man-luring curves, walked around the Volvo to the driver's side. She got behind the wheel and pulled into the street.

As Cristina drove through Golden Gate Park, she said, peppy and upbeat, "It's such a gorgeous day. Look at the daffodils around the pond. Spring's finally here."

"Right," Lila said, trying to sound enthusiastic. But the bright springtime sun made her a more visible target for someone to shoot at, and she'd have been glad for tinted one-way windows.

When Cristina approached the San Francisco Bay, she pointed through a stand of pines to the fluttering sails of boats. "Look. Beautiful!" She glanced at Lila as if she hoped for an eager reply.

"Right," Lila said again. She kept her eyes on the road so she could warn Cristina if she started to swerve. If they crashed into the water, Lila would be unable to swim with her arm in a cast. She'd drown.

Cristina raked her fingers through her dark hair, which she wore free and sexy to her shoulders. She nudged Lila's knee. "Earth to Lila. Come in, Lila."

Lila was supposed to laugh, and she wanted to. But a slight curve at the corners of her mouth was all her uneasiness would allow. She, who used to love to ride her bike in this very place, would have preferred today to travel in an amphibious tank. Lila and Cristina crossed the Golden Gate Bridge in silence.

Cristina drove through a tunnel and turned off the freeway toward Mill Valley, the small town where she lived—and where she'd invited Lila to stay for a week till she was well enough to go alone to her apartment. Rising in the distance was Mount Tamalpais, known as the "Sleeping Lady" because of her reclining human form against the sky. But in Lila's mind she wasn't sleeping; she looked like someone had shot her, and she was lying, wounded, above the hills.

Lila and Cristina traveled down Miller Avenue, past flowering plum trees and businesses that whizzed by in a blur: Tam Market, Closet Transfer, Oil and Water Art Store, Elsa's Chocolates, the Framery, and Jenny's Chinese Kitchen. After Cristina drove across Mill Valley's main street, where baskets of petunias hung from lampposts, she and Lila headed down Emerson Avenue and followed a stream into a forest.

Cristina turned onto a winding, narrow road and traveled up the mountain to her house. Lila had always thought it was charming, the kind of place Hansel and Gretel might have left a trail of crumbs through the forest to reach. Today, however, Lila felt apprehensive, so the ivy-covered stone walls and leaded-glass doors and windows made her think of a castle that a witch had cast a spell on; and the gnarled old wisteria entwined in the porch's iron railing looked choked.

As Cristina pulled into the garage, Lila glanced back across the bay at San Francisco, which, before, had always seemed like a far-off shining jewel. Now, though, the city had lost its magic; it was a place of shootings and murders, a tangle of troublesome buildings crowded on hills.

Cristina guided Lila to the front door, which had ten panes of streaky, antique glass. Cristina's two toy poodles were clawing their needly toenails on the bottom ones, and a scruffy golden retriever with a red bandana around her neck was smudging her nose on the pane next to the doorknob.

Lila stiffened when she saw the retriever. She had to be Grace, and she was far scarier in the flesh than she'd been in the poster. She had mange on her back, which had not been visible in the photograph; mange could make her irritable and, therefore, more prone to attack. Her troubled face, with forehead furrows and dark, mistrustful eyes, looked like she was contemplating bites. Though her fangs were hidden, they had to be sharp.

"Isn't Grace adorable? I'm fostering her for a little while," Cristina said.

"I thought she'd be with your friend. The one in the photo."

"You mean Adam. He couldn't take her, so I agreed to it."

"You didn't tell me she was here."

"If I had, you'd have insisted on going home. You forget how well I know you." Cristina smiled. "You'll love Grace. She's a sweetheart."

"Menace" was the word Lila would have used. She steeled herself for sharing a house with an animal who at any time might bare her teeth and lunge. You could never tell what a dog like that might do.

Cristina worked her key into the lock. When she opened the door, the poodles yapped and jumped on her. Grace had the decency to move aside, but something was wrong with her left front leg, so she hobbled into a corner and slouched. Her glower informed Lila that she'd picked up Lila's fear of dogs and disapproved of her invasion of the house. If dogs could talk, Lila was sure Grace would have said, *This is* my *house, you odious toad. Why don't you leave?*

Cristina must have noticed Lila's frown. "Don't be afraid. Honest, Grace is very shy. She wouldn't hurt a flea."

Lila walked sideways through the door, the better to look the dog straight in the eyes and dare her to turn savage. Lila and Grace sized up each other with mutual suspicion. When Lila passed, Grace yawned and exposed her fangs, along with two horseshoes of teeth a shark might have envied. Then she went back to slumping. Lila kept her distance.

5

For her first couple of days at Cristina's, Lila lay on the guest room bed and willed her strength to return. But she learned that strength wasn't something you could will, demand, or control. It was a gift, and it took its own sweet time, as did peace, of which Lila had little. During the day she sweated through flashbacks, and at night she woke yelling for help in a recurring nightmare of men hacking down her apartment door and stepping through the rubble to kill her.

Also unsettling was Cristina's scheduled departure. The day after Yuri shot Lila, Cristina's husband, Greg, an environmental lawyer, had started a six-month consulting job with the EPA in Washington, D.C. Cristina had stayed behind to pack and look after Lila, but Cristina and her daughter, Rosie, would leave to join him. They were as close as Lila had to family—and she dreaded how much she would miss them.

Many times each day she leaned against a blue corduroy bolster and took deep, steadying breaths. She stared at the trees out the window to receive what Cristina called "redwood therapy," which was supposed to calm her and lift her spirits, and she dozed and listened to jazz on the radio.

In the afternoons Rosie came into Lila's room after kindergarten, and they played Go Fish. Or they sat on the bed and took "trips," as they had before in Cristina's Volvo; and Rosie, wearing sunglasses and a baseball hat, her ponytail threaded through the back, drove Lila to the North Pole to see what Santa was up to and to the moon for apple juice and cookies.

Lila and Rosie also played with Gerald, her imaginary lion friend, who had antelope breath. They made up special menus to feed him: flamingo beak soufflé with sunbeam muffins; sautéed ostrich toes on a bed of marsh grass; zebra tail in peanut butter sauce, accompanied by a tomato and hippo-eyelash salad. While Lila drew Gerald a pride of mates, Rosie drew a portrait of Lila with fingers sticking out of her cast like an electrocuted spider's legs.

Occasionally, as Lila and Rosie passed the time together, the poodles ran lawlessly up and down the hall. Once in a while, Grace shuffled by, her fangs glistening more brightly than Gerald's, her gold fur rumpled, and her plumed tail sagging. She was on her way to and from her favorite hiding spot under Cristina and Greg's antique four-poster bed. Grace never came into Lila's room. She seemed to know she wasn't welcome. *Thank goodness.*

Late one afternoon Cristina was making dinner in the kitchen, and Rosie was chasing the poodles around the backyard. Lila was surfing TV channels with hope for information about Yuri Makov, as usual, though in the last few days coverage of the shootings had waned to almost nil. Nevertheless, the TV kept her company, which she welcomed as the sun slipped behind the mountain and the forest darkened. Uneasy in the shadows, Lila turned on her bedside lamp and kept the TV volume high so the reporters would seem like they were in the room.

As she flicked the remote control from a weatherwoman to a sportscaster, footsteps heavier than Cristina's thumped on the hardwood in the hall. Out of the corner of Lila's eye she saw something move. She whipped her head around to look. A broad-shouldered man in a moss-green sweater was standing in her doorway. He was taller than she by a good four inches. He had to outweigh her by seventy pounds.

Lila's stomach pole-vaulted to her throat. Common sense would have told her that the man had not shown up to kill her. But her frayed nerves canceled logic, and an image of Yuri Makov in her office entry flashed through her mind. She couldn't run to Cristina in the kitchen because the man was blocking the way and trapping her as surely as Yuri had. She jumped out of bed to protect herself, then froze like a deer in headlights.

Finally, she managed, "Who *are* you?!"

"I'm . . ."

"What are you *doing* here?!" As Lila curled her good hand into a fist, her nails dug into her palm.

"Cristina sent me to meet you. I'm Adam Spencer."

"Oh." The sun rose on Lila's mental landscape. The man in the dog poster's photo. If he'd not frightened her so badly, she might have recognized him.

She rested her hand over her heart to slow the pounding, but that hardly helped. Coming down from an adrenaline rush of fear would take a while. Lila's brain raced as quickly as her pulse, so she couldn't settle on the right response to Adam, such as "Nice to meet you" or "I'm Lila." In an accusatory tone, she blurted out, "You scared me half to death."

"Nothing scary about me," he said, as cool as lettuce. "I'm an ordinary person."

But he wasn't ordinary. Besides being big, he had a handsome face you might expect to see chiseled in stone. A straight patrician nose. Strong chin. Full lips. Intelligent eyes. You could tell nothing got by them, including Lila in her faded flannel nightgown with its arm slit for her cast. Today she'd not yet washed her face or brushed her hair.

"You should have knocked or warned me you were coming," she said.

"Sorry." But his remorse did not seem especially sincere.

He wasn't sensitive enough to understand her anxiety, Lila decided, so she didn't bother to explain herself. As she searched her mind for what to say next, Grace hobbled in, wagging her tail with exuberance. She whined and whimpered and threw herself at Adam.

As he bent down and hugged her, plastered against his knees, her ecstatic drool polka-dotted the floor. He murmured "good dog" and petted her shoulders with big sweeps of his hands. She trembled and nuzzled his neck, and her eyes, which had always looked troubled, were shining.

Lila grabbed the bedpost and shrank back from Grace, though shrinking put only an extra inch between herself and that dog. Lila had almost gotten used to being in the same house with her, but not in the same room. And now that the dog's mood had flipped from dejected to ecstatic, Lila knew that Grace was bipolar—and more unpredictable than Lila had thought.

"Grace isn't supposed to be in here. Will you please take her away?" she asked.

"She won't hurt anything. She's just being herself. After all she's been through, it's great to see her happy," Adam said.

"I don't want her here."

"Why *not*?"

"I'm not wild about dogs."

Adam narrowed his eyes as if she'd just mentioned the leprosy she'd picked up while serving her term in San Quentin.

"I had a bad experience with a dog," Lila said, defending her position.

Without bothering to ask what it had been, he said, "Grace should help you get over it. She's wonderful." There was judgment in his voice. Clearly, he thought she was as worthy as a dust mote.

Anyone could see that Adam was a dog fanatic. Lila pictured him living with a pack of hulking Irish wolfhounds, who licked spilled milk off his kitchen counters and slobbered over raw hamburger in metal bowls. Huge wet noses streaked the back window of the pickup he hauled the brutes to the park in every day. To get across his living room, he had to hopscotch over dog beds as big as barges. His kitchen walls were covered with dog-show ribbons.

He ruffled the fur on Grace's forehead so it looked like a rooster comb. "Come on, Grace. Let's go. You shouldn't stay where you're not wanted." Adam stood and gently slipped his fingers through her bandana. Without saying goodbye, he led her away.

The next morning before Cristina drove Rosie down the hill to kindergarten, she brought Lila the *Herald*. With hungry eyes, she skimmed the front-page headlines—mostly about mayhem in the Middle East and scrapping in Congress—and she combed the news section.

She was looking for an article about Yuri Makov or anyone else who had gone postal and who might help her understand him. But the only story that came close to workplace violence was two paragraphs on the last page, about an armed robbery in a San Francisco grocery store. The Korean owner had come around the counter and grabbed the criminal—about five-six, in a black ski mask and blue fleece hoodie. He'd shot the owner in the thigh, and so far the police had no suspects. At least Lila was lucky to know who'd shot her, but the article brought her no closer to learning why Yuri had done it.

She looked through the *Herald*'s entertainment and business sections and found nothing related to going postal there. Disappointed, she folded the paper and pressed the crease along the middle extra-hard. Once she got back to her apartment, she could search the Internet for information about Yuri Makov, and she wouldn't have to dodge Cristina always insisting, "He was nuts! Let it go!" If Lila mentioned his name more than twice a day, Cristina lectured her about obsessing and said, "Get some more redwood therapy."

Except for the grandfather clock's chimes in the living room and a distant whoosh of a street sweeper down the mountain, the house was silent. Ever since Adam Spencer had frightened Lila, she listened for footsteps. Cristina's house was across a wooded gulley from the nearest neighbor, and Lila could yell for help till she was hoarse—and no one would hear. She wrapped her good arm around herself, but it was paltry protection. Two weeks ago, she'd have said the only thing that frightened her was large, erratic dogs, but after Yuri Makov, nothing seemed secure.

6

Without Cristina's feminine touches, Greg's den would have looked like a Victorian lawyer's office. He had an antique partner's desk, a wall of leather-bound books, a dark green leather wingback chair and sofa, and a painting of a ship cutting through the froth of a stormy sea. Cristina had added peace lilies, poodle statues, needlepoint pillows, and a wild-goose-chase-pattern quilt, under which Lila was curled up on the sofa. Today was her first time out of the guest bedroom and bath since coming here. The change of scene freed her.

That morning Cristina had cut the sleeve of Greg's oldest flannel shirt and guided Lila's cast through, then buttoned her up and helped her into a pair of jeans. Though Lila had resisted the assistance, she had to accept it until she could manage buttons and zippers with only her right hand. Just as she'd learned to tie her shoes as a child, she'd have to conquer simple tasks—changing her chest bandage, squeezing toothpaste onto her brush, pulling a nightgown over her head, showering with her left arm in a plastic bag, washing and drying her hair. Sometimes the list seemed daunting.

Still, Lila felt better being up. Though the shirt and jeans were frumpy, sitting, dressed, in Greg's den helped her feel less like someone who'd been shot and more like a normal person. The only drawback to being in the den was Grace, sprawled on a pillow across the room. She looked like she'd been poured there, a gold puddle of a dog. Though she pretended to sleep, occasionally she opened one large, dark eye and aimed it at Lila, who was sure it had a malicious glint. She eyed Grace back, and on the windowsill she noted a large wooden poodle that could serve as a club, if needed.

Grace was resting her chin on her vile, bacteria-ridden tennis ball. She'd dug it up in the backyard, where it had probably been buried for two hundred years. Though Cristina never seemed to mind Grace's bringing the ball inside, it dripped slobber and contaminated the house as surely as her mange did. As usual, however, far more unsettling than mange and germs were her teeth, only ten feet away.

Cristina set a tray with napkins, cups of tea, and a plate of sweet rolls on the glass-topped table that, thankfully, stood between Lila and the dog. Cristina kissed her fingertips the way Italian waiters do to say something is delicious. "Come on. *Mangia!* I didn't bake these for nothing. I don't want you to waste away." As the den filled with a rich, cinnamon smell, she picked up a roll and took a bite.

Though Lila's appetite had run off with the use of her left arm, to please Cristina, she took a roll. The vanilla icing melted in her mouth. "You're dear to do all this for me, Cris, but you don't need to work so hard. Really, I'm all right."

"You are not. You've got black circles under your eyes. You look like someone just let you out of a dungeon." Cristina kicked off her loafers and eased into the wingback chair.

"I don't think I look so bad," Lila said.

"Maybe not as bad as last week, but you've got miles to go." Cristina polished off her roll in four bites and blew at the steam curling from her tea. "On the phone last night Greg and I decided you can't go back to your apartment this weekend. You're not well enough."

"Don't worry about me. I'll be fine."

"That's not true. You couldn't make it up the stairs to your front door. You need to stay here till Rosie and I leave, and then you should house-sit for us."

Lila shook her head. "I couldn't commute to work."

"You wouldn't have to go back to work. Greg and I will pay for your utilities and food so you won't have any expenses."

"I could never let you do that."

"We want somebody in the house while we're gone. It should be you."

"You've never said you wanted a house sitter before."

"We decided we need someone to water the yard. This summer's supposed to be dry."

"I can't pack my stuff and move it here."

"I could do it in a day. Look, you'd be doing us a favor. We need your help." Cristina took a swallow of tea and set her cup on the table. "If you stay here, you can paint full-time. I know you want that more than anything."

A direct hit to Lila's heart. She couldn't argue with that, as Cristina well knew.

It went without saying that Lila wanted to help her, especially after all Cristina had done for her for eighteen years—and more than ever since Yuri had shot her. There were hundreds of small kindnesses, such as birthday cakes, Christmas dinner invitations, and chicken soup for Lila's colds. And there were hundreds of times when Cristina had given moral support. After Lila's parents had died two days apart from an infection in Peru, Cristina went with her to pick out cemetery plots. When Lila's income as an artist had dropped below anemic, Cristina commissioned a portrait of Rosie; and after Lila had walked out on Reed, Cristina invited her home till she found an apartment. Besides owing Cristina, Lila loved her like a sister.

Still, house-sitting for six months would be complicated. A banner saying BE INDEPENDENT traveled across Lila's inner sky. Though Cristina had said she and Greg needed help, Lila had a nagging sense that they wanted to help *her*. Though well meant, their subsidy was hard to accept. Every day in Cristina's house, Lila would have to talk her pride off a tenth-story window ledge.

Also, secret longings made Lila hesitate to house-sit.

Five years before, she'd been with Cristina and Greg when Rosie had refused to be born. After nine hours in labor, Cristina was gripping her watermelon stomach, and despite the counting and breathing they'd learned in birth classes, she was moaning with pain. Nevertheless, as Lila draped Cristina's shoulders with the Italian flag she'd bought for her, Lila would have traded places with her in a finger snap. Greg was massaging and kissing her arms and telling her he loved her, and she was about to have his baby—and Lila was living with baby-disdaining Reed, with whom her good judgment had been urging her to break up, but she had not yet gathered the conviction to do it.

After seventeen hours, Rosina Patrizia Harrison presented herself for their devotion. Her eyes were puffed closed, her hands looked like small starfish, and her skin was an extra-deep shade of rose madder. When she howled at being squeezed out into the world, her lips curled up and exposed endearing little gums. To Lila, she was the anointed queen of the universe; she would rule the sky and wind with one nod of her charming head. As her godmother, in the next few years Lila would buy her princess costumes at the thrift store, invite her teddy bears to tea, paint her face like a cat for Halloween, and play five thousand games of Go Fish with her.

But Lila was not Rosie's—or anybody's—mother, and she had no husband. Reed was out of her life for reasons she didn't think she could ever forgive. She also had no financial security or beautiful home of her own, as did Cristina, whose life was a sophisticated version of a Norman Rockwell painting

If Lila stayed in Cristina's house for six months, everything around her would be shouting about what she longed for but was missing. The photos in every room would underscore this feeling: Cristina and Greg stuffing wedding cake into each other's eager mouths and sledding down a hill in matching red parkas. Rosie toddling across the living room or sitting in a Shaker rocking chair in her pink sweat suit and looking cute enough to smother in a hug. Rosie was everywhere—in the mouse drawing on the refrigerator, the step-up platform to the bathroom sink, the tiny green galoshes with frog-face toes in the mudroom. Evidence of a happy marriage was also all over the house. You couldn't miss it in the silver Victorian tea set that Greg had bought Cristina just because she liked it.

Lila's envy came to life only when provoked, such as during Rosie's birth or on the afternoon when Cristina showed Lila a dime-size clamshell that Greg had given her.

On its smooth interior, Greg had written with a ballpoint pen, "I love you."

Cristina said, "We were on the beach. He acted like he found the shell in the sand like that. Isn't it the dearest thing?"

Indeed, it was. Envy flew into Lila's face like a hornet, but she swatted it.

Despite Lila's longings for security and family, though, Cristina was right: Lila wanted to paint. It was essential for picking up the pieces of her life. For months she'd been planning a series of doors, gates, and windows. When a new idea for a painting came to mind, her fingers ached to curl around a brush. Painting had been the heartbeat of her life, and she had to get her heartbeat back. Cristina was making an offer Lila could never refuse.

"You'd take the poodles?" she asked.

"We'd never leave behind those preciouses," Cristina said.

"And that golden retriever?" Lila pointed across the room at Grace, who was lying on her back with her legs flopped out, like she was working on her stomach at a tanning salon. The fur there was more sparse than on the rest of her so pink skin showed through.

"Adam's put up posters. She'll have a home in no time. Everybody loves goldens," Cristina said.

Everybody minus me.

"So you'll house-sit?" Cristina asked.

"Whatever you need. I'm glad to help."

Cristina clapped her hands together. "Fabulous!"

For the first time in months, Lila's heart brimmed with hope.

7

When two strange men walked up to Cristina's front porch, Lila's breath caught in her throat. She told herself they were selling or campaigning for something, but the reality check didn't neutralize her fear, which was stark because Cristina had taken the dogs to get Rosie at school. Lila was alone.

If the men hadn't seen her through the front door's glass, she'd have gone to her room and pretended no one was home. One, in a dark suit and wide, lime-green tie, was about to knock; when he saw her through the panes, he dropped his hand to his side and waited for her to answer the door. The other, in a rumpled blazer, scowled as she approached. She scowled back because the last thing she wanted was to talk with men she didn't know.

She cracked the door an ultra-wary four inches, narrow enough to slam shut. Not that slamming the door would do any good when the men could knock it down like the ones did in her recurring nightmare.

"Lila Elliot?" the man in the rumpled blazer asked.

"Yes." She cleared her throat. It was tight, as if she were

squeezing back a cry for help and holding it in reserve in case she needed it, though neighbors were too far away to hear.

The man in the lime-green tie flipped open a leather case and showed her a badge. "Rich Mason. San Francisco PD. We want to talk to you about Yuri Makov."

His name hit Lila like a cloud of pepper spray. She studied the badge. She'd heard of men impersonating police, then robbing or killing people. But the badge looked real, and the men knew who she was. With resignation, she opened the door.

Rich stepped into the entry and thrust out a large, friendly hand, like a dog's paw, for a shake. His clammy hand made hers feel clammy too. He said, "Sorry to bother you. You must be upset about what happened." He was tall, slim, and clean-cut. Lila could picture him jogging along a beach or drinking wheat-grass juice at a health bar.

The other man was pudgy and dour. He introduced himself as Joe Arruzzi and grunted something about how hard it had been to find her. His clothes smelled of cigarette smoke. He had thick, bushy eyebrows, and the bags under his eyes looked like small hammocks filled with fat people.

Lila led the men into the living room. As her mother had taught her to do when visitors came, she offered them a Coke. They declined. Rich settled into one of Cristina's red club chairs, and Lila sank into the other. Joe leaned against the oak fireplace mantel, jingling the coins in his pockets and surveying Cristina's poodle sculptures on the tabletops and windowsills.

When Rich leaned forward almost close enough for his knees to touch Lila's, his coat fell open; at his waist the handle of a gun stuck out of a leather holster. She winced—his gun was the first she'd seen since getting shot—but Rich seemed not to notice her discomfort. Smiling, supportive, and sunny, he uncapped his pen and flipped open a notepad. Clearly, he was going to take the lead, and Joe was going to stand by watching.

"You were new at Weatherby, weren't you," Rich said, not so much a question as a fact.

"I'd worked there three months," Lila said.

"Did you know Makov very well?" Rich asked.

"No. We just talked once in a while."

"How would you describe him? Outgoing? Secretive? Troubled?"

"Maybe a little odd. He didn't know much English. He was quiet."

"Withdrawn?"

"No. Just hesitant to talk."

"So you tried to talk to him?"

"Not exactly. I was polite. I thought he wanted his words to be perfect."

"Anybody give him a hard time about his English?"

"Not that I know of."

Rich scribbled something in his pad without taking his eyes off Lila. "Was he close to anybody in the office?"

"I have no idea." She shifted her weight in the chair.

"What else can you tell us about him?"

She thought for a second, wanting to help. "He dressed really well for a janitor."

"So you noticed what he was wearing?"

"Because he seemed like he was trying to look prosperous. Janitors don't usually wear sports coats and ties."

As Rich made another note, a delivery truck sped around a curve on Cristina's winding mountain road. Her grandfather clock struck two.

Joe crossed his arms over his paunch. His shoulders brushed Cristina's silver candlesticks on the mantel. "Tell us about your conversations with Makov," he said, like he was trying to nudge Rich to more fruitful questions.

"There's not much to say," Lila said.

"You must've talked to him," Joe said.

"Rarely. When I started working at Weatherby, I was more aware of him as a service than a person."

"So when did you notice him as a person?" Rich asked.

For a second Lila searched her mind. How was she supposed to answer that? "A couple of months ago, I guess. He showed up in my office after work."

"What'd he say?" Rich asked.

She leaned deeper into her chair and wrapped her good arm around her chest. She told herself there was no reason to hide the truth. "He asked if I liked his valentine."

Rich's face stayed blank. Joe's caterpillar eyebrows arched their backs toward the cathedral ceiling, and his earlobes turned pink. "Whadaya *mean*, valentine? You . . ."

"Tell us about it," Rich interrupted.

Lila squirmed and wished she were at her easel, mental miles from these men. A plane flew overhead with an irritating hum. For days she'd been wondering about the card. Should she have responded to it differently? "I found it on my desk."

"Makov write anything?" Rich asked.

"Just 'yours always' or something like that. I had no idea who'd left it."

"Makov must've had some reason to think you'd know it was from him," Joe argued.

"I don't know what he thought." But now, thanks to this interrogation, Lila did know how an animal felt when men poked sticks at it.

"You still have the valentine?" Rich asked.

"I threw it away."

"That's too bad." Rich glanced at Joe.

"I had no reason to keep it. It meant nothing to me."

"Yeah, sure." Rich leaned closer, as if he were about to have a whispered, confidential chat over a beer. "Makov have any reason to, uh, think you had a . . . relationship, or something?"

The question soured Lila's stomach. "I hardly knew him."

"He must've thought you'd be glad to hear from him. Why else would he leave you a valentine?" Joe demanded.

Even though Lila wanted this conversation to go smoothly, she did not have the energy to speculate. Her head felt like a small crowbar was prying off her scalp, and the questions were making her woozy. "I'd really like to help you, but there's no more I can tell you. Honestly," she said, then wished she'd not said "honestly," like she was guilty of something.

"You said you talked to Makov several times. What about the others?" Joe asked.

Lila pulled Greg's flannel shirt tighter over her chest and looked out the window at the redwoods, whose soothing power was gone. "There's nothing to say about the other times. They were no big deal."

"When did you last talk to him?" Rich asked.

"A few weeks ago. I don't know exactly."

"*Surely* you can remember," Joe pressed, as if Lila were a criminal he didn't believe.

"I didn't pay attention to the exact day."

"You must remember what the conversation was about," Joe insisted.

"It couldn't have been important," Lila said, sounding more defensive than she intended. Being badgered when she was feeling weak, she could hardly keep her mind straight or think of what to say.

Joe squeezed one of Cristina's candlesticks like a turnip he wanted blood from. "You're too young to be so forgetful."

"I'm telling you the truth. I probably thanked him for emptying my trash. I don't know." When Lila shrugged, pain shot from her wounded shoulder down her arm. "I've been thinking about getting well. Yuri Makov hasn't been the center of my life." But, then, that wasn't exactly true, since Cristina had accused Lila of obsessing about him.

"Can you tell us about any beef he might've had with any-one?" Rich asked.

"I didn't know him well enough to know about a beef." Lila pressed the nails of her good hand into piping in the club chair's armrest.

"Anybody beside you in the office have much contact with him?" Rich asked.

"I didn't have much contact. I told you I hardly knew him." Lila paused, pressed her lips together. "What beef do *you* think Yuri Makov might have had with somebody?"

"Don't know yet," Rich said.

"Have you ever had a case like this before?"

"Yeah, a couple," Rich said.

"What made the people kill? Did you find out?"

"It can be complicated." Rich tapped his pen on his knee like a small walking stick. "We had a guy shoot up a drugstore where he worked. He had an abusive dad who humiliated him all the time, kinda like another employee who kept calling him 'fag.' He lashed out, or so we decided."

"Remember Michael O'Toole?" Joe asked Rich.

"He got wigged-out when he lost some big law case, so he killed four people in his firm. One sick puppy. Angry about everything." Rich put his pen in his pocket and closed his note-book. "It can be hard to tell with these psychos, but we'll figure out what made Makov tick."

"He didn't come across as some violent freak," Lila said.

"Gotta have been provoked somehow." Rich got up to leave. "Try to think of anything else to help us figure this out."

"There isn't anything else." With effort, Lila struggled to her feet.

"If we need to talk to you again, how can we reach you?" Rich asked.

Not pleased at the prospect of seeing the men a second time, Lila said, "I'll be here."

Rich handed her a business card and started toward the door. Joe followed. When he stepped on the porch, sunlight glared on the bald spot crowning his head. Jingling the coins in his pocket, he turned around and muttered, "Shit happens."

"Tell me about it," Lila said.

8

Lila wiped Cristina's kitchen counter around tote bags and boxes overflowing with cookies, paper towels, dog toys, games, and CDs. As she squeezed out the sponge at the sink, a box slammed on the garage's concrete floor. Cristina was out there packing the van and muttering to herself. Tomorrow she and Rosie would drive to Sacramento to pick up a cousin and travel with her to Washington.

At dinner Cristina had stabbed her fork into a green bean. "I'm a pathetic camp follower. If my boss hadn't agreed to let me telecommute, my career would be ruined because Greg wants to make tideland policy."

"He'd never have taken the job if you and Rosie couldn't join him. You're giving him a gift," Lila said.

"I don't want to go to D.C. It's not fair to disrupt my life. Rosie's, too." Cristina got up, scraped wilted lettuce leaves off her plate into the garbage disposal, and disappeared into the garage.

Lila believed Cristina was not so opposed to leaving as she seemed. The stress of packing made her cross. And her grumpiness was a good sign, really, because it meant she believed Lila was healing. Since Lila had been shot, Cristina had held back anything that might cause distress. Seeing her be herself again, cranky or not, was a relief.

At the table, Rosie, in robin's-egg-blue coveralls, was humming "Three Blind Mice" and shoving her meatloaf around her green beans.

"Gerald would want you to finish dinner," Lila coaxed. She'd set a place for Rosie's lion at the table and served him klipspringer flank with marinated crocodile scales and giraffe-tail pudding.

Rosie screwed up her face. A strand of dark hair, free from her ponytail, fell into her eyes. "Can't I feed my meatloaf to Gerald? He's still hungry."

"He told me he's allergic to meatloaf. It makes him break out in a rash."

Rosie looked so disappointed that Lila would have crossed the kitchen and kissed the top of her head if Grace weren't hunched under the table like a bird of prey, waiting for treats to fall to the floor. Though persnickety about her own food, her quest for Rosie's was relentless. At breakfast Grace hung around for Cheerios that Rosie dropped, and at lunch Grace waited for bits of sandwich, which she grabbed with a snap of teeth. Aware of the dog's location, Lila used the kitchen island as a barricade. Thank goodness someone would pick up that dog tonight and Lila would never have to worry about her again.

When Rosie rested her cheek on the table, Lila gave in. "Okay, you can go."

Rosie clapped her hands and jumped down from the chair just as someone knocked at the front door. Involuntarily, Lila flinched—Dr. Lovell had been right that she was edgy. When she went to the entry hall, she expected to meet the unfortunate soul who would be Grace's new owner. But smiling and waving from behind the front door's panes was Adam Spencer, who seemed to have forgotten that Lila had said she didn't like dogs.

As she opened the door, he said, "Hi." Obviously at home in Cristina's house, he stepped, uninvited, across the threshold.

"Hi," Lila said. She noted his charcoal Dockers, light blue sweater, and damp hair, which he must have just washed. Wavy and thick, it was parted on the side and combed back from his face. He'd probably gotten cleaned up to sit with his Irish wolfhounds at an outdoor café, Lila thought. He was holding a cellophane bag of what looked like gingersnaps, tied with a raffia bow. Maybe he'd stopped to give them to Rosie for the long drive ahead.

She must have heard his voice because she ran to him and threw her skinny arms around his waist.

"How's my favorite kid?" He hoisted her up over his head, and she extended her arms and legs like a helicopter propeller. As he spun her around, she shrieked with delight and her ponytail danced. He let go and caught her mid-drop, and she shrieked even harder.

Grace appeared, whimpering at Adam as happily as she had the week before. He set Rosie down, and they fussed over Grace, who panted, her eyes half closed in ecstasy. Lila backed toward the kitchen so as not to be too close to her. When Christina called Rosie to winnow down her stuffed animals for the trip, she ran to the garage. Grace padded across the entry toward Lila.

As she was about to step farther away, Adam said, "I want to talk with you."

"Me?" Lila said.

"I need to make sure you know how to take care of Grace."

A gulp lodged in Lila's throat. "I assumed somebody was going to pick her up tonight."

Adam's eyes narrowed as if he were confused. "Cristina didn't tell you?"

"Tell me what?"

"I thought you agreed to keep Grace."

Lila gritted her teeth. She knew how General Custer felt, having a perfectly acceptable day and suddenly out of nowhere getting trapped.

As her face clouded, Adam said, "We tried to find someone to take Grace. We called all our dog rescue friends, but nobody had any room."

"Why can't *you* take her?" Lila's tone sounded like she was accusing him of mugging someone in a wheelchair.

"I'm still living next door to the man I stole her from."

Do you rob banks in your spare time? "You *stole* her?"

"Well, rescued. She was living with a sadist. He chained her to a tree."

As cruel as that sounded, it was no excuse to railroad Lila. She shook her head in disbelief that her dearest friend would manipulate her into keeping that dog. She, who Cristina knew was afraid of Grace, who had just one good hand to defend herself, who was trying to put her life back together and had no energy to waste. No wonder Cristina had stayed in the garage, out of the way when Adam sprang the news.

On the other hand, though rushed to pack her own belongings, Cristina had persuaded Lila's landlord to let her break her lease and had moved her apartment's contents here. The hours of work had been one more example of Cristina's eighteen years of kindness to Lila. For Cristina, she should have been willing to take on not only a potentially vicious golden retriever, but even a radioactive goat. Just as Lila had concluded when she'd agreed to house-sit, she owed Cristina.

As Grace nosed Adam's hand to ask for more petting, Lila shook her head and told herself not to be resentful. She needed to be as gracious and helpful as Cristina had been the last couple of weeks. Lila said, "You've taken me by surprise. Cristina never asked me if keeping that dog would be okay."

"She must have forgotten. She's bound to be distracted. She has a lot to do before she leaves tomorrow." Adam looked maddeningly sincere. "I'm really sorry. I wish we had another solution. We'd never ask you to keep Grace if we had a choice, but we couldn't help how things worked out."

"Well . . . So . . . ," Lila said, apropos of nothing. She knew defeat when she was surrounded and there was no escape.

"Goldens are quick to get adopted. Grace'll only be here a few days."

"That's what Cristina said when I came here last week."

"You can't tell how people will respond to posters. Calls come in waves. Someone will be glad to have her."

Adam fixed Lila with his eyes, which she noted were intensely blue. He was the kind of man you had to rally strength to argue with, and she hadn't gotten hers back.

"I've looked after Cristina's dogs here at least a dozen times. It's easy," he said.

"I guess," Lila said. But her enthusiasm would not have filled a gnat's shirt pocket. Her few days of dog-sitting stretched before her like a road through a jungle with pythons and leeches.

In the kitchen Grace settled, drooling full blast, at Adam's feet. He, apparently, thought nothing of dog drool. Lila shuddered to think what his Irish wolfhounds did to *his* floor. "Slimy" would be too charitable a word for it.

"How can anyone not love this wonderful girl," Adam said.

"Easy. Look at her teeth," Lila said.

"They scare you?"

"Well, yes, if you really want to know."

Even if he didn't want to know, she felt compelled to justify her attitude. She told him about the dog who'd lunged at her when she was nine. "The fur on his back bristled like a stripe of nails," she said.

"That doesn't sound so bad," Adam said.

"It was when he *bit* me."

"Was it a serious bite?"

"Five *stitches*. In the emergency room."

"Could have been a lot worse."

"It was horrible. Blood everywhere. I was just a girl."

When no hint of sympathy appeared on Adam's face, he made clear whose side he was on. But, then, she already knew he cared more about dogs than people.

"It wasn't the dog's fault. He was telling you to leave him alone. You woke him up and startled him. If someone did that to you, you'd get just as upset," Adam said. He set his cellophane bag on the counter as if his verdict about the loathsome mutt was final and the subject was closed.

Lila refused to relent. "The dog was out of control. It was terrifying." He'd been as violent and unpredictable as Yuri Makov, but she didn't feel like explaining that to Adam.

"It's not fair to damn a whole species because of a single incident," Adam said.

"Why not? Dogs can be dangerous."

"Not if you treat them right."

So they were back to him as judge and Lila as wayward underling. She was wasting her breath defending herself.

From his back pocket Adam got a piece of yellow legal-size paper, unfolded it and moved close to Lila so she could read it with him. As the clean smell of his shampoo drifted toward her, she saw "Dog-Sitting Duties" printed with a felt pen across the top. Below, he'd outlined with numbers and letters what the duties were.

No doubt he was an engineer, born with a calculator in his hand and an obsession about efficiency and organization. He would keep his Irish wolfhounds on a strict bathroom schedule and name them alphabetically—Alice, Bruno, Cooper, Daisy.

He'd go to work with a row of mechanical pencils clipped to his shirt pocket.

Adam opened Cristina's walk-in pantry door and pointed out Grace's plastic kibble bin and cans of Nature's Best chicken in gravy. He explained that Lila should feed her two cups of kibble and three heaping spoonsful of chicken in the morning and evening. He partly filled a measuring cup with water and held it out to Lila. "Pour exactly three-fourths of a cup over her food and break up the chicken in the kibble. Too much water and she won't like it. It'll be too much like soup."

In a drawer by the sink, Adam found a rectangular brush with steel bristles, which he swept along Grace's chest, leaving tiny trails in her fur. She leaned against his legs with her eyes half-closed again, as if she'd reached the Mount Everest of pleasure. "You don't want somebody coming over here to meet her and finding her unkempt," Adam said, and then he moved on to Grace's exercise program to strengthen her hurt leg. "A walk three or four times a week ought to do it."

"You said you'd find her a home in a few days," Lila said.

"I'll do it as fast as I can."

She exhaled the weary breath of someone who'd been mopping floors since dawn. "I can't handle that dog on walks. I've got an injured arm." She held up her cast as if it were a courtroom exhibit.

Adam shrugged, like the cast wouldn't hinder her from Olympic backstroke competition. "Grace won't give you any trouble."

"How can you presume it would be so easy for me?"

"All I'm presuming is she's a sweet dog. She'll do anything to please."

Maybe for you, not me.

Adam glanced at his list. "The most important thing is to keep Grace away from Marshall. He's the sicko she lived with over the hill about three miles from here. Grace belonged to his son. Marshall's wife left him and took the boy to Santa Barbara."

"So why would Marshall care if you stole Grace?"

"Power. He's mad I got the best of him." Adam untied the raffia bow of his cellophane bag and handed Lila a small cat-shaped cookie. "Want to give Grace a biscuit? See how gentle she is?"

The last thing Lila wanted was to get her hand near that dog's fangs, but she was too proud to refuse and stand there like a quivering violet. Pinching the cat's paws between her thumb and index finger's tips, she held out the biscuit toward Grace, who must have sensed that Lila was recoiling. Obviously offended, Grace gave her a disapproving look, as if she were foaming at the mouth with rabies Grace didn't want to catch. She turned her head away.

"You have to act like you're enthusiastic." Adam took the biscuit and beamed at Grace. "Look what I've got!"

She whined and her face lit up. She chomped down on the cat, crunched it to rubble, and swallowed. Anyone could tell she was thrilled.

Adam stroked her floppy ears. For a man his size, his touch seemed gentle. "See. Nothing to fear."

"You're never going to change me into a dog person. I want you to know that," Lila said.

"Can't help but try. You don't know what you're missing."

"Yes, I do." *Bites. Bloody hands. Stitches.*

9

On Cristina's street early in the morning, Lila fumbled with the buttons of Greg's flannel shirt to fasten them up to her chin. For two days she'd practiced with buttons, zippers, and snaps so she could dress herself when Cristina was gone.

The cold, damp air smelled of bay trees. Fog inching over Mount Tamalpais looked like gray fingers reaching out to clutch the Sleeping Lady's shoulders. On any other day, the pink banners festooning the sky would have lifted Lila's mood, but she felt sad as Cristina backed out of the garage. In minutes she and Rosie would be gone, and Lila's only company would be that dog.

When Lila had been packing lunch, Cristina came into the kitchen and squeezed her hands together in a guilty, worried way. "I'm sorry you have to take care of Grace for a few days," she said. "The last thing I wanted was to bother you with her, I swear."

Her apology was surprising because last night after Adam had left, Cristina and Lila tiptoed around the eggshell of Grace without mentioning her name. It was as if they had an unspoken agreement to part without strife. At breakfast Lila had stretched the truth and said the dog would be no problem.

Now in a cloud of exhaust, Cristina rolled down the van's window. Mascara on the lashes of only one eye signaled how frazzled she was. "I'll miss you. Greg's dumb job. I hate leaving you."

"You'll be glad once you get on the road." Lila's heart felt heavy, like it had gained a pound. She bent down and waved to Rosie, who was belted in a car seat in the back. "I'll draw Gerald some more animal friends."

"He wants a giraffe." Rosie waved, and crushed goldfish crackers in her hand flew into the front seats.

"Oh, God." Looking stressed, Cristina brushed them to the floor. As she changed gears, the poodles, incarcerated in matching carriers next to Rosie, whined and pawed at their barred doors, searching for a way out.

"Don't forget Adam's on my contact list. You need anything, call him," Cristina said. "He's a good person. You'll like him if you get to know him."

"Possibly," Lila said, as neutral as beige, "but he doesn't like me much." To win his approval, she'd have to become a wolfhound zealot.

"I'm sure he likes you. He just broke up with a leech. He's about to be happy for the first time in years, but he doesn't know it yet. You and Adam could be friends."

"We'll see."

Lila reached out and squeezed Cristina's hand. As Lila watched the van's taillights travel down the hill, become red specks, and disappear, tears leaked from the corners of her eyes. Loneliness engulfed her. That was how she'd felt four months before when she had learned the truth about Reed.

He was tall and blond and handsome in a craggy, weathered way. His skin was ruddy; his nose, sharp. When a friend had introduced him to Lila in the grocery store, she liked his faded jeans and blue work shirt—the same clothes she wore to paint—and his tan from working as a contractor on construction sites.

She wished she'd known. She wished she'd seen the train wreck waiting down her track. The pro bono carpentry Reed did for St. Anthony's Shelter, or the cups of tea he brought her, in bed with the German measles, were only a cover-up for future betrayal.

The tee shirt Lila found wadded up behind the passenger seat of his Ford pickup last September should have tipped her off. As she and Reed were driving to Berkeley for dinner with friends, she held up the shirt by the shoulders. "Whose is this?"

"Must be yours."

"It's not mine."

"Should be. You'd look great in it." His stroking of her thigh had been like hot buttered rum on a cold winter night.

Lila told herself that the shirt must have been one of the many she bought for a quarter each at the Turnaround Shop to use as turpentine rags for her brushes. But she could not explain away the picture at the PhotoMat.

She was standing in line behind a woman whose Chanel Allure perfume wafted from her body in sultry waves. The skin on the back of her neck was porcelain white, and she swept her chestnut hair back from her face with gold barrettes, curved in the shape of satisfied smiles. When she got to the counter, she pulled a five-by-seven color photo from her purse and said she wanted an eight-by-ten for a silver frame she'd bought.

Curious, Lila looked over her shoulder at the photo. The woman was sitting behind Reed on his new motorcycle. Her arms were wrapped around him, and her siren-red polished nails spread out on his chest like two small fans of exclamation points. The siren of her nails matched her moist lips, which, like his, were parted in a smile that could have run New York City air conditioners for an entire summer.

Lila felt as if someone had jumped on her stomach with both

feet. In two seconds, the photograph had broken her life into pieces; she could never crawl around on the floor, find them all, and glue them back together. Later, however, she realized that putting her life back together with Reed wasn't what she wanted anyway. For years she'd considered breaking up with him, as you'd work up the resolution to quit a bad habit, like smoking.

Her mismatch with Reed had gone on too long; their relationship was worn out, a fizzless Coke. Still, that rational conclusion could not cancel her anger at him and her shock that he'd found another woman without having the decency to break up with Lila first. And Reed had nicked her self-esteem. Perhaps something about her had not been enough. Was she not pretty enough? Pleasing enough? Easy enough to get along with? Had her father been right that she was too stubborn?

Cristina had said that what Reed did was about him, not Lila, and she was better off to have learned he was a weasel before marrying him and staring divorce in the face. But Lila's confidence was tarnished. After wasting five years with Reed, she was thirty-five without a partner. For all she knew, she'd missed out forever.

Her mother had always told her, "Look for character in a man." On the subject of boyfriends, her father had kept up his crusade for independence. "Make sure you don't need a man," he'd told Lila. "Nobody can make you happy but yourself. It's up to you to make your life the way you want it."

To make her life the way she wanted it, Lila went to Cristina and Greg's bedroom, where she would be sleeping. She took Greg's navy terrycloth robe from the chrome hook behind the closet door and put it in his dresser drawer—one less reminder that she had no husband. She went into Rosie's bedroom and glanced one last time at the stained-glass turtle nightlight on her dresser, and she closed the door. Now Lila wouldn't pass by and see the turtle, or Rosie's angel collection, or the moon and stars Cristina had painted on the ceiling above Rosie's bed—and risk a wilting spirit because she had no child of her own.

To dispose of other signs that she missed having a family, Lila went downstairs to the mudroom and took Rosie's, Greg's, and Cristina's coats from the antique brass doorknobs attached to the wall for hooks. Lila folded the jackets and parkas and set them in a cabinet above the washing machine. She put the boots and gardening shoes lined up against the wall into the water-heater closet.

While downstairs, Lila checked that the door to the back-yard was bolted and all windows that murderers could reach were locked. She reassured herself that the bolt and locks were sturdy and she had no reason to be afraid. When Grace shuffled to her water bowl upstairs in the kitchen, though, apprehension about the dog—and men with guns—rippled through Lila. To be sure of her safety, she checked the door and windows again.

Grace was lying by the front door in a dismal heap, like a large yam. She pressed her nose against a sidelight and bristled her eyebrows, looking puzzled, perhaps about why Lila was there after everyone else had gone. As Grace stared through the glass, her body tensed; she could have been waiting for a T-bone steak to fall to her paws like Rosie's Cheerios. Surely Grace was hoping Rosie, Adam, or Cristina would appear on the porch. The dog was waiting for someone she was attached to, to come home.

Grace's apprehension was sad to see, but for now she'd have to tough it out with her people gone, as Lila was doing. The dog was not the only one in the house who felt alone.

Wanting to stay as far from her as possible, Lila headed to-ward the kitchen. As she passed Grace, she closed her sad brown eyes and cut off Lila, who got the point: Since she'd been ignoring Grace, the dog was going to ignore her. Their playing field would be even, and the match would be Invisible Dog vs. Invisible Human.

Lila stopped at the kitchen door and looked back to check that Grace hadn't changed her mind and decided to sneak up behind her, brandishing her fangs. Grace was staring out the window and seemed miles away. She looked innocent huddled at the door, but the little-lamb act might be a ploy, and at any time Grace could turn savage. Her gimp leg was no guarantee she wouldn't charge.

Grace turned her head and glanced at Lila. The fur along Grace's spine was rumpled like spikes along a stegosaurus's back, and the usual wary glint was in her eyes. Lila was sure they said, as clear as a bugle blast, *I'm not the only potential savage in this house. You could turn vicious. I'm keeping tabs on you, you rampant rat fink.*

Lila poured granola and milk into a china bowl and set it on the kitchen table. As she eased into a chair, her foot hit something round and squishy—Grace's tennis ball.

Lila got up and grabbed five paper towels off the roll hanging below the kitchen cabinet, the better to protect her hand. With the towels, she picked up the ball like it harbored typhoid. "Let's get one thing clear, Grace. No ghastly ball allowed in this house."

Grace closed her eyes as if Lila did not exist.

With care, she threw the ball off the back porch into the ferns, where she hoped Grace would never find it. Back in the kitchen, as Lila crunched her granola, she had the feeling the dog was watching her, and she got a brief attack of the shivers.

Adam called when Lila was shivering. If he'd been sensitive, he'd have known she was anxious about Grace, and phoned to dispel her fears.

"Just checking on our dog," he said.

Our *dog?! No lukewarm "how are you?" or a verbal nod of recognition that I exist?* "Grace is fine," Lila said.

"Have you fed her yet?"

"Cristina did before she left."

"Did Grace eat okay?"

"Her bowl's still full."

"You've got to encourage her to eat. Does she seem upset because Cristina's gone?"

"Grace is always sad unless you're here."

Adam chuckled. "A walk would make her feel better. She shouldn't be cooped up."

Before Lila could remind him of her inability to walk the dog with just one hand, Adam ordered, "Get her to eat. That's the most important thing." He said he was late for a meeting.

Feeling used, Lila hung up the phone.

With her foot, Lila nudged the kibble bowl across the kitchen floor and stopped at the open doorway to the entry, where Grace was lying on her stomach with her head raised and her front legs stretched out like a sphinx. Extra pounds would make her more appealing to adopters and remove her more quickly from the house.

"Eat your kibble and chicken!" Lila commanded in the tone of lion tamers ordering their charges to leap through burning hoops.

She may as well have mentioned the Dow Jones to a being from Uranus. When Grace yawned and looked out on the front porch, she said clearly that obedience was a foreign concept, and, further, she was not eager for breakfast. She studied oak grains in the threshold.

"Grace," Lila said.

The dog continued observing the wood.

"Adam wants you to eat. We're talking about the Great Divide here. You gain some weight or you'll never get a home."

Grace seemed to find the warning tedious. She hobbled to the living room, flopped down, and toward the wall pointed her nose, which looked like a licorice gumdrop colored pink on top.

"If you don't eat, no one will adopt you," Lila warned again.

Grace stuck to her guns as a Uranian. She glanced at her food as if it were a personal affront.

Had Grace been more receptive, Lila might have encouraged her to eat by pointing out the starving dogs in Bangladesh and the dangers of anorexia. But Lila saved her breath. "All right. Whatever you want. I was trying to help." She walked through the living room to Google Yuri Makov in the den.

Grace averted her eyes.

"Have it your way," Lila said. "I'm not too thrilled about you, either."

10

As Lila typed with only the fingers on her right hand, her wrist stiffened. Her left hand's fingers itched to jump in and help Google Yuri Makov, but they sat on the desk chair's armrest weighed down by her cast. As she hunted and pecked, she blamed Yuri for another limitation—until 347 citations for him popped up on Greg's computer screen and a current of excitement ran through her.

As Lila scrolled down, however, she saw that the citations were for the newspaper articles that had flurried like a blizzard after Yuri had gone postal. They mentioned "rampage" and "carnage" and the same facts she already knew, such as Yuri's occupation and Russian origin. Occasional articles questioned why he might have gone on a rampage, but the newspaper reporters provided no answers. The dead ends frustrated her as much as her typing limitations, and she exhaled a discouraged breath.

Then a different citation leapt out at her. Yuri had posted a message on NICOclub.com, a site for Nissan car owners. Lila clicked on the link and found his forum name: Goodlife. It suggested that he must have longed for one, but so did everyone else on the planet.

In a small window at the left of the screen was information he had registered for the site. He lived in San Francisco—no surprise. His age was thirty-seven, and his e-mail address was russman75@gmail.com, probably meaning he was a Russian man born in 1975. Lila ached to e-mail him and demand, *Why did you do it?*

Under interests, Yuri listed music and art—but didn't say what kind—and boxing. *Boxing?* Did he watch or pound fighters in rings? To Lila, the interests conflicted and indicated a dissonance inside him. Out of the soil of his soul, the flowers of music and art had grown along with a testosterone-driven, down-and-dirty, thorny cactus of destruction. How had he reconciled the opposites? Maybe he *hadn't.* Maybe that was the problem, and boxing had been one step away from shooting. For half an hour, Lila stared out the window at nothing and wondered.

The English he'd posted was as garbled as the English he'd spoken. "Own 1994 Nissan Maxima. How get catalitic cheap converter? Must okay in California. I highly thank anything of this subject information."

So for his Nissan Maxima, Yuri wanted to find an inexpensive catalytic converter that measured up to California standards. A reasonable request. It contained no hint of a motive for murder.

Since cars people drove were supposed to reveal their identities and values, Lila looked up images for 1994 Nissan Maximas. But the car seemed plain and ordinary—a fender here, a bumper there. Headlights. Doors. A windshield. The best the car could say was, *I'll get you there.*

Only one person on NICOclub.com had replied to Yuri's message: "Unfortunately, I don't think there's such a thing as a cheap Cali-spec converter." Lila stared at the person's forum name until her eyes blurred: the Minister of Doom.

An irony like Goodlife vs. Doom had to contain a cosmic message. Was the universe tugging at Lila's sleeve to underscore opposites, such as art and boxing? Or was it pointing out a linear progression in Yuri's life—from happy boy to tortured killer? Or was the message about her *own* life, changed by a bullet from a tolerable and healthy struggle like everybody else's to a painful string of challenges? Whatever the meaning, one thing was sure, and Cristina and Lila had discussed it many times: The universe could sprinkle tantalizing signs around you. You had to be on the lookout for them and try to understand.

Side by side on the living room sofa across from Lila, Rich and Joe looked like a pair of buzzards until Rich set his elbows on his knees and gave Lila one of his eager Boy Scout looks. Joe leaned against the pillows, jingled the coins in his pockets, and hooded his eyes at her as if he didn't feel like opening them wide on what he didn't like. The week before, he'd seemed to want more from Lila than she could give, and flowing out of him had been an undercurrent of disapproval. It kept Lila off balance, though maybe that had been Joe's aim.

He glanced at Grace lying in the corner on her side so he couldn't miss her protruding ribs. He gave Lila an accusatory look. "Where'd that pathetic dog come from?"

She couldn't tell him that Grace was stolen. "She came with my house-sitting job."

"She needs some decent food," Joe said, seeming to suggest that Grace's scrawny body was Lila's fault.

"I tried to get her to eat this morning. She wasn't interested."

"Change her diet."

"I'm supposed to feed her what my friend left her," Lila said politely. She sat back farther in her chair, recrossed her legs.

Grace seemed to know she was being discussed, and she wanted to wring more sympathy from Joe. She hobbled to the kitchen and, with a wrenching sigh, plopped down on the oriental rug under the table where he could see her.

Joe shook his head and muttered, "Damned shame."

Rich flashed Lila a smile like sunshine. "Forget the dog. We want to talk to you about the case."

"Fine," Lila lied as Grace slumped into the position of a roosting chicken, rested her chin on her paws, and groaned like she had crippling arthritis Lila also needed to attend to.

Rich said, "We've talked to your colleagues. It sounds like something personal was bugging Makov."

"That could be," Lila agreed.

"Since he sent you a valentine and you knew him so well, we thought you could tell us . . . was he mad at anybody at work?" Rich asked.

"I told you last time—I didn't know him well." *Why wouldn't this simple fact sink into the policemen's brains?*

"Was he mad at anybody?" Joe pushed Lila back to the question.

"Not that I know of."

"Could he have been mad at you?" Rich asked.

Lila swallowed against the tightness in her throat. "I don't see how. I was always polite to him."

With his eyes, Rich pinned her wings to cotton. "Is there anything you haven't told us, Lila?"

She didn't like the familiar way he'd used her name—or the implication she was holding something back. But, then, maybe she was. Since Rich and Joe's last visit, she'd been thinking about something she should have told them – not that it made any difference, but she needed to be open and honest.

Lila sat up straighter, took a breath. "Yuri Makov called and asked me out once. I turned him down. We talked for two minutes, and that was the end of it. He never called again."

Rich cleared his throat. Joe widened his eyes as if Lila had just confirmed his suspicions. On the sofa he leaned toward her so he looked like he was about to lunge. She backed farther into her chair.

"Did he call before or after the valentine?" Joe demanded.

"After."

"So the relationship was getting to be a bigger deal to him," he said. "Why didn't you tell us this a week ago?"

"The call meant nothing. It was as unimportant as the valentine."

"Makov obviously liked you."

"If he did, it was all one-sided. I hardly ever talked with him."

Joe's caterpillar eyebrows arched. He thrummed his pudgy fingers on the sofa's arm. "One of your colleagues claimed Makov hung around outside your office. She thought he was waiting for you."

Lila felt sullied that anyone would suggest that. "I didn't see him hanging around."

"Never?" Joe demanded.

"Well, maybe once in a while. I didn't think anything of it. He was cleaning the hall," Lila said. "What colleague told you that?"

"She asked us not to use her name," Rich said.

"Because she's wrong. Yuri Makov would only have been there to vacuum." *Surely that's true. But what if it isn't?*

Like Joe, Rich moved forward so he was barely sitting on the sofa cushion. The sun in his smile had set. "We're gonna ask you straight out . . . Were you and Makov having an affair?"

"No! Honestly!" Saliva gathered on Lila's tongue. Her mouth tasted like tin. "How can you *ask* me that?"

"It's a logical question," Rich said.

"It makes my skin crawl." She pressed her unhurt arm against her stomach.

"An affair's no crime. Admit it. We need to wrap up this case," Joe said.

"I'm sure there's some other explanation for what he did. It can't have anything to do with me. I've told you I hardly knew him." How many times did she have to say that to make them believe her?

"You're sure you never went out with him?" Joe asked.

"Positive."

"Ever meet him away from the office?" Joe asked.

"Never."

"Ever flirt with him?" Rich asked.

"Of *course* not." The points of thumbtacks protruded from Lila's words.

The men's questions made her writhe as if she were guilty of something, when she insisted to herself that she'd done nothing wrong. Yet she couldn't shake the excruciating questions: What if she'd played an unintended role in Yuri's shooting everybody? Could that be possible?

As these questions lingered in Lila's mind, she wished she'd never asked them. And she was angry at Joe and Rich for even suggesting she might be responsible for what Yuri Makov had done. As she told herself she wasn't to blame, she squeezed the club chair's arm. Her face flushed, and a bead of sweat trickled down her spine.

Rich and Joe watched her with hard-set faces. For a long, silent moment, they let her hang in the wind.

"Okay," Rich finally said, looking as dark and mistrustful as Joe. "There's no point wasting more time here, but we want you to do some serious thinking about what was going on between you and Makov."

"I told you, there was nothing. And if there was, it would have been in his head." Lila wanted the men to leave. Desperate for a cool, clean breath of air, she gripped the chair's arm tighter and said politely, "I'm sorry I can't help you more."

"You could if you wanted." Joe's eyes were hooded with suspicion again.

"I'm sure this case is hard for you."

"You could put it that way," Rich said. He and Joe got up and headed toward the door. "We may be back."

I hope not. "Fine."

Lila locked the deadbolt behind them. Usually a healthy eater, she hurried to the kitchen for some reassuring chocolate chip cookies that Cristina had left in the freezer. As Lila took a bite, Grace lay under the table and turned her face toward the wall to avoid eye contact. Lila could have offered her one of Adam's biscuits, but she was tired of trying so hard to be nice to everybody.

As much as Lila wanted to learn about Yuri Makov, she'd had enough of him for one day. Instead of returning to the computer, she went to the deck and, exhausted, flopped down on the white canvas chaise lounge.

Clouds had blown in and covered the sun. In a bay tree by the street, blue jays were squawking the way they do when the weather is about to change. Wind swayed the redwoods and unsettled them to their roots. Nothing seemed soothing.

As Lila rested her head against the pillow and festered over Rich and Joe's questions, she felt a stirring of the members of her mental family, the facets of herself who lived, like relatives, inside her head. Sometimes they presented themselves as characters in her imagination, and the first one to appear on that distressing afternoon was her Crazy Aunt, whom Lila rarely let out of her mental attic because she was angry and out of control, as most women were taught not to be.

She roared into Lila's thoughts in her bashed Ford Explorer and bared her tobacco-stained teeth. Her bleached hair was cut in a Mohawk, a safety pin pierced her earlobe, and the head of a fourpenny nail stuck out from the middle of her forehead.

Those cops are fools. You don't have to take their garbage, she bellowed. *Your life is a screwed-up mess because of Yuri Makov, and they're trying to make you take the rap. That's ridiculous! It's time for you to rip out their hearts!* Lila's Crazy Aunt snarled like a dog gone mad, and her safety pin quivered.

Her brief, furious outburst in Lila's mind was a clue to how tired she was of being civil when she didn't *feel* civil. She wanted to fight back against the men who had caused her grief—Yuri, those policemen, Reed, and even Adam Spencer for saddling her with Grace.

Admitting her anger forced Lila to take an unflinching look at another mental-family member, diametrically opposed to her Crazy Aunt and instilled in her by her mother, who had valued graciousness. That mental-family member was the Pleaser, the part of Lila who pranced around in a pink jumpsuit and lavender tennies, blowing bubbles and handing out roses on street corners. Eager for no one's feathers to be ruffled and awkward situations to be smoothed, she controlled social interactions by lubricating others' rusty feelings and ensuring that everyone was happy. She had taken Grace without protest and been polite to Rich and Joe. She soothed and cosseted people so they felt comfortable and liked her—a way to dodge conflict and keep relations on an even keel.

Maybe she had soothed and cosseted Yuri Makov. Shrinking back, Lila told herself that couldn't be. *But maybe it could.*

Lila retreated to the bedroom, where Grace was hiding under the bed. If she decided to wriggle out and bite Lila, she could run into the bathroom and lock the door.

Grace's leg was sticking out from under the bed skirt like an errant drumstick that had fallen from the ceiling. Her foot was bent back at an odd angle, and her paws' pads resembled a fedora hat's gray felt. Her nails curled down like commas written with a black, felt-tip pen; wisps of gold fur stuck out between her toes. If Lila had found Grace's leg on display in an art gallery, it would have interested, not threatened her.

Lila stepped over Grace's foot, and in the middle of the day she climbed into bed and pulled the covers over her ears. Now she and Grace were stacked on top of each other with a mattress between them, double-decker refugees from the world.

11

"Come on, Grace." Standing by the open back door, Lila pointed to the yard.

Under the claw-footed kitchen table, where Grace had been keeping her distance all morning, she blinked at Lila as if she were addressing her in Coptic.

"You need to go out." Lila pointed again. But after ordering Grace to eat and getting no response, Lila didn't expect the dog to carry out her wishes. "Look, I want to paint. I'm going to sit at that table. Nothing personal, but I refuse to get so close to your teeth."

Grace rested her chin on her paws, closed her eyes, and announced that she did not intend to interrupt her morning lounging.

Refusing to let her Pleaser bow to a dog, Lila snapped her fingers. "Out."

Probably tired of being nagged, Grace limped through the kitchen, out the back door, and down the steps toward the tree ferns. Lila was ready to start a watercolor study of the first painting in *Openings*, her oil series of windows, gates, and doors. She pulled a chair to the table and told herself to focus, as she'd never have been able to do if Grace's teeth had remained under the table.

Today's painting would be of clouds through Cristina's kitchen window. But unlike René Magritte's fluffy white clouds, the ones in the sky that morning were stormy and dark. Thor was up there, swinging his hammer and thirsting for a fight, as lightning and thunder gathered to express themselves. Maybe Lila was drawn to the clouds because they reflected her dark, hostile grudge against Yuri Makov.

She fumbled with a roll of masking tape and anchored corners of paper to her pine watercolor board. Then she sketched the kitchen window's rectangle with a soft-lead pencil that made a comforting scratching sound. She unscrewed the caps of crimson, black, and Prussian blue paint tubes and squeezed pea-size lumps of watercolor on her palette—and the kitchen filled with an earthy smell of hope. When she dipped her brush in a mason jar of water, the handle clinked against the glass, as cheerful as a ringing bell. She sloshed water on her palette, pushed in small amounts of paint, and mixed till she had swirls of interesting colors.

As Lila slid her brush's bristles across the rough watercolor paper and painted a delicate trail of purple wash, she slipped into the vast, exquisite world of creativity and listened for the urgings that would tell her where to put on color and what to leave alone. Her inner guide nudged her to layer on more purple and show the clouds' dark mood, but leave contrasting patches of the paper white to define shapes. Finally, after more dabbing and swishing with her brush, she spritzed on water to haze the clouds' edges, and a cool mist blew in her face.

For a more blurred image, she spritzed again—but she misted too much and her clouds puddled. She put down the bottle, wishing she'd not lost control. Painting was a safe place to let loose, and nothing terrible happened; yet you had to rein in the freedom, or you could wreck your work—as the puddles showed.

So many things could hijack a painting. As an artist, resistance had been Lila's constant companion. She'd first been up against it when her father tried to stop her mother from registering her in an after-school art program in junior high. He'd bought Lila encyclopedia software and a lacrosse stick and insisted, "Look up the Krebs cycle and the Weimar Republic. You're drawing in your room too much. Go outside more."

Lila looked up the Krebs cycle and the Weimar Republic, and she played lacrosse. But she painted and drew, and her father grumbled and stood in her way. When she was in high school, he explained why: Artists starved, and he wanted to protect her from crawling home, impoverished, with an empty rice bowl in her hands. Still determined to be a painter, though, she got an art degree in college—and he turned out to be right, because poverty became another obstacle.

In Lila's low-rent apartments, mice were her roommates, and she ate daily hot dogs—boiled, deep-fried, simmered with chili or cabbage, buried in a sweet-and-sour sauce, wrapped in crescent rolls and baked. Furnace heat in winter was Lila's distant dream; health insurance, a mirage. She got used to deprivation because she loved what she was doing. Still, her father disapproved.

When Lila started dating Reed, she painted a slightly surreal series, *Odd Juxtapositions*, which joined incongruities on canvas. She painted a 1968 Thunderbird parked on a lily pad, a watermelon slice zooming through the Milky Way, a diamond-scaled Chinese dragon curled up in a laundry basket. Next, she depicted flowers, and, true to odd juxtapositions, she painted cherry blossoms floating in a giant cup of tea.

By then Lila's paintings were selling in galleries but not earning enough to live on, so one hot summer afternoon she took her work to a Palo Alto fair. She spread a quilted blue bedspread on the dirt and set out her cherry blossom painting with others in the series. Gnats buzzed around her eyes as the sun beat down and filled her head with visions of lemonade, which she couldn't afford. In her pocket was $18.29, all the money she had in the world.

A woman in jeans and pointy-toed red sandals looked down at Lila's work, darkened by her shadow. "Could you make those flowers orange?"

"Orange?" Lila bent back her head to look into the woman's pie-shaped face.

"You know, like the fruit."

No one had ever asked Lila to compromise her work. "Why orange?"

"I have orange chairs in my dining room."

"Those flowers are cherry blossoms. They're pink."

"You could paint over them. If you don't have to start the painting from scratch, that would keep the price down, wouldn't it?"

Lila could relate to how a flat tire felt. She heard her father whisper in her ear, "Orange? Pink? What difference does the color make when your rent is two weeks late?" But she'd intended for the petals to be a pink flash of beauty before the tea muddied them brown. She'd wanted to capture a vision of grace that was vulnerable and easily ruined. Only pink could convey that; orange would be too harsh. She couldn't bring herself to change the color.

Lila pictured the woman's dining room, a meeting place of Sears and the Alhambra: Ornate, velvet-upholstered orange chairs would circle a matching ornate Moorish table. In its center, on dark walnut veneer, a wicker cornucopia would spill out shriveled squash left over from Thanksgiving—under a chandelier raining down plastic, sawtooth-edged teardrops.

Lila stood to her nearly six feet, muzzled her Pleaser, and frowned down at the woman, a moral pygmy who was baiting her to lower her standards and who didn't understand the importance of integrity in art. In her head, Lila heard her father urge his usual, "Don't be stubborn! Yield!" Nevertheless, she said with a blink of determination, "Maybe you could match your chairs with a sunset painting. This one isn't *about* orange flowers."

As the woman turned away, Lila shook hands with destitution. The woman's footsteps made puffs of dust, but Lila refused to let them cloud her spirit. The woman called back, "Forget it." But Lila would not forget it. She told herself that she would fight resistance harder to keep doing the work she loved, and she would wear the fight as a badge of courage. She would never go down in defeat.

Now at Cristina's table, Lila picked up a sponge and resolutely mopped the puddle to salvage her clouds.

Absorbed in painting, Lila barely noticed the raindrops pinging on the skylight. She went to the window to check on Grace, sitting by the ferns. Apparently, rain had been falling on her for a while, because her fur had matted and darkened to a dingy, sodden ash. Her red bandana, now maroon, had drooped around her neck.

Grace must have known that Lila was at the window, because she turned and looked at her. Though Grace was drenched, her eyes had the proud glimmer of spaniels in eighteenth-century portraits, sitting on velvet pillows beside ermine-dripping kings. Her eyes announced, *You may think I look like an urchin, but I can take any cold and wet the world has to give. Far be it from me to beg to come inside.*

Lila could never leave Grace shivering in the yard. If she'd been chained to a tree, she'd endured rain and cold. Though sharp-toothed and bipolar, she did not deserve to suffer more. Lila went to the door and called her. She climbed the stairs slowly, as if to let Lila know that bounding gratefully into the house was beneath her. When she came through the door, she brushed against Lila's legs and got wet gold fur on her black twill jeans. Grace walked through the kitchen and left muddy paw prints, like calling cards, across the floor.

"How does anybody live with a dog?" Lila moaned.

Grace bristled her eyebrows, which consisted of a few coarse hairs. With what looked like indifference at the trouble she'd caused, she lapped water from her bowl and ignored Lila wiping up the paw prints with a paper towel. Uncouth was what Grace was. An unmannered beast, like Adam Spencer's Irish wolfhounds.

Grace padded to her living room outpost, which was an oriental rug beside the sofa. She closed her eyes. The stage curtain dropped, and she geared up for a production of her one-act, solo performance piece: *The Napping Dog*. She began to snore. In minutes she was really into it, fully committed to a loud, blockbuster rendition of "Adenoids in Trouble." As she inhaled, she sounded like rusty machinery grinding in a Jean Tinguely sculpture. When she exhaled, her lips puffed out with a blast of air.

Grace often changed sleeping positions, each of which showed that moping was her art form. First, she curled into a ball and pressed her nose against her tail, as if she were trying to disguise herself as a dejected pumpkin. Next, she lay on her side with her legs stretched out in front of her so her body made a large, despondent *U*, perhaps for melancholy "underdog." Finally, she rolled onto her stomach and closed her eyes so she looked like she was contemplating life's sorrows. No matter how she sprawled, her body always seemed to say, *I am sad.*

Though she'd messed up the floor and Lila's jeans, Lila wished Grace had had a better life. But when Lila went back to painting, Grace's snores distracted her; then Lila realized she was breathing in sync with Grace, like they were connected, two parts of a whole. Unwilling to let Grace interfere not just with her art, but also with her breath, Lila stalled it to alter her rhythm and breathe to the beat of her own drum.

Lila could have blown a hair dryer on her clouds to get back to painting, but she did not want the loud, metallic whine to startle Grace awake and put her into bite mode like the mutt at Walmart. While Lila waited for the paper to dry, she went to the computer, surrounded by peace lilies in the den. With single-minded right-hand fingers, she typed "going postal" for a Google search.

One article began with Patrick Sherrill, who in 1986 shot and killed fourteen employees, wounded six others, and shot himself at a post office in Edmond, Oklahoma. Though a few workers had killed people in post offices before, Sherrill was the first to murder on such a grand scale. "Going postal" was coined for what he did.

Lila leaned toward the computer screen and stared at his photo. In a checked sports shirt, he smirked at her. He had jug-handle ears, his eyes made him look sneaky, and his eyebrows turned up at the outer ends like a villain's twirled mustache. Yet just like Yuri Makov's photo on TV, this picture did not hint at what Patrick Sherrill would become.

According to the article, when he was growing up, neighbor-hood kids had called him "Crazy Pat," and he'd started going bald in high school. He lived alone with his mother until her death, after which he was caught peeping into neighbors' windows and making obscene phone calls. Acquaintances labeled him an "odd duck" and believed he was lonely, but shy and gentle, the last person to kill anyone. That was exactly what Lila might have said about Yuri Makov before he shot ten people.

Sherrill's boss had reprimanded him for spraying Mace on a barking dog behind a locked fence, and then suspended him for leaving parcels and mail unattended and delivering five hundred letters late. On the day before Sherrill went postal, his supervisors also criticized him, and he had felt they were documenting his mistakes in order to build a case to fire him.

Sherrill was a classic example of what Dr. Leibowitz had described on the TV news. Had Yuri also been? If he'd been upset about his job, though, Rich and Joe would have discovered it and not come after Lila for an explanation.

With bitter resentment, she glared at Patrick Sherrill's rodent face. *What were you thinking? How could you have done something so awful?* If Sherrill had never existed, Yuri might not have thought of shooting people.

According to the article, soon after Sherrill shot his Oklahoma colleagues, other U.S. postal workers copied him. One hostile postal employee commandeered a light plane in Boston and shot up his workplace with an AK-47. Another employee wounded three and killed two, including himself, in a Dearborn, Michigan, post office on the very same day that still another postal worker killed his mother, then two colleagues in Dana, California. The article theorized that all those murders boiled down to rage.

Could rage have driven Yuri? Once again Lila asked herself, what was he so mad about? And what about her own anger at him for shooting *her*? If he were standing in front of her, would she be mad enough to kill him? Probably not, though she might not be sorry if someone else did.

She leaned back in her chair to put distance between herself and the photo of "Crazy Pat." What were you supposed to do with anger? You couldn't burn it because it was already fire. Burying it wouldn't do you any good, because it would just dig itself out one day and come after you, stronger than ever. If you tried to drown it, it would pull you below the water's surface too. There didn't seem to be any way to get rid of anger. For the rest of your life, you had to live with it, or work around it, or pretend it wasn't there.

Just then, something exploded like a cannon fired off the deck behind the house. Lila jerked with a start. *A gunshot. It had to be.* In a flash, Yuri Makov was running down the hall to kill her, and she was shaking like an aspen leaf in the wind.

Lila broke out in a sweat. Her heart beat like it was trying to crack her ribs. Her head was ringing. Doors slammed up and down the hall. People shrieked outside her cubicle. She smelled gun smoke. She had to run to protect herself.

When Lila looked for a place to hide, she saw Greg's den. His law books. Peace lilies. The wild-goose-chase quilt folded on the sofa. The wingback chair.

Lila mentally grabbed herself by the scruff of the neck and shook herself to bring back reason: *Get control of yourself. This was a flashback. You're safe. The explosion was thunder. The shrieks are coming from Grace.*

Wrenched out of sleep, Grace was making anguished, panicked cries. She ran into the living room, crouched down, and buried her face in her paws. Apparently finding no reassurance, she got to her feet but didn't seem to know in what direction to run—so, confused, she hobbled around the room in a circle. Then howling and whining as her crippled leg buckled under her, she zigzagged down the hall to Greg and Cristina's bedroom.

Lila knew firsthand how terror could pulverize you. Grace was as scared as Lila had been. Seeing Grace fall apart added to Lila's distress, yet it also made her feel sorry for the dog.

Since Grace could not be a threat when she was so afraid, Lila rushed into the bedroom and found her hiding under the bed. Lila kneeled on the floor and raised the bed skirt. In the darkness, Grace's haunted eyes glowed like hot coals. Quivers from deep inside her rolled out in waves. Her meaty breaths were jagged, and her ears were pressed back in fear.

"Grace, it's okay. It was thunder. It won't hurt you."

When more thunder rumbled in the distance, Grace's body

vibrated. Her whimpers seemed to be more than sound; they brushed Lila's face like cobwebs.

She kept repeating Grace's name. "You've heard thunder before, haven't you?" Of course Grace had—when chained to a tree. Storms must have terrified her. Lila had not realized that dogs could have such intense and primal feelings.

But comforting Grace exhausted Lila. So recently shaken herself, she had little strength to help the dog. Lila dropped the bed skirt, leaned against the wall, and closed her eyes. As the neediness in Grace's whimpers overwhelmed her, Lila identified with the vulnerability and anguish.

Grace and Lila stayed in the bedroom until the thunder stopped. Eventually, Grace crawled out from under the bed and looked at Lila with glazed eyes that asked, *Who* are *you? What are you doing here?*

"You poor thing. I'm so sorry. You're going to be okay," Lila whispered.

She, the former dog distruster, patted Grace's shoulder.

12

Lila started down the mountain road toward town. The forest smelled of redwood fronds and bay leaves. Fuzzy shafts of morning sunlight shone through the trees onto clover, ferns, and miner's lettuce and dappled them like camouflage. Around a bend, the road passed through a patch of brighter sun and thickets of blackberries and Scotch broom, behind which murderers could hide. Lila searched for them in each clump of vegetation. She peered into a passing car.

Three years ago when she and Cristina had been hiking in the Mill Valley woods, a man with a rifle had stepped out from behind a redwood trunk. His overalls were filthy, his waxy dreadlocks brushed his shoulders, and a lens in his glasses was cracked. He shoved his rifle toward Lila and Cristina and looked like he was a breath away from taking aim and shooting them. Cristina screamed. She and Lila tore down to the creek bed and ran home.

That was when Cristina told Lila about David Carpenter, the Trailside Killer. Nearly thirty years before, he'd sneaked up on three women and stabbed or shot them to death on Mount

Tamalpais, practically in Cristina's backyard. Eventually, he was caught and convicted of seven murders, and Lila would never forget him because he'd begged the police who arrested him, "Please, don't hurt me!" After what he'd done, who could forget such audacity and cowardice?

Because of him, Lila had had to convince herself this morning to walk to the store. If she hadn't needed yogurt and tofu, her staples, and if she'd had two working hands to drive a car, she'd never have set out by herself on a road where another human being passed by only every few minutes—and the human being could shoot her.

After breakfast, she'd Googled David Carpenter to make sure he wasn't preying on women anymore. Though he was a serial murderer, not a mass shooter, she hoped he might give her insight into Yuri Makov—and one sadistic brute might have something in common with another.

As Grace snored in the kitchen, Lila read an online article about Carpenter, who'd worked as a salesman, ship's purser, and printer. Though he'd been condemned to death, he was still alive and well in San Quentin, across the freeway just a few miles north of where Lila was sitting, she thought with a pang of fear.

In a mug shot, Carpenter, dressed in a coat and tie, looked like he was going to a dance instead of to prison. His nose was as wide as a gorilla's, and one eye seemed larger than the other, making him look off balance and disturbed. He was mostly bald, and probably to compensate he'd grown long sideburns, which curved toward his mouth. That was an unfortunate emphasis, since at his arraignment he'd stuttered so badly that he could hardly answer "yes" when the judge asked if his name was David Carpenter.

He'd stuttered since age seven, maybe because his alcoholic father had beaten him and his near-blind, tyrannical mother had forced him to take ballet. The article suggested their cruelty might also have caused his bed-wetting, torturing of animals, flying into rages, and retreating behind a carapace of shyness. At seventeen, he molested two of his cousins. Later, he drove a woman to the woods, straddled her, and told her he had a "funny quirk" she had to satisfy—and then attacked her with a hammer. Intending to rape another woman, he slammed his car into hers to get her to climb out—and stabbed her when she fought him.

He killed six people whom he found in isolated places like Mount Tamalpais, but he lured his last victim to him by promising to sell her a used car. He had been teaching her to use computer-typesetting machines at Econo Quick Print, where he worked, and it was rumored that he had driven her home several times and tried to date her.

Lila imagined his furtive glances at her, sitting with her legs tightly crossed in his passenger seat and feeling unease that she could not yet fully understand. He would radiate violent lust and plan how to prey on her, and he would stutter, red with shame, a dinner invitation. Maybe she would feel sorry for him, living with a speech impediment like that, yet she would recoil at his fat lips, which might be all over her if she accepted. Her "no, thanks" would make him seethe. Those two simple words would unleash death for her, an unintended consequence like the butterfly flapping its wings in Brazil and starting a hurricane.

When Lila studied Carpenter's photo, the computer screen seemed to darken, as if the computer itself were repulsed to bear such slime. She wondered if Yuri Makov had molested, raped, or attacked anybody before he shot her and her colleagues, and if he'd been a troubled child whose parents had abused him.

What kind of parents would raise a killer? What mistakes would they make? How much could you blame parents for what their children did, anyway? Weren't choice and free will part of the picture?

No matter what Yuri's parents might have done to him, Lila could not dismiss his violence as just their fault. Still, she pictured his father as a stern, flinty man—in a beaver hat and tall black boots—who might have learned torture methods working for the KGB. He might have hauled Yuri to the basement of their apartment building, where no one could hear him yell, and slid his belt out of his pants' loops and whipped Yuri till he bled. Maybe his father had said that Yuri's insolence gave him no choice but to beat him. Maybe when the leather crackled on Yuri's skin, his father smiled.

Yuri's mother may have been as sadistic as his father or too submissive to intervene. She could have encouraged the violence to discipline and strengthen Yuri. Lila imagined her in a babushka's kerchief, waiting in line for bread with Yuri, age six. As they inched toward the baker's counter, she would make him stand as still as a soldier at attention, allowed only to stamp his feet in the cold. He would not know till later that children could be happy and free; but then it would be too late, and the damage would be done. He would murder to calm his anger, as the Trailside Killer had. Yet that was no excuse.

The Mill Valley Library was a shingled wood-and-glass structure with a roof that looked like a gently sloping wing. Since Cristina had canceled her *Herald* subscription, Lila stopped there and scanned the previous week's newspapers for going-postal stories. Finding nothing of interest, she went back to the street. She passed a church with arched windows, and houses behind tall fences, one of which had wooden frogs nailed to the top of each post.

On Mill Valley's main street, cherry trees were planted along the sidewalks, and redwoods grew in clumps around the town square. The windshields of cars, parked at an angle, reflected the sun. A bus chugged by. Most important for Lila, people were milling around.

Though she now knew you could never tell what psychopaths might be sharing your street and you couldn't count on safety in numbers, at least there was comfort in them. If someone shot her, she wouldn't die alone, as she would when walking down the mountain. She breathed more easily.

Lila passed geeks in a computer café, aging hippies in a head shop, and well-coifed women knitting around a table in a yarn store. A man in a business suit and wing-tip shoes climbed out of a Jaguar as a Buddhist monk in a magenta robe and Reeboks walked by beating a drum. Ahead of Lila, a missionary handed out brochures on Darfur, and a gray-haired woman in a tennis skirt loaded bags of kitty litter into a Volkswagen bus, whose license plates said, "Cat Power."

At the Wayfarer's Market, which was crowded with people, Lila bought yogurt and tofu, and to celebrate her victory at venturing out alone, a gourmet black bean sauce—all she could carry home, one-handed. Then she went to browse in the Second Time Around Shop.

It smelled of aging furniture polish, crumbling paper, and milk that someone had soaked china plates in to hide craze. The light was dim, and dust motes traveled through the air. The manager was eating lunch behind a tattered red velvet curtain. He clinked a fork on porcelain and tuned a radio to NPR.

In the housewares section, Lila's hope always abounded because you never knew what you might find. Her breathing quickened with the joy of the chase, like a hunter galloping on horseback behind a beagle pack. Once for a dollar she'd bought a spoon and polished it—and discovered "sterling" stamped on the back. She paid $18.95 for a tiny engraving of the Greek Pythius, galloping on horseback; at home with a magnifying glass, she read that the artist was the famous English painter William Turner.

The Second Time Around Shop had a thrift store's usual baskets and mismatched dishes and glasses, one of which was cranberry red and would have made an interesting vase, but it was chipped. The only "painting" was a landscape print, on which someone had brushed varnish to try and fool buyers into thinking the varnish strokes were oils and the painting was original. Lila found rusty bread and yogurt makers; a bin of sheet-and-pillowcase sets held together with masking tape; and a sign with GRANDMA'S KITCHEN carved in wood.

Nothing beckoned to her to buy it. Like a disappointed fox hunter, she turned her horse around and called the beagles home.

When Lila got halfway up the hill, she sat on a curb and rested. Her fatigue reminded her that she had far to go to get her body strong, and her chronic fear of attack said that her post-traumatic stress was alive and well. But after rarely leaving Cristina's house for weeks, being out among people had buoyed her spirit, and her cast seemed to weigh less than before. The sun felt like it was shining straight into her brain and brightening the dark, threatened corners. Being away from Grace for a couple of hours felt like she'd set down a burden.

When she got up and moved on, her footsteps were lighter. But the closer she got to home—and to Grace—the more her feet shuffled. Grace had been with Lila for almost two weeks. Lately, she'd put on a little weight, and someone would be more likely to adopt her. But not once had Adam reported on his search for her home. As far as Lila knew, he wasn't searching at all, and even her Pleaser would say he was inconsiderate. Lila stared at the pavement's cracks. If they'd been Rorschach inkblots, she'd have seen trouble in them.

She didn't need more trouble. She needed to take charge. If Adam wasn't going to call her, she'd call him when she got home.

13

As Grace pressed her nose against the front door's sidelight, the wood around the window framed her face so it looked like a portrait of sorrow. She could have been standing in line at the pharmacy for her prescription of Zoloft. Mourning crepe would have been more fitting around her neck than her red bandana was.

But when Lila started down the path toward the door, Grace saw her coming and brightened. Grace got to her feet as if she were president of the Welcome Wagon, and her breath fogged the glass pane by the doorknob. When Lila unlocked the door, Grace moved only enough to let Lila step into the entry. Since she'd comforted Grace out of her panic attack from the thunder, Lila had clearly risen a notch in Grace's estimation. So she no longer kept a distance.

"How's it going, Grace?" Lila no longer kept a distance, either, and she and Grace had been getting along well enough to pass the time of day.

Grace's panting said, *I'm fine!* Her eyes shone as brightly as when she'd run to Adam. She padded behind Lila to the kitchen and watched her put away the groceries.

Lila could have sworn that Grace's slouch had grown less droopy than before. Her back and shoulders seemed straighter; someone might have tied an invisible rope around her middle, pulled it up, and taken out her slump. She also held her plumed tail out straight and swished it back and forth, as if she were a slave fanning an imaginary sultan lying on the floor.

Lila couldn't be sure, but the slow swish of Grace's plume might have been a wag of pleasure that Lila was home. Though she was glad Grace was improving, Lila felt burdened all over again because Grace might want more from her than she was able to give.

When Lila went to the bedroom, Grace followed and plopped down next to the dresser so her bottom and front legs made a small tripod that was reflected in the TV screen. A sliver of her tongue hung below her charcoal-lump nose. She panted slightly, like she was asking about Lila's trip to the store. If Lila were a dog, Grace would have expected her to pant a reply.

As Lila shrugged out of her fuchsia jacket, a stab of pain traveled down her injured arm. "*Ow!*"

Grace shrank back like she'd felt the pain too.

"I can't help it. This awful man shot me, and my arm still hurts." What was Lila doing telling her troubles to a dog?

Grace blinked and cocked her head with rapt attention; she looked like she was listening with all her heart. If Grace had been a person, Lila would have believed she was concerned. But surely dogs couldn't feel empathy or pick up people's feelings.

After lunch Grace's eyes followed Lila as she pulled the sheets off the bed with her right hand. She unfolded a clean bottom contour sheet and tossed it over the mattress the best she could, then wrestled, one-handed, with the sheet's lower right corner. When she got it in place, she tackled the lower left corner, but the sheet's right one snapped off. No matter how hard Lila tugged, her injury prevented her from fitting the lower corners at the same time.

Finally, struggling till her forehead was sweaty, she worked a safety pin through the sheet and mattress cover to hold the lower left corner, and then she yanked the second into place and pinned it, too. Though she pulled till her right hand trembled with fatigue, she couldn't get the sheet over the upper left corner—and she had to admit to herself that fitting the upper right one would also be impossible. For now she was going to have to sleep in a rumpled, sheetless bed.

Flopping onto it, she told herself that having no sheets wouldn't kill her, but it would remind her how gravely she'd been hurt and how limited she was. Frustration sidled up to her, as if it planned to be a permanent guest at her table and there wouldn't be room for anyone but the two of them. With her good hand, Lila squeezed part of the sheet into a frustrated ball.

When Grace limped over and pressed her body against the mattress, Lila was about to shoo her away so she wouldn't get fur in the bed. She pressed her cheek against Lila's hand so the silky tufts of fur above her ear brushed Lila's wrist. To her surprise, the softness felt soothing; she released the sheet and stroked Grace's fur with the backs of her fingers.

Perhaps Lila had been wrong about empathy in dogs. Grace seemed to have come to console her, just as Lila had consoled Grace during the storm. If she couldn't hug or speak, she might be comforting the best she could by presenting a part of herself for Lila to hold. Astonished that Grace might be offering solace, Lila stroked Grace's ear again.

Grace rested her chin on the mattress and looked at Lila with eyes that said, *I care! I really, really care!* But slowly they got a troubled slant, as if she were thinking about something that hurt her.

Soon Grace's eyes gave Lila a gut-wrenching speech that no one would need words to understand. Grace said that she sympathized with Lila's distress. And even though Grace had lately been putting on a chipper front, deep down she was distressed herself, and she needed someone as much as Lila did to encourage her out of sorrow. Grace had had a miserable time at her cruel, sick owner's hands, and she was desperate to be with someone who would love her.

Can't you be that person? Won't you give me the home I want more than anything in the world? Grace's sad eyes begged. *Please, please, I'll do anything if you'll let me be your dog. Please, love me.*

Grace's eyes were moist with longing. She could have been a street urchin, looking in the window of a candy store and clutching a penny that could not buy a single chocolate-covered cherry wrapped in gold foil. Lila closed her own eyes to cut off the emotions pouring out of Grace, but her neediness was too compelling to escape.

Lila's sympathy urged her to help Grace. The dog wasn't bad; Lila hadn't minded being around her nearly as much as she'd expected. But she couldn't possibly keep Grace when she couldn't even change her sheets. Lila still had months to go before her life's dust would settle and she'd be herself again. She didn't have the time or strength for Grace, who was a constant distraction when Lila needed to focus on healing.

For both their sakes, Grace and Lila needed to get on with their lives and go their separate ways. The sooner Adam found Grace a home with people who'd love her, the better. Lila removed her hand from Grace's shoulder and sat up in her rumpled bed. She sighed. "I care about you, but I have to do *something*. It's time."

* * *

"Adam?" Cristina's contact list was on the desk next to the phone. Grace was at Lila's feet. "This is Lila Elliot."

"I recognized your voice."

He sounded welcoming. An artful ploy to coax Lila into keeping Grace for another month?

"How are you and Grace getting along?" he asked.

"She's growing too attached."

Adam ignored the negativity implied in "too" and said, "I told you she was a loving dog."

"She is," Lila conceded and set her hand on Grace's head, a natural resting place. "I've been waiting for you to call. Isn't it time for you to come and get her?"

Adam's pause told Lila that his engineer's brain was outlining ways to dodge her request. "I can't get Grace now."

"You've quit looking for her home?!"

"No. I'm asking around all the time."

"Is asking around enough? Can't you do more? What about the posters?"

Lila's Pleaser urged, *Don't be pushy!*

"You don't have to get upset," Adam said.

"You told me Grace would be gone in a few days, and it's been two weeks. Don't you think you're being thoughtless?"

Lila's Pleaser hopped around and shrieked, *Don't talk like that, for heaven's sake. Your mother taught you to be gracious.*

If Lila had listened to her Pleaser, she would have clamped her hand over her mouth and told Adam that something must have gotten into her; she was never so blunt. But her Crazy Aunt jumped out of her Ford Explorer and snarled, *You have a right to speak your mind! I'll smack you in the chops if you apologize to him.*

"It can't be so hard to feed a gentle dog," Adam said. In his words, again lurked judgment.

"Feeding Grace is only part of it. Having her around is difficult," Lila said. "I'm scared I'll trip over her. I got shot. I can't do half of what I used to."

"I remember. The broken arm."

The broken arm? "It's not a simple broken arm." *You could be more understanding.*

"I know you've had a hard time," Adam said.

Lila would not allow that concession to sway her. "Before you left Grace with me, you never asked if I could manage a dog."

"I thought your injury might be too personal for me to mention. I didn't want to pry."

"You could have asked. You could have made sure Grace wouldn't be too much for me."

Adam exhaled, loud enough for Lila to hear. "Actually, I thought Grace could help you heal."

"Heal?!"

"By keeping you company. Being there for you."

"It's been the other way around," Lila said.

But, then, she wasn't being honest. Grace had just tried to comfort her when she was distressed about her sheets. And Grace had kept her company and tempered her distrust of dogs. Lila didn't know what else to say to Adam, and suddenly she felt too tired to argue. Walking to town that morning had sapped her strength. She wanted off the phone.

Grace's chin rested on Lila's toes as if claiming her as her very own. Grace's closed eyes gave her a proprietary look, which notified anyone else who might want Lila that Grace had gotten title to her first, and negotiation for her was impossible.

14

Lila's new physical therapist, Betsy McKibbon, had an encouraging, gentle manner, and her smile exposed a tiny gap between her front teeth. Her eyes were the blue of an autumn sky on a cloudless day. Silver dolphins cavorted at her earlobes just below salt-and-pepper curls, which rested, flat and soft, against her plump cheeks.

In her consulting room, Betsy settled on a metal stool opposite Lila, who was sitting on a padded table, and Betsy's knees protruded under her long purple skirt. A pair of lavender-framed bifocals hung from a silver chain around her neck. Her wide hips and large breasts made her look like she'd birthed and nursed eight children.

"I've got to tell you. You're the first person I've treated who's been shot," Betsy said. "It must have been traumatic. You can't snap your fingers and get over something like that."

Her empathy contained a kindly hug that put Lila at ease. "It's been hard," she admitted.

"I can imagine."

Betsy put on her bifocals and flipped through the records

from Dr. Lovell, who had removed Lila's cast the day before. When he'd sent her to Betsy, he said she was slightly unconventional, but good with distressed patients—Lila's category, he inferred.

As Betsy glanced through Dr. Lovell's notes, Lila looked around the room. The carpet, walls, and curtains were violet; in a tabletop fountain, water splashed from a copper fish's mouth onto an amethyst geode. Feathers and peace pipes hung on the walls beside papier-mâché angels with heavy Frida Kahlo eyebrows. On a rolltop desk in the corner was a framed photograph of towheaded boys jumping on a trampoline —probably Betsy's grandchildren.

From the desk, she pulled out a printed form with the outline of a body, the arms and legs extended like Leonardo's Vitruvian Man. She unscrewed the cap of her purple fountain pen. "Okay, so tell me . . . what happened? How did the bullet hit you?"

When Lila explained its path from her breast into her arm, Betsy marked an *X* on the body for each wound. "What about pain?"

"I still hurt."

"Where exactly?"

Lila pointed to places on her shoulder and arm, and Betsy noted them on the drawing of the body too.

"What kind of pain? Burning? Aching? Throbbing?" she asked.

"Aching. It comes and goes."

"Any particular movements that bring it on?"

"Mostly reaching up and forward."

"On a scale of one to ten, how would you rate the pain today if ten's the worst?"

Lila thought for a moment. "Maybe seven. Mostly when I move my arm."

As Betsy wrote "seven" under the body's left foot, she said, "We're going to get that number down to zero."

Lila wanted to believe her, but faith eluded her, especially when Betsy examined Lila's arm, which was pasty and shriveled. As Betsy moved it back and forth at the elbow, though, she acted like she'd seen plenty of injured arms and Lila's wasn't unusual. Betsy bent down and looked closely at the wound; healed like the one on Lila's breast, it resembled an angry crimson centipede.

Betsy ran her fingertip over its legs, where stitches had been. "You've got 'proud flesh.' The name comes from the swelling."

"Maybe my flesh is swollen and red because it's still mad at the bullet."

Betsy chuckled. "And you're still mad at the man who shot you?"

"I hate him. I can't help it."

"That's not helpful for your spirit. The only person your anger hurts is you." When Betsy smiled, she exposed the gap between her teeth again. "You can calm down the scars with vitamin E oil. Skin is very forgiving."

Like Lila should also be, she figured Betsy was implying. But that would be impossible. You couldn't walk away and forget someone who'd tried to kill you.

As Lila fidgeted, the papier-mâché angels on the wall looked like they were frowning at her.

Betsy left the room while Lila took off her shirt and bra and climbed between the padded table's sheets, which were striped lavender and white. When Betsy returned, she draped a pillow of warm flax seeds around Lila's neck—a delicious comfort. Next, Betsy put gel on Lila's injured arm and ran the flat metal surface of an ultrasound head over her sore, tight muscles to reduce pain, though Lila guessed that Betsy was talking long term, because Lila couldn't tell a difference. Finally, Betsy rubbed cream on her hands. As the smell of lavender filled the room, she gently kneaded Lila's flesh from shoulder to elbow, to reduce swelling.

The massage made her as limp as gauze. More relaxed than she had felt in months, she closed her eyes and listened to the water from the fish's mouth splash on the geode. Outside, a motorcycle roared down Mill Valley's main street. But Lila ignored it because she was soaking up the peace in Betsy's office.

When she stretched out Lila's arm as straight as she could coax it, it stayed stiff and partly bent. But it tingled, as if Betsy had opened a dam in Lila's veins and persuaded new blood to flow through. Betsy put more cream on her hands, reached under Lila's shoulders, and massaged with heavy sweeps. Over the years Betsy's powerful hands had surely removed pain from legions of needy people.

Lila pictured her slapping reins on oxen and rumbling across the prairie in a Conestoga wagon. Strong and sturdy, she would not flinch at snakes or blink at dust; she would bake huckleberry pies on campfires. Stability also seemed lodged in her touch, and it made Lila feel as close to safe as she'd felt since getting shot. Betsy was like Mother Hubbard, peering at the heavens through a shoelace eye and reassuring Lila, one of her many children.

Betsy gently pressed her fingers against Lila's shoulder blades. "You've got a lot of tension here. Your shoulders are still cringing from terror."

"I can't help it."

"It's involuntary." Betsy pushed them down as if she were encouraging them into a straight, more trusting line. "Our bodies show what we're feeling in the present, but they also hold emotions from the past. I'd say you're carrying a lot of stress."

"I can't get rid of it."

"Sometimes it's difficult." Betsy kneaded Lila's shoulders again. "When my husband died, I went around hunched down with grief. It took me a couple of years to push my shoulders back and stand up straight again."

"How did you get yourself to do that?"

"Thinking things through. Seeing my life was still good. Even though I was alone, I had lots to be thankful for."

"I have things to be thankful for, but I've got reason to be mad, too," Lila said.

As the muffled voices of passersby filtered through the window, she told Betsy about her flashbacks and nightmares. For good measure, she threw in Reed and Adam and Grace.

"Sometimes challenges come in groups," Betsy said.

Lila didn't see challenges. She saw Yuri's violence, Reed's disloyalty, and Adam's inconsideration. "All I want is to get my life back in control."

Betsy's laugh came from her belly. "You think we can control our lives?"

"We can clean up messes. We can straighten out things."

"Oh, honey. Seems to me it's more important to accept them. Then they usually straighten out themselves." Betsy pushed Lila's shoulders down again and gently put them in their place. "The best way to fix your life is to go after what makes you happy. Forget the rest. I tell everyone who comes in here that joy is the greatest healer."

"Uh-huh," Lila said. But where were you supposed to find joy after a maniac shot you?

Betsy moved to the side of the table and massaged Lila's arm again, then pulled it up and forward. "Look! Your range of motion is already better."

Lila had to admit she was right.

"Your life is going to be better too. This injury is going to be the best thing that ever happened to you."

Before Lila could say, "That's crazy!" her Pleaser leapt in and gagged her.

Betsy covered Lila with a Navajo blanket that had brightly colored stripes of triangular trees, stylized eagles, and zigzags of lightning. Betsy said they symbolized Native Americans' values: The trees meant growth; the eagles, independence; and the lightning, power. The heavy wool weighed down on Lila and smelled of mysterious sheep.

"I want you to lie here for a few minutes and think about your injuries. When your body got hurt, so did your mind and spirit," Betsy said. "Those three parts of you are related, and one influences the others. I can help put your body back together, but only you can heal the rest of you."

"How am I supposed to do that?"

"You could start by not seeing yourself as a victim."

"I am a victim. It's a fact. I got shot."

"There's more than one way to look at things. Your job now is to get your power back."

Power, as in the blanket's lightning, Lila guessed.

Betsy adjusted the venetian blinds so the room got as shadowy as a church, and she left and shut the door behind her. As Lila closed her eyes, the American flag in Mill Valley's town square snapped in the wind so wire clinked against the pole. She asked herself: *How do you stop seeing yourself as a victim when you are one?*

A movie started playing on the screen behind Lila's eyelids. It starred Mrs. Podolsky, her favorite high school English teacher, who was all angles and no curves; chopsticks through her bun kept even it from looking rounded. She'd just had the class read *The Diary of Anne Frank*, and she asked what they thought of it.

Billy Axelrod, who always acted like he thought he was so smart, spouted off, "Anne seems like a goody-goody."

Mrs. Podolsky narrowed her eyes at Billy, like he was Santa Fe High School's biggest twit. She rested her palms on her desk as if she were about to leap over it and squash Billy as flat as plywood. "Anne was heroic. She could have simpered and hated up there in that Amsterdam attic, but she chose to be brave and kind," she said.

Betsy would have wanted Lila to raise her hand in that class and side with Mrs. Podolsky. Betsy would have urged Lila to add that Anne Frank's stomach must have growled from hunger, and fear crept into her thoughts. But though the Nazis harmed her body and mind, she refused to let them victimize her spirit or diminish the quiet power of her courage.

Lila guessed everyone could make that choice to keep their power for themselves. Ultimately, not even Yuri Makov could take away her inner strength. Still, the only way she could feel like she had it back was to stand up to him—but she couldn't shake a fist and demand an apology from a dead man.

Somehow Lila would have to confront him in her mind. But to do that, she needed answers. Since her Internet search had not yielded much fruit, Lila decided to go straight to the horse's mouth.

15

The horse whose mouth Lila went to was Agnes Spitzmeier, Mr. Weatherby's stern and stocky office manager, a long-toothed Clydesdale of a woman and a former Marine recruiter. Lila offered to take the bus to San Francisco to talk with her, but she insisted on coming to Cristina's house that very afternoon. "The least I can do," Agnes said on the phone several times. She seemed to want to make up to Lila for getting shot when she herself had not been hurt.

Lila was relieved not to go to the office. Before, it had been a cheerful place, but now it would represent tragedy. The bullet marks would be patched in the walls, the broken windows replaced, the bloodstains washed out of the carpets. But the smell of disaster would linger, and the karma would be black. Lila wanted never to face that office again. By coming to Cristina's, Agnes was doing Lila a favor.

Agnes arrived in a tailored navy suit, a white shirt with a button-down collar, and sensible flats with rubber soles and a spit-and-polish shine. Too much hairspray made her hair look like a motorcycle helmet. She carried a boxy briefcase with snaps that twanged when opened. It was probably her purse.

When Grace set eyes on Agnes through the front door's glass, she barked the first barks Lila had heard from her—ferocious and determined protests to run off Agnes. Lila got Grace to calm down. But as Agnes stepped into the entry, Grace refused to resume her role as a Walmart greeter. The fur on her back bristled like an agitated skunk's stripe, and she stiffened her legs and glared.

"Be polite, Grace." Lila gave Agnes an apologetic look. "I'm dog-sitting. She's not mine. She's never been protective before."

"Looks like a nice dog." Agnes's voice tended more toward booming than conversing. Fearless, she extended a beefy hand for Grace to sniff.

Grace was more inclined to sniff Agnes's ample thighs and bottom, as if she were a fire hydrant. Grace could have been patting down Agnes to decide if she could board a plane into the house.

When Lila tried to push Grace back, she wouldn't budge. "I'm sorry."

"No problem. I grew up on a farm with four dogs a lot more aggressive than she'll ever be." Agnes stooped down and gave Grace an affectionate chuck on the chin.

Grace wanted none of Agnes's chucking. Clearly repulsed, Grace stepped back so Agnes couldn't chuck her again, then glowered as Agnes followed Lila into the kitchen, where she poured boiling water over teabags in white mugs.

While Lila and Agnes waited for the tea to steep, they mentioned the freeway traffic and spring weather. Agnes filled her in on how people at the office were faring. Grace sat under the kitchen table and beamed huffiness with her eyes, which said in no uncertain terms, *I'm not going to let you be Lila's entire focus this afternoon, you unwelcome slug. Don't forget for a minute that she's mine.*

Ignoring Grace, Lila put cream and sugar in Agnes's tea and handed it to her. They carried their mugs to the living room and set them on the coffee table, under which Grace immediately crawled. Through the table's glass top, she frowned at Agnes with resentment and watched her settle her heft onto the sofa adjacent to Lila's chair.

"She's sweet," Agnes said.

As if on cue, Grace groaned her loudest, most disdainful groan and shut her eyes.

Agnes lifted her briefcase to her lap, twanged the snaps, and got out a mechanical pencil and yellow pad. She looked like she was about to take notes. "Okay, you wanted to talk about Makov."

"I wanted to know if you had any idea why he shot everybody."

"Why do you care?"

"I want to make sense of what happened. I need to get over it."

"Why come to me?"

"You hired him. I thought you might have known him better than anybody in the office did."

"That's not true. Nobody knew him very well, at least not that I know of."

Agnes didn't seem to want to discuss Yuri, though she'd come to Cristina's house to do exactly that. Something was wrong. Lila asked, "Is there any reason we shouldn't talk about the shooting?"

"No. Not unless you're planning to sue."

"I'm *not*." Lila's cheeks burned. She felt as insulted as Grace had when Agnes had chucked her chin. "I'm not after money, if that's what you mean. That was the last thing on my mind."

Agnes gave Lila a long, hard look and apparently decided she was telling the truth. Agnes's conciliatory smile revealed horse teeth. She took a swallow of tea and clunked her mug on the table. The noise rousted Grace, and her eyelids sprang open.

She clambered out from under the coffee table, plopped in front of Lila, and smacked her paw on her knee; clearly, she wanted Agnes to know that Lila was hers and not to be shared. When Lila brushed her paw away, she returned it and, whining, dug her nails into Lila's skin. Grace's eyes had lost their anti-Agnes cast and now seemed to plead, *Love me! Please, please! Pay attention to me!*

When will Adam Spencer come and get her? Lila's resentment toward him filled her mind. No matter how understandably needy, Grace was annoying and out of control. "I'll put her away, or we'll never get a chance to talk," Lila said.

When she grabbed Grace's bandana, the dog whimpered, but Lila led her to the kitchen anyway. Lila closed the door, behind which Grace groaned, like she was auditioning for the melodrama *The Perils of an Abject Dog.*

Ignoring Grace took concentrated effort, but Lila eased back into her chair. "Sorry."

Agnes gulped her tea as if Grace had never interrupted them. "Mr. Weatherby feels horrible about what Makov did," she said. "What happened wasn't Mr. Weatherby's fault. Mine, either. We treated Makov better than he deserved. It's all documented. We can't be responsible for somebody going crazy."

"Why did he go crazy? That's all I want to know. Did anybody come to an official answer?"

"The police report was inconclusive. Maybe a shrink might have an idea, but I don't know what it would be."

"What about you? What do you think?"

"He was screwed up. Simple as that."

"How?" Lila asked as Grace whined behind the kitchen door—and Lila wanted to bind her muzzle shut with baling wire.

As Agnes crossed one knee over the other, her stockings strained against her flesh. She shook her head with obvious dismay at Yuri Makov, and her jowl quivered. "Lemme tell you, his references were great. When I interviewed him, he was polite. He seemed, well . . . prissy or something. I thought he'd fuss over the office."

On her stout fingers, Agnes counted examples of the subtle, civilizing changes Yuri had made at the firm in his first weeks on the job: He'd straightened photographs on walls, set wastebaskets out of sight behind desks, left a bowl of peach potpourri in the women's restroom, fertilized the hall's schefflera plant so it quit shedding leaves.

"I thought he was going to work out great, but a month or two after you started working for us, he slacked off," she said. "He left toothpaste on the bathroom mirrors and ham scraps in the staff lounge sink's drain. His idea of a vacuumed hall was a clean path down the middle and filth around the baseboards. The morning I found Mr. Weatherby's trash can overflowing, I decided Makov was being a slob on purpose. Angry about something. Passive-aggressive. Know what I mean?"

Lila nodded that she understood. "Do you think he wanted a promotion? Or a raise?"

"No, his problem was bigger than that. After the trash can, Mr. Weatherby told me to give him another chance, so I did." Agnes's frown made clear she'd gone along to get along with Mr. Weatherby, but she'd thought that *semper fi* was not in Yuri's character.

"He showed up one day and announced 'I not wet clean.' He was too good for toilets and sinks. Can you believe that?" she boomed. "I offered to get him rubber gloves and a plastic apron, but that wasn't good enough. I told him we weren't the Soviet Union, and he wasn't going to get a free ride here."

"Did that make him mad?"

"He was already mad. Something was bugging him."

"What was it?"

"Who knows?" Agnes shrugged. "You probably noticed how bad things got toward the end. The bathrooms were like nasty porta-potties at construction sites. Never saw such a mess in an office."

Agnes explained that on the afternoon she hired a janitor to replace Yuri, she waited for him to arrive for work so she could fire him. Instead of showing up at three, as contracted, he stepped off the elevator at nearly six, wearing a dark suit, a tie patterned with fallen red leaves, and a rose boutonniere—"of all the damned things." Agnes rolled her eyes and mocked him. "He was holding a symphony program. He'd gone to some matinee.

"Thank God he didn't make a scene when I fired him. He got back on the elevator and left," she said. "The next day I told Mr. Weatherby I'd send Makov's last paycheck in the mail, and he'd never come to the office again. The impudent jackass. He thought he was better than the rest of us and the world owed him a living."

"If he didn't want the job, getting fired couldn't have made him shoot a bunch of people, could it?" Lila asked.

"He had a damned chip on his shoulder. If you'd known him, you'd have seen it."

"I knew him. Sort of." Lila's stomach fluttered slightly as if goldfish were swimming around and brushing her insides with their fins.

"How'd you know him?" Agnes asked.

"Oh, the same as everybody. I saw him around."

"What did you think of him?"

"He seemed needy and shy."

Agnes narrowed her eyes in what looked like suspicion. "How'd you ever come to that?"

Lila squirmed and searched for an answer.

One afternoon Yuri had come to her office in a tweed jacket

with black suede patches on the elbows. He had smiled at her as if he liked what he saw, and that gave a small boost to her confidence, which Reed and his girlfriend had sullied.

Yuri dug lined yellow paper out of Lila's wastebasket. "Beautiful . . . uh . . . shirt," he said, nodding at her old Lands' End pea-green turtleneck.

"Thanks," she said.

He pointed at Lila's abstract painting, leaning against the wall. "You do?"

"Yes, a few years ago."

"Beautiful." He gathered the last yellow paper from the wastebasket as if he were picking a daffodil. "I." He pointed proudly to his chest. "Moscow University . . . architecture . . . study."

"Good! Good for you!" Lila felt sorry for his talk in clumps and halts. He was obviously embarrassed about his English. Wanting to take control of the awkward situation, her Pleaser stepped in and beamed at him. "Maybe you can go to school and be an architect here."

He nodded like he needed time to process her words. "Yes," he finally said.

"I'm sure there are good architecture programs in San Francisco." Lila spoke extra-slowly so he could understand.

"I . . . uh, hope." He pronounced it "hop." He was backing toward the open doorway. Her wastebasket's papers were folded in his long, sensitive fingers.

"Thanks for taking my trash," Lila said, like he'd just done her a great favor. *Would my Pleaser just shut up?*

"I . . . here . . . clean?"

"It's okay. It's clean enough."

"Tonight . . . I good floor . . . for you."

"Oh, just your average vacuuming would be fine." Lila's Pleaser smiled too broadly.

"Lady nice . . . you." He nodded formally and backed into

his dustbin, which clanged against the wall. His face clouded with shame.

Lila flinched for him. "You're doing a good job. Thank you so much!" She said it extra-loud and with a little too much gratitude.

How could Lila describe to Agnes her initial sympathy for Yuri? What could she say about his insecurity and eagerness to connect? Their encounter had meant nothing to him, or so she told herself. *It couldn't have mattered, could it?* All she'd meant was to be polite.

Lila tugged her shirt's cuff, as if at least she could control her sleeve. "I don't know why I got the impression Yuri was shy. I guess it's just that he was quiet. I never picked up he'd kill anybody."

"None of us did. Nobody saw it coming. The police said experts find the warning signs almost impossible to read." Agnes took another gulp of tea. "You don't know how many nights I've been in bed asking myself what if I'd never hired him. Or fired him."

As Lila shrank back into her chair, she played her own secret round of the What-If Game. What if her Pleaser had been cruising the Caribbean when Yuri showed up in her office that day? What if she'd not felt sorry for him? What if she'd been a hunchbacked, knock-kneed gnome whom he never would have noticed?

"If Yuri was mad about getting fired, he'd have gone after just you and maybe Mr. Weatherby, not the rest of us," Lila said.

"He could have been mad at me and Mr. Weatherby and gone after the rest of you to pay us back." Agnes pressed her knuckles on her eyebrows as if she were trying to push all the tragedy out the back of her head. "I keep going over every time I talked to him and looking for something I should have seen.

Getting fired must have frosted him, but we don't know if that set him off. Nobody knows what it was."

When Lila swallowed, the muscles in her throat were tight. The neatly wrapped package of answers she'd hoped for from Agnes receded into the distance, out of reach.

16

Lila heated leftover split pea soup for supper and set Grace's kibble and chicken on the floor. When she didn't cross the kitchen to eat, Lila thought perhaps she wasn't hungry. Lila pushed her paints aside on the kitchen table and sat down for her soup. But she wasn't hungry, either, because her mind was on Yuri Makov.

Agnes had raised two important questions without providing answers: Why had Yuri shot people after being fired from a job he didn't want? And what had been troubling him before Agnes fired him? When Lila so badly wanted answers, not getting them was hard. A fog of unknowing darkened her thoughts as she twirled her soup spoon between her thumb and index finger.

She swallowed some soup and noticed that Grace was staring at the kitchen floor's heater vent like she expected stray cats to leap out. That was odd. Lila got up from the table and looked through the metal grille to see what was so absorbing, but all she saw was darkness. Grace glanced at her, then returned her focus to the depths below the floor.

Lila had almost forgiven her for being a pest with Agnes. Grace probably couldn't help being possessive after never having a decent home. If someone visited again before Adam came and got her, Lila would lock her in the bedroom. But he'd better come soon, because every day Grace seemed to feel less like a foster dog and more like a permanent resident.

She kept staring into the heater vent while Lila finished her soup and carried her bowl to the sink. She was relieved that Grace was taking a break from her new clinging-vine impersonation and seemed to have found something besides Lila to be interested in. She sloshed soap and water into the soup pot and scraped a spoon against the bottom's crust. While Lila was cleaning the sink with a sponge, Grace got up and left the room.

The paintbrush she'd set to dry on a paper towel near the dish rack was gone. All that remained was a pale gray tinge on a pucker in the paper, where the wet bristles had been resting. Needing the brush to paint that night, Lila searched the counter. Nothing. Perhaps she'd knocked the brush to the floor when making dinner, she thought. She got on her knees and looked around the sink, but there was no brush—and she began to worry.

At Lila's high school graduation, her mother had given her the brush in an antique Chinese box. The brush was from France, made of Russian sable bristles attached to a smooth oak handle that felt like a beloved friend's hand. When Lila shook water from the bristles, they returned to a perfect point, which encouraged the precision that had won an award for *Wind Song*, one of her first paintings in college. To Lila, the brush was a tool for a lifetime, a symbol of her mother's belief in her—and it had meant all the more after her mother's death.

That was why Lila cringed when she crawled under the kitchen table and found oak splinters scattered like matchsticks beside the gold ring that had once held the bristles in place. Now the ring was a curved metal scrap, pocked and stippled by dog teeth. The missing bristles had undoubtedly made their way down Grace's gullet.

A lump of sadness rose in Lila's throat. Not getting answers she'd hoped for from Agnes had been disappointing, but Grace's destroying Lila's prized possession was worse. Maybe it was only a material object, but losing it felt like her mother had died a second time. Lila scooped up the metal and splinters and got to her feet. "Grace! Damn you! Grace!" Lila hurried down the hall.

When she didn't find Grace in the den, Lila went to the bedroom and lifted the bed skirt. Plastered next to the wall, Grace was resting her chin on her front paws. She blinked at Lila and knitted her eyebrows. Even Lila, who'd never been close to a dog, could read the emotion behind Grace's expression and recognize guilt in her frown.

Still, Lila couldn't muffle her anger. Grace had earned it. "You did this while I was talking with Agnes, didn't you? You were seeking revenge because I put you in the kitchen."

Grace pressed herself against the wall. Her eyes begged, *Please, don't be mad! I couldn't help myself. When you banished me from the living room, I was very upset.*

"I was upset too. You were being rude to Agnes."

In my heart I meant no harm, Grace's sad eyes said.

If dogs could speak, Lila was sure Grace would say she'd thought the brush was a stick, and all dogs chewed sticks, especially when the dogs were stressed. What was she supposed to do when a tempting piece of wood lay on the counter, asking for teeth? Couldn't the person who left the stick where a dog could reach it be to blame, at least a little?

Please, please, won't you love me? Grace's sad eyes pleaded.

Lila dropped the bed skirt. She did not believe she was to blame; the demolished brush was Grace's fault. Lila had been responsible in caring for her, and look how she'd repaid the patience and goodwill. It wasn't fair that a dog forced on Lila had caused so much trouble.

"I've tried to get along with you, but it's not working," Lila said.

Leaving Grace to stew in her transgression, Lila went back to the kitchen. She told herself that she had a right not to mollycoddle the dog orphans of the world. Adam was being maddeningly unreliable, and Lila had a long way to go to be healthy and strong. She had no time for Grace when she was trying to get her work and life in order.

Lila had to find a way to be dog-free. If her Pleaser objected, Lila would call on her Crazy Aunt, who would push the Pleaser off a ship with her hands tied behind her back, or banish her to Tokelau, or strangle her with Grace's red bandana.

When Lila woke the next morning, Grace had wriggled out from under the bed, but she wasn't waiting for Lila in the kitchen as usual. Lila didn't bother looking for her because she was still upset about her brush, though her annoyance at Grace had been tempered overnight. Now Lila's feelings leaned more toward hurt at Grace for betraying their temporary friendship and toward resentment at Adam for taking advantage.

Wrapping her resolve around her, Lila found Cristina's contact list in the kitchen drawer and phoned Adam's house.

After four rings, he greeted Lila on his answering machine. "You've reached Adam Spencer," the recording said, as if she needed to be told. "Leave a message, and I'll call you back. Or try my cell." Sounding more solicitous than he'd ever been with her, he gave the number.

At the beep, she said, "This is Lila Elliot," then added, in case he'd forgotten, "I'm Cristina's friend . . . the one with Grace." Lila's Pleaser made her sugarcoat her pill of resentment with a friendly tone of voice. "Would you call me? It's a little urgent, actually. I need for you to get serious about finding

Grace a home." She gave Cristina's number in case Adam didn't have it handy. For good measure, Lila called his cell phone and left the same message.

At the latest, she expected to hear from Adam by noon. If Cristina had been right that he was a good person, he would call Lila back quickly and show his good side. Trying to be positive, she pictured him stopping by in the late afternoon, eager to help her, and leading Grace to his pickup, where his Irish wolfhounds would be waiting. They'd all drive off together, slobbering and happy.

When Lila hung up the phone, Grace padded into the kitchen like a vandal returning to the scene of the crime. She sniffed the tile floor, sat down next to the table, under which she'd committed her atrocity, and gazed out the French door as if she were meditating on the backyard's Gravenstein apple tree. She must have hoped Lila's annoyance had cooled and they could make up and hang around together, a peaceable kingdom of two. By Grace's quiet presence, she let Lila know she was waiting to reconnect.

But Lila didn't feel like doing that. She steeled herself. It was time for Grace to go.

Lila's missing brush was like a pulled tooth that the tongue keeps going back to look for. All morning as she painted, she kept reaching for the brush and remembering with sadness that it was gone. She was working on a door from *Architectural Digest*, with a brass handle shaped like a dolphin and a window framed with scallops, like waves. When the phone never rang, she kept getting up and making sure it was securely in its cradle—and her frustration at not hearing from Adam slowly mushroomed into huffiness.

At noon, no matter if Lila seemed desperate, she left messages at both of Adam's numbers again to remind him of the importance of her call. When he did not phone back by two, she was certain he was too arrogant to stoop to returning messages. By four, she imagined him out cold in a hospital bed after an auto accident—having lost the use of his arms and legs and become brain damaged and incapable of speech—and her huffiness morphed into despair. By five, she called his numbers again but got recordings, and still another time she left messages, which now edged toward hostility.

Cristina used her cell phone only for crises because, she said, it might give her a brain tumor, and she had to live to see Rosie married. Normally, Lila would not have called Cristina's cell because she'd think there was an emergency and be alarmed. But she hadn't answered at her D.C. apartment, and she was indirectly to blame for Grace's brush atrocity. That warranted Lila calling her cell, alarm or not.

"What's *wrong*?!" Cristina asked. She must have thought Lila was about to tell her that the house was sliding down the mountain.

"Everything's fine. Don't worry. I just need to talk to you."

"Are you okay?"

Lila sighed to introduce her despondence. "Adam's never found Grace a home. I've left messages all day, but he hasn't bothered getting back to me."

"He must be busy."

Lila doubted that. "What am I supposed to do with Grace? She's been with me almost a month."

"How's the precious getting along?"

Through gritted teeth, Lila explained Grace's criminal act.

"She didn't mean to cause trouble. She was just being a dog," Cristina said. "I'll buy you a new brush."

"It can't be replaced. My mother gave it to me. I loved it." Then Lila dug deeper to the root of the problem. "I can't worry about my arm and try to paint again when I'm being forced to take care of Grace. I wanted to help you, but it's not working.

You've got to do something. I don't see how you could have left her here with me." Lila's voice sounded shaky.

"I didn't want to leave her with you. I swear we tried to find a place for her. I told you that."

"I know, but out of the gazillion people in the world, I can't believe I'm the only one who could take her."

"We *asked* a gazillion people. Adam can tell you how hard we tried."

"Maybe he could if he'd be decent enough to get back to me."

"Call him again."

"I'm willing to beg only so much for someone's help." Lila watched a woodpecker go after a redwood trunk outside the kitchen window.

"Don't be mad at Adam. He's either out of town or busy. He's considerate."

"Not that I've seen."

"You'd see it if you knew him better. Really . . ."

As if Lila were interested—which she wasn't—Cristina described the care he'd taken when breaking up with his last girlfriend. On her freelance writer's irregular income, she'd racked up huge bills for an iPad, a BlackBerry, and expensive clothes. Adam bailed her out, but she wouldn't stop spending. "She was totally irresponsible. She didn't care," Cristina said. "Adam was upset when he broke up with her, but he didn't pressure her about moving out of his house till she found a good place to live. He was thoughtful . . ."

"He's not being thoughtful to me, and he's being just as irresponsible as his girlfriend." Lila pressed her hand over her eyes, the better to hide in some dark corner of herself, free of Adam and Grace.

At least Lila now knew he'd judged someone besides her, and he was an equal-opportunity spreader of his disapproval. If his ex-girlfriend told her side, she'd explain that she'd shopped believing she could pay but had run out of money. No compassionate person would end a relationship over a human mistake like that. As a miser, Adam probably spent days comparing prices for his wolfhounds' kibble.

"Can I do anything to help you hang on till Adam figures something out?" Cristina asked.

"That could take years. I need you to help me find a place for Grace *now*."

Again, Cristina urged Lila to call Adam, but how many messages did Cristina expect her to leave? Finally, spiraling down in what Lila vowed to herself would be only momentary defeat, she asked, "Where are you anyway?"

"On my way to the grocery store with Rosie. What I wouldn't give for some California fruit right now. I want to come home."

"You'll be back before you know it," Lila said. "Is Rosie okay?"

"Her PlayStation died a little while ago. I'm keeping her occupied with the alphabet game."

"Tell Lila about the snakes," Rosie chimed in.

"Oh, yeah . . . We went to the zoo. This man was demonstrating how to milk venom. It was scary," Cristina said. "Hold on, Lila . . . Look, there's a *P*, Rosie! In the billboard. On the Pepsi can . . ."

Cristina seemed as far away in thoughts as in miles. The Pepsi's *P* underscored in bold that Grace was Lila's problem.

After Lila hung up the phone, Grace turned away from the apple tree and gave her a sad, heartrending glance. She limped over, wagging her feathery tail, and sat in front of Lila. As Grace ratcheted up her glance to a stare of longing, sweet, starry-eyed adoration flowed out of her. Though Lila had locked her in the kitchen yesterday, Grace seemed to view her as her personal potentate; Lila had hung the moon with her own hands and invented chicken skin and beef gravy.

"How can you be loving when I'm annoyed at you?" Lila was talking as if Grace's illicit behavior were forgotten, though Lila remembered every splinter under the kitchen table.

Grace responded with a tail thump to the tile floor. She got up and rested her head in Lila's lap.

No doubt Grace was trying to hug her again and make up for what she'd done. She was begging Lila to reassure her that she wasn't upset and letting Lila know that she'd never stop pouring love on her. Forgiveness, like adoration, was an expression of Grace's nature. Lila could rail at her, but she'd never hold a grudge.

Betsy would have said to take a lesson from Grace about forgiving, Lila thought as Grace nuzzled her hand with her wet nose and asked Lila to pet her. Though Lila didn't want to, she broke down and obliged. Then she wondered if Grace's love-bug behavior was a ploy to make her feel guilty for wanting her gone. Lila's Crazy Aunt jumped in and cut off the guilt with a quick conk to its gizzard.

She curled her lip and hissed at Lila, *Forget the Good Samaritan act. The Humane Society is just down the freeway!*

It's not that simple, Lila mentally replied. *Grace is needy. She shouldn't be cast away.*

Yeah, sure. *Are you a simpering coward, or* what? Lila's Crazy Aunt snarled. *Who comes first? You or Grace? You've got to end her damned starring role in* The Dog Who Came to Dinner.

You're right, Lila conceded. She was. Really.

17

Lila's mother often told her that necessity gave birth to invention, and she was stirring miso noodle soup at the stove when inspiration for an invention struck. It would be a promotional campaign, like those she'd helped devise at Weatherby to get publicity for products. But her objective would be a home, and the product would be Grace.

If Cristina and Adam wouldn't help Lila, then she would find someone who needed a golden retriever. There was no reason why she shouldn't be proactive. She wouldn't hand Grace over to just anyone; the person would have to be decent and respectable. But Lila would know she'd stopped being exploited and she'd gotten back some power.

Though Lila had sworn she'd never groom Grace, she got out the dog brush and started on her fur, which was sticking out as if it had been starched. Lila took swipes at Grace's head, skipped her neck, which was covered by the bandana, and worked her way down Grace's haunches and back. As Lila brushed, Grace's tongue hung from her mouth like a wet camellia petal. She half closed her eyes with a look of ecstasy, as if she were mentally zooming off to an opium den. When Lila got to her tail, she had to chase the wag. Grace accidentally thwacked her mouth. Repulsed, Lila picked fur off her lips as fervently as she'd picked it off her black jeans, and she added the thwack to Grace's other transgressions, such as the vile tennis ball and demolished brush.

Lila fluffed up the pointed tip of Grace's bandana to give her an extra-bright and fetching look. With her fingers, Lila pushed Grace's fur over the bald patches above her tail and partly hid her skin condition. If Lila squinted just right, Grace looked almost kempt, and her long, wavy fur invited hands to pet her.

"You're not ready for prime time, but you're presentable," Lila said.

Grace swished her tail fervently enough to blow the turban off the imaginary sultan she fanned on the floor.

Her wag made clear that she did not know that Lila was about to turn into Benedict Arnold with steps two and three of her campaign: taking Grace on a walk, and persuading some unsuspecting but acceptable passerby to adopt her.

When Lila herded Grace toward the front door instead of the back, where she usually went out, she looked up and bristled her eyebrows, as if she were confused. They asked, *Why are you altering my routine when it's been working fine? Where are we going?*

"We're going for a walk!" Lila lilted her voice with excitement at "walk," so she sounded like she and Grace were about to romp across a yard where dog biscuits pushed through the grass like tulips.

Grace quickly taught Lila that dogs read minds.

Though Lila had not mentioned her campaign, Grace seemed to sense that something deceitful was going on, and she did not like it. She stared at Lila with a suspicious look in her eyes. When Lila opened the door, Grace refused to step onto the porch. She acted like she'd never been taken on a walk and disdained setting out on one now, especially with someone she'd begun to believe might not be trustworthy.

"Come on! Let's go!"

Lila pushed Grace's haunches over the threshold. Lila had expected her to bound outside and explore the forest, but she pressed against Lila's legs. She couldn't tell if Grace was being insecure or protective, but Lila urged her off the porch and they started up the path toward the street.

The sun filtered through redwood branches and dimly lit the forest. The air smelled of miner's lettuce and acacia. Ahead of Lila and Grace, crows sat like Christmas ornaments in a bay tree but flew away, cawing, as dog and human encroached on their safety zone.

Wary, Lila checked blackberry thickets for another Trailside Killer. But, surprisingly, with Grace beside her, fear ruled her less than it had on trips alone to the store. Though another murderer could shoot Lila as easily as Yuri had, Grace's company shored up her confidence and slightly dulled her anxious edge about being on the road.

Knowing that those pluses could never persuade her to adopt Grace herself, though, Lila stopped at the house next door, where Virginia, as fair and big-boned as a Viking, was sweeping her driveway. She was wearing a sari embroidered with tiny gold flowers, and humming something you'd hear plucked on a zither in a coffeehouse.

"Your yard's looking great." Lila tugged Grace close to Virginia so she could witness the gut-wrenching longing for love that was always in Grace's eyes.

Virginia stopped midsweep but did not notice her. "Blasted redwood fronds. I've got to keep at them, or they clog the drain." She stooped down and poured her dustpan's contents into a green garbage bag.

"I need to find this dog a home," Lila said.

Virginia gave Grace an evaluatory glance. "I've seen her at the window. She looks out on the road."

"She always waits for me to come home."

"The poor thing." Virginia came over and patted Grace's head.

Acting increasingly certain that something disadvantageous to her was going on, Grace distrustfully hooded her eyes and flashed Virginia her most hangdog, antisocial expression.

Virginia could not have missed Grace's sullen face and bald spots. "It might be hard to get someone to take her. Makes you sad."

Lila said good-bye and left without asking Virginia if she'd take Grace herself because she knew what Virginia would say. Grace and Lila headed down the road.

They came to a man in a fleece vest and hiking boots, depositing a Gatorade bottle in his green recycling bin. His Santa Claus beard made him seem like he'd be warm and friendly, the very qualities that Grace would respond to. Lila brought her to a halt, so he wouldn't see her limp, and sat her at an angle, so he wouldn't see her bald spots.

"Hi," Lila said.

When the man looked over at her and Grace, his lips parted in a smile. "Morning."

"Interested in adopting a great dog?"

As he peered down at Grace, she glowered even worse than she'd glowered at Agnes Spitzmeier. Nevertheless, he reached out his hand for her to sniff and get acquainted, but she got up and slunk away. Perverse was what she was being.

"Why are you giving her up?" he asked.

"I'm house-sitting for a friend who rescued her. She left Grace with me till we could find her a home."

"You could keep her."

"I'm too busy. I don't know much about dogs anyway. I've never had one."

"You ought to. They're lots of fun."

"Right!" Lila said to hint that maybe Grace would be great fun for him.

But he didn't take the bait. "I've got a snippy Yorkie. She'd never tolerate another dog in the house."

Lila's disappointment tasted like unsweetened lemonade sucked through a charcoal straw. "Do you know any nice person who might want Grace?"

"Not offhand."

Lila gave him one of the index cards she'd written her phone number on, in case he thought of somebody. As she and Grace walked away, Lila said, "She's such a wonderful dog!" She wanted to leave him with a final, positive thought to spur his search for Grace's new home—but Lila wasn't hopeful he'd bother.

Slowly, she and Grace worked their way down the street. Looking sulky, Grace sat at Lila's feet while she talked with an elderly woman planting pansies in her window box, a man with slumped shoulders emptying the trash, and a woman in a pantsuit lifting groceries from the trunk of her burnt-orange Alfa Romeo. Lila stopped a pair of sweaty joggers who ran in place while she asked if they might want Grace, and a UPS delivery-woman who pulled her truck to the curb with a metallic squawk of brakes.

Lila's offer was always the same, delivered with as much enthusiasm as she could rake out of her put-upon heart. But Grace kept acting grumpy and withdrawn, like her only friend was Prozac. And everyone had a polite excuse for not taking on a misanthrope:

"I'm allergic to dogs."

"I'm a cat person."

"I'm never home. It wouldn't be fair to a dog."

"My wife's pregnant. A baby's all we're going to be able to handle."

Lila's campaign was a bust. By evening, all the index cards she'd handed out would be wadded up next to sour cream containers and wilted spinach leaves at the bottom of everybody's garbage can.

On the way home, Lila wrestled with discouragement, made blacker by knowing she could have spent the afternoon painting or searching the Internet for more going-postal cases. And Grace's sudden attitude reversal added to the frustration. Instead of acting like a crank, she apparently concluded that Lila had given up the search for an adopter and Grace was safe. She hobbled along, acting beatific, flashing Lila worshipful glances, and turning up the ends of her mouth in what looked like a smile. Was it possible dogs *smiled*?

In her head, Lila replayed her failed sales pitches. She wished she'd bowled everybody over with red-letter zeal. "I'm trying to find a home for this gorgeous, fabulous, friendly golden retriever!" Lila could have said in the beginning. When someone asked why Grace needed a home, Lila could have stretched the truth to something compelling, such as, "Her owner fell off a ladder in his backyard and had to go to a nursing home, the poor, poor man. He's beside himself that he can't keep his beloved dog."

When anyone resisted, Lila could have iced more drama on her duplicitous cake with a Grace-as-hero tale. "Grace went absolutely wild when her owner fell off the ladder," she might have said. "She yowled till a neighbor came over to see what the commotion was about, and he called an ambulance. This smart, sensitive, loyal dog saved her owner's life. Isn't that amazing? She's sure golden in more ways than one."

Cristina and Lila used to have lying contests when they were bored studying for finals. For instance, they once described to each other trips to places they had never gone. Lila quickly mentioned a bus ride in Kazakhstan and a campout in

Mali, but Cristina went on and on when it was her turn. She related chilling images of the yak who almost gored her on a trek in Nepal—his ferocious horns, the iron muscles in his legs, his breath that could wilt cactus. When Cristina described the sunburn that had turned her skin cranberry red on the Costa Brava—and the hotel owner's wife who rubbed vinegar on her back and arms to soothe the pain—Lila's own skin hurt. That was how good Cristina was at lying.

"If you want someone to believe a lie, you have to throw in feeling and detail," Cristina said. For fun, she embellished Lila's Mali campout with bandits who had yellow teeth and spears with poisoned metal tips—so Lila never wanted to travel there for real.

Maybe today Lila could have given a pitch as emotional as Cristina's lies, but, then, just as effective as a lie for finding Grace a home might have been the sympathy-yanking truth: She was desperate for someone on whom to shower her devotion. If she loved you, she glommed onto you like she had a barnacle in her genetic heritage. It wasn't fair for even a brush-chewing delinquent like her to be sad when she had so much love to give.

Still, those weren't reasons for Lila to keep her.

18

Because Lila believed that Adam Spencer was avoiding her on purpose, she was hesitant to contact him again. Yet even if he didn't want to talk with her, he was responsible for Grace still living with her, and he owed her his help. One last time Lila swallowed her pride and phoned him, though she did not expect him to answer. Like whistling for a dog, she called her determination.

She told herself that if Adam had cared enough to rescue Grace, he'd want to make sure she found a good home. Lila would appeal to his concern for Grace and count on her Pleaser to make her cordial and her Crazy Aunt to help her stand her ground. Since she was miffed that Adam was taking advantage of her, however, she'd sprinkle into the conversation a few references to virtues Adam clearly lacked, such as reliability, trustworthiness, and compassion. He probably wouldn't get the hint, but she'd give it anyway just to enhance her self-respect and get back her power.

As Lila picked up the phone in the den, Grace leaned against her ankle and panted, like she was talking to herself. Lila called

Adam's home number. He didn't answer, wouldn't you know? She hung up, imagining him slinking around in Timbuktu so she couldn't find him to ask for help. She tried his cell.

"Hello?" he said.

After all the failed attempts to reach him, she was shocked to hear his voice. Noise in the background told her that he was in a public place; she quickly wished it were a meeting hall whose floor joists were sagging under the weight of dog adopters.

"Errr . . ." She was off to a robust start. She identified herself. "I've left you six messages." *Since you like dogs better than people, maybe I'd have heard back from you if I were a dachshund.*

"Sorry. I haven't called my voice mail. I've been at a conference in Chicago. I'm at O'Hare, about to fly home," he said.

What sounded like a CNN newscaster mumbled stock quotes in the background. Grace's damp breath warmed Lila's foot.

"I'm sure you'll be glad to get back. The weather's great here," Lila's Pleaser made her say.

"Nothing's wrong with Grace, is there?" Adam asked.

"As a matter of fact . . ." Lila cleared her throat. "I need you to come and get her. I've had her over a month."

"We've been through this before." He sounded irritable and tired. "Can't you hold on a little longer?"

"I've held on for too long. It's not right. I just walked Grace around the neighborhood and asked people if they wanted her, and . . ."

"You did *what*?"

Lila's hackles rose. "I took her around the neighborhood . . ."

"That was absolutely irresponsible."

"I hate to say this, but I think you're the irresponsible one here. Since you wouldn't help, I had to do something. Somebody has to find Grace a home."

"You might have handed her over to a dog torturer," Adam

said. "I told you Marshall doesn't live that far away. If he found out you had her, it would be a nightmare."

"Okay, so do you want me to put an ad in the paper? Free dog to good home?"

"That would be worse." When Adam exhaled, his breath contained scorn. "Crazy people search the ads for dogs every day. You wouldn't know how to screen callers."

Lila rankled at the put-down. "I can tell a sicko if I talk with one." But, then, she hadn't recognized how disturbed Yuri Makov was.

"You have to protect Grace. She's already gone through more than any dog should. It would be criminal if something bad happened to her again." Without pausing long enough to blink, Adam launched the same kind of emotional appeal that Lila had wished she'd used on the neighbors for Grace: Marshall bragged he'd locked Grace for months in a dark garage as a pup to teach her that he was her master, Adam said. One night as he watched from his bedroom window, Marshall dragged Grace to an oak tree in his backyard and wrapped one end of a ten-foot chain around its trunk and the other around her neck. In a week she wore a small circle of dirt around the tree, which on freezing winter nights showered acorns on her, and she curled into a ball to protect herself or stood for hours to keep her body off the icy, muddy ground. And Marshall practically starved her. She'd have died if Adam hadn't thrown food over the fence to her when Marshall was at work. He beat Grace too, and that's when Adam broke into Marshall's yard and stole her.

"Imagine a wonderful dog like her living such a horrible life. Sometimes she cried all afternoon because she was so lonely. Look at how loving she is despite that jerk," Adam said. "Grace didn't deserve any of it. Through no fault of her own, she got put in the hands of a sadist. She's like you. You both suffered from a random act of fate."

"Well, I . . ." Till then, Lila hadn't been sure that Yuri's shooting her had penetrated Adam's mind. "I didn't know about Grace's life. It's terrible. But it's not fair you haven't come to get her. You said you would."

"You ought to understand better than anybody that Grace needs to be protected. Can you imagine how bad it would be if some cruel person got hold of her again? Is that what you want?"

"Of course not. It would be awful . . ."

"United Flight 197 is now boarding at Gate 9." On the intercom, the woman's voice sounded scratchy.

"I have to go," Adam said. "If you'll just be patient for another month, I'll take Grace myself."

"I can't keep Grace another month!"

At hearing her name, though Lila's voice was shrill, Grace looked up at her expectantly and said with her eyes, *I love you!*

"A month is not long," Adam argued.

"It's twenty-nine days too long. I have to get back my life. Grace is siphoning my energy. I need to get well . . ."

"Just listen, okay?" Adam interrupted. "I bought a house. It's in escrow. I'll be moving in soon. The house doesn't have a fenced yard, so it might take me a while to get ready for Grace, but I'll do it as fast as I can."

As Lila was about to cave and agree to keep Grace longer, her Crazy Aunt, who'd just dyed her hair green, stomped into Lila's mind. *Keep your trap shut,* she snarled at Lila. *That oaf may have made you pity that dog, but he's steamrollering you. You're not the only dog sitter in the world. Don't let him push you around.*

"If you'll wait for me to come and get Grace, you'll never have to see her again," Adam pressed. "I'm counting on you to keep her for me just a little longer. I'm asking you to have some heart."

As far as Lila was concerned, he'd fed his own heart to his wolfhounds for breakfast. Her heart was fine. She'd shown plenty of it taking care of a dog who'd been pushed on her by an insensitive man as untrustworthy as Reed.

When Adam hung up, he hadn't seemed to notice that she'd not agreed to anything. The fence was just another of his ploys to stall—and she'd never hear from him. If he ever did contact her, he'd say that he'd gotten a consulting job in Antarctica, and after the work was finished, he had to visit his consumptive cousin for a few months on the Yangtze River. And by the way, he'd ask, couldn't Lila keep Grace just a tiny bit longer, like another year? By then he'd be back in town, happy to take her off Lila's hands.

Grace rested her chin on her paws and sighed with contentment. Apparently sensing no potential change in her living arrangements, she closed her eyes and began to snore.

19

Lila clicked on the Safari icon at the bottom of the computer screen and Googled the white pages directory. As she held her breath, she typed, "Yuri Makov, San Francisco, California." She wanted his phone number so she could call his roommate, who'd been on the TV news two months before and might help her understand why Yuri had been angry. But Yuri wasn't listed. As that door closed in Lila's face, her heart drooped, like it wasn't wild about beating anymore.

Certainly, she wasn't as angry as Yuri had been, but she was mad. Resentment had been nesting in her soul since she'd met Reed's lover at the PhotoMat. When Yuri shot her, the resentment had multiplied like cancer cells and turned into anger. Her last conversation with Adam had added anger's cousin, annoyance. Staring at the computer screen, Lila brooded about his taking advantage and not caring if Grace disrupted her life. What was she supposed to do? Keep a dog she didn't want until it died a natural death? The more Lila thought about her phone conversation with Adam, the more hostile she felt.

Anyone could understand emotions sometimes piling up

and taking you hostage. As Lila's anger filled her mind, it elbowed aside her decency, compassion, and pity for Grace. Lila's Crazy Aunt boomed into her thoughts, stomped on her Pleaser's toes, and took over. *For God's sake, cut the wimp act. Get rid of the dog. Do what you have to do.* Lila's Crazy Aunt curled her lip.

As Lila swallowed pomegranate green tea, she glanced out the window at a dead bay tree branch's jagged twigs. She told herself, *I will* not *be used. Not for another minute.*

She got up, called the Humane Society, and wrote down directions to their shelter. She folded the paper and stuffed it in her pocket. The staff vetted anyone who wanted to adopt an animal. Grace would be safe. They'd find her a good home. Let someone besides Lila solve the problem.

Lila called Grace. Again she proved that dogs read minds, and she refused to come. She might not have known Lila's plan, but she must have sensed a new impetus in Lila's resolve to be dog-free and recognized that something unsavory was about to happen to her.

Lila went to the kitchen and jingled the keys to Cristina's station wagon to hint at the joys of riding in a car. Grace didn't move. By the door Lila rattled the dog biscuit box to lure her to the garage. Finally, she hauled herself to her feet, then slumped back to the floor and closed her eyes, which said, *What a drag. Car rides are not my thing. I want to stay right here.*

Ignoring the ennui, Lila said with feigned enthusiasm, "Grace! Let's go!"

Their find-a-home walk around the neighborhood the week before must have alerted Grace that Lila could act as if pleasure lay ahead when it didn't, and Grace had honed her dishonesty radar. She got up, limped to her pillow in the living room, and curled up in her pumpkin position, ready to launch another production of *The Napping Dog*.

Lila followed. "Come on, Grace! Let's go have fun!" Jingle. Jingle.

Grace's look was as dark as a Yankee dog's trying to make a go of it at Andersonville. The smile that had lately curved up at the outer edges of her mouth now dropped to a bleak, straight, you-can't-fool-me line.

"Don't you want to go for a ride?" Lila raised her voice at "ride" as if it were the pinnacle of dreams at the Dog's Make-A-Wish Foundation.

Grace told her unambiguously and forthrightly that she did not want to go for a ride: She got to her feet and hobbled toward her hiding place under the bed. As she passed Lila, Grace's scowl informed her that she suspected Lila's motives. Her scowl back told Grace that her patience was frayed and she wanted this difficult trip behind her.

If Lila couldn't persuade Grace to come willingly, she would drag her to the car. "Come *on*." Lila blocked her in the hall, forced her to turn around, and pushed her from behind toward the door. "You can't blame me. This is Adam Spencer's fault, not mine."

Grace seemed not to care whose fault it was. Lila had to nag her into the garage. When Lila opened the back of the station wagon, Grace stared at the license plate and made no move to jump in.

Lila patted the carpeting to encourage her. "Here, Grace."

Breath wasted. Deaf ears.

Thinking perhaps Grace's injured leg prevented her from jumping, Lila led her to the door behind the driver's seat, where she could step into the car. "Get in."

Grace did not budge. She seemed to be infused with the spirit of Gandhi, and "passive resistance" was inscribed between the toes of her intransigent paws. When Lila pulled her bandana toward the backseat, she must have concluded that she had no choice but to comply. Nevertheless, she made it clear that she was not amused by the coercion. Giving Lila the cool, steady look of Queen Elizabeth sizing up a peon, Grace climbed into the backseat. With regal dignity, she might have set her scepter on her lap and smoothed her paw over her brocade train's seed pearls.

When Lila got behind the steering wheel and looked at Grace in the rearview mirror, she was watching the garage wall. Lila could tell Grace sensed misfortune coming. Guilt tapped Lila on the shoulder and said "ahem," but her built-up anger— and her Crazy Aunt—knocked him to the garage floor. Lila started down the mountain.

Lila had not driven after breaking up with Reed because she didn't have a car, and she'd not driven after coming to Cristina's because of her cast. Now she could use her left arm well enough to get behind the wheel, but she had not factored in how stressful driving for the first time in many months would be. On the freeway, her forehead was damp, and perspiration trickled between her breasts.

Focused on a bus painted like a loaf of bread, Grace ignored Lila. Grace made clear that until her suspicions were proven unfounded, she was pulling up her drawbridge and withdrawing to her throne room.

If Lila hadn't been eager to deliver Grace to the Humane Society, she'd never have been willing to drive so soon. She owed Grace for indirectly nudging her to get behind the wheel and jump another hurdle toward a normal life. To be honest, Grace had helped her sometimes, Lila thought with an unexpected pang of regret at what she was about to do. But her Crazy Aunt pushed the regret out of the car. *Keep driving,* she growled.

Grace acted like her entire existence depended on the Bekins moving van in the next lane.

* * *

The Humane Society, a compound of concrete buildings half an hour north of Mill Valley, looked like a campus where important lessons could be learned. As Lila drove into the parking lot, a bronze sculpture of a mother bear and two cubs greeted her and Grace. Across the main building's front wall, mosaic deer, raccoons, and rabbits marched in profile like figures on an Egyptian frieze. In the windows of a smaller building next door, cats sleeping in baskets exuded peace. Yet from somewhere inside, frantic barks and howls seemed to zigzag through the roof.

Grace must have heard them. Dispensing with her regal stance, she panted and shifted her weight from her healthy to her injured leg so the front half of her was marching in place. She frowned at the building as if she were certain that frenzied dogs were throwing themselves at kennel walls to escape incarceration—and she emphatically did not want to join them. She whimpered and pawed the back of Lila's seat to convey this preference. Her entire demeanor urged, *Please! Let's get out of here!*

Though Lila wanted to regain her power by standing up to Adam and getting free of Grace, her resistance made Lila wince. She assured herself that she'd gone extra miles to take care of Grace and find her a home, and not even Lila's Pleaser could expect her to have done more. She didn't need to feel bad about leaving Grace there. But she did. Very bad.

Lila turned around in her seat. Grace was huddling against the door. "Look, I'll tell you what. If nobody adopts you in a week, I'll come back and get you. Either way it'll work out fine," she said. "Lots of nice people might come along. You might find a family with kids. It could be great! You'd be a lot happier living with them than with me."

Grace did not seem impressed. Her face looked grim.

Lila got out of the car and opened the door for her. When Lila called Grace to jump out, she planted her legs in front of her like iron stakes and dug her toenails into the upholstery. "Grace, let's go inside."

She sank to her stomach and stretched out her front legs in her sphinx imitation. Her anxious drool splotched the upholstery. When she gazed up at Lila, the whites below her pupils looked like beseeching commas on their backs. *Please, please, don't make me go in there.*

"Everything's going to be okay," Lila told herself as much as Grace.

Keep moving, Lila's Crazy Aunt ordered.

As Lila nudged Grace to stand, yowls traveled from the building. Grace shrank back against the seat. Finally, she climbed out of the car and took a few leaden steps across the parking lot toward the sign that said ADOPTION CENTER, pointing to the building with the sleeping cats. But she must have thought better of coming with Lila because she turned around and limped back toward the car. Lila tugged Grace's bandana. She tugged back.

Her tugs urged Lila to reconsider: *I've tried my best to get along and shower you with love. I'll do anything if you'll keep me. All I want in the world is to be with you. Oh, please.* Tug. Tug.

Lila felt like a wretch. She reminded herself that Adam had put her in this terrible position, but she still felt like a wretch. She disliked him more than ever.

Stop the sniveling, her Crazy Aunt bellowed.

As Lila forced herself to lead Grace into the building, guilt, who'd recovered from being knocked to the floor, trailed them through the door and poked Lila's bottom with his cane. He said, "Tsk-tsk. You're taking out your anger on an innocent dog." He pointed out that in the last couple of weeks Lila had not minded Grace; sometimes her company had been pleasant. "If you're truthful with yourself, you know you'll miss her."

Who cares about truth? Lila's Crazy Aunt snapped.

Lila gripped her purse's shoulder strap and herded Grace through a crowded reception area to a swarthy man with lambchop sideburns and shaggy eyebrows. He was cleaning off a counter covered with brochures. From the shoulders up, he looked like a Minotaur, but his spindly arms and legs were pure satyr. He should have been prancing on small hooves across a Greek urn.

"Hi! I'm Tony" was written on the name tag pinned to his maroon tee shirt. "Need some help?" he asked.

"I can't keep this dog." Lila nodded down at Grace.

Tony stepped from behind the counter to get a closer look at her, and a frown of disapproval creased his forehead. Anyone could tell he thought Grace's poor appearance was Lila's fault. As if to help foster that impression, Grace gave him a desperate look and slouched more dismally than she ever had.

"Her name is Grace," Lila said.

"How long have you had her?"

"About six weeks."

"Where'd you get her?"

As a woman passed by with a sheltie on a red leash, Lila explained that someone had left Grace with her—but she discreetly omitted Adam's theft.

When Tony kneeled down and patted Grace's shoulder, she panted like she was about to keel over with neediness and he was her last hope. With all her heart, Grace begged him to love and protect her since Lila had become the Judas of the Western World.

"You're a sweet dog." Tony stroked the feathery tufts above Grace's ears.

"You'll find her a good home?" Lila practically begged.

"We'll groom her and make her available to people looking for a dog," Tony said.

"If nobody adopts her, I'll come and get her."

"Sure. Lots of people say that. We never hear from them again."

"I swear I'll come."

Tony didn't answer as he fumbled with the knot on Grace's bandana. When he pulled it off, Lila gasped, along with half the people in the room.

Around Grace's neck was a ring of skin, speckled with gold fuzz. Clearly not long before, her neck had been shaved, and her fur was growing back—over a thick, blackish-red, perforated line that Lila could hardly bear to look at. Angry welts circled Grace's neck, and from the red welts on Lila's breast and arm, she knew a scar when she saw one. Grace's neck said that something terrible had cut into her, and she'd known pain like none Lila could imagine.

Tony shrank back and shook his head like he was trying to shake off the hideous sight of those welts. He dropped Grace's bandana to the floor. "Just a minute." He reached for the phone on the counter and punched in a three-digit number. "Send Bill down here pronto."

While they waited for Bill, who Lila thought would be a helpful vet, Tony explained in clipped, harsh words that the welts were signs a too-tight chain had bored into Grace's neck. Perhaps the chain had originally fit her, but she'd grown too big for it. Or maybe someone had deliberately forced it around her neck to torture her. Whenever Grace had barked or pulled at the chain, the links had cut deeper till they were embedded in her flesh. Removing them had required surgery. "In eight years here, I've never seen a dog in this appalling condition," Tony said.

Lila was blinking back tears when Bill arrived and kneeled in front of Grace for a closer look. "Holy shit." His voice was a dark, bruising purple.

As he stood up, he gave Lila a look that said she should consort with worms. His gold-framed glasses were slipping down the bridge of his nose, and sweat semicircled his uniform's armpits. "I'm an animal control officer. You tell me how this dog's neck got turned to goddamn hamburger," he demanded.

"I didn't know it was like that."

"We hear that excuse around here a lot." Bill exchanged a glance with Tony.

"It's the truth. Grace has been wearing the bandana since I got her. I never took it off." Behind Lila's back came harsh murmurs from people in the reception area.

"If she's your dog, then who do you claim abused her like that?" Bill asked.

"She isn't my dog. I don't know who hurt her. I've only been taking care of her a little while."

"You've done a rotten job."

Lila flushed from unearned shame. "She came like that."

"I thought you said you didn't know she was hurt."

"I didn't." It was hard to get out words when Lila's teeth were clamped together.

On the green linoleum floor, Grace's bandana looked like a red badge of courage pinned to army fatigues. But standing beside it, surely believing she was minutes from abandonment, Grace looked desolate. She seemed to shrink, then crumble, as if small, quivery pieces of her body were sprinkling on the floor and there'd soon be nothing left of her. Though she refused to look at Lila, Grace might as well have shouted that the tie between them was broken as far as she was concerned, and she was steeling herself for what lay ahead. She seemed to be hiding in her deepest, most shadowy recesses.

Grace had been cruelly victimized, but she'd also been brave to allow herself to trust and love Lila and to come so far. Grace's welts said more about her misery than anything Adam could have told Lila. No matter what her Crazy Aunt said, giant fissures ran through Lila's resolve to leave Grace. Lila's insides hurt for her, a courageous Anne Frank dog.

Tony handed Lila a clipboard with a printed form and a ball-point pen and looked at her as if blood were dripping from her fangs. Clearly, he'd been trained to stay calm while getting animals away from sadists. "Fill this out. Bill can take Grace to the kennel."

Lila could hardly think straight. Numb, she took the clipboard, and Bill threaded one end of a leash through the eye of the other to make a small noose, which he gently slipped around Grace's neck. Lila glanced at the form. After blanks for her name, address, and phone number were questions: Why was she giving up the dog? Was it current on shots? Did it have any physical problems?

Lila stopped reading. What did the questions matter when she felt like sumo wrestlers were rolling around on her heart?

"Let's go," Bill called to Grace and started toward the swinging kennel doors.

"Wait!" Lila followed them. "I'm keeping her."

Bill's glower might have melted Arctic ice. "You've had your chance. This dog is better off here."

"No." Lila would show her power. She mentally shoved her Crazy Aunt away and said to Bill, "Grace is coming with me. She's mine. I'll take good care of her."

"We don't trust you as far as we could throw you," Bill said.

Lila wouldn't listen. "I'll call the man who left her with me. He can explain how her neck got that way."

"Yeah, sure," Bill said.

"Do you have a phone book?" Lila asked Tony.

He glared at her as he got one from behind the counter.

With sweaty hands, Lila looked up Adam Spencer, and, relieved, found his number. If only he'd be honorable enough to answer.

20

As Lila drove Grace away from the Humane Society, you'd never have known she'd been trembling with distress. On the front passenger seat, she smiled and panted as a sliver of her camellia-petal tongue hung from her mouth. Lila had retied the bandana around Grace's neck to cover the scars, and her face filled with trust. *Hurrah! We're going for a ride!* her expression shouted. Grace seemed to have forgotten that Lila had almost left her at the shelter.

Lila was not so carefree as Grace, because Bill and Adam's phone conversation clung to her like harsh soap. Standing next to Bill, she'd heard Adam explain in a steady voice that he'd volunteered in the Humane Society's education department and the staff could vouch for him. He claimed he'd found Grace on the street with the chain embedded in her neck, and he'd rushed her to a vet. Adam urged Bill to let Lila keep her until Adam could bring her home. A kennel would be traumatic after all she'd been through, he said.

With words that sounded bitten off of sheet metal, Adam called Lila "irresponsible," "insensitive," and "that damned flake." Lila steamed at those words, which applied to him more than her. Her Crazy Aunt had urged her to grab the phone from Bill and yell at Adam. But, for Grace's—and Lila's own—sake, she stood there, docile, waiting till they could leave together.

Now she and Grace followed a black Humvee off the exit into Mill Valley and turned down a main road to town. As they passed ranch-style homes and a shopping plaza, Grace leaned against Lila so their shoulders touched. Grace seemed like she was trying to let Lila know, as far as she was concerned, they were a team, and it was the two of them against the world. As far as Lila was concerned, maybe they could be traveling companions on a road called Healing. But she never thought she'd have a dog.

She patted Grace's shoulder. Touching her felt different now that she was Lila's, not just a dog she was sitting for Adam. Grace didn't seem as burdensome or foreign as before, and her meaty breath did not seem so offensive, either. That, Lila couldn't explain.

What mattered was that something had changed. When she and Grace got home, Lila would give her compensatory dog biscuits, take her for walk, and let her lead wherever she wanted to go. Lila would wash the covers on the dog beds. She would rub her vitamin E cream into Grace's welts and hope her skin was as forgiving as she was.

Pet Stop smelled of fish food, rawhide chews, and hamsters' cedar chips. A cockatiel screeched from her perch by the window. Half the overhead fluorescent lights had burned out, so the store was shadowy and the crowded aisles felt like a homeland for moles.

Grace hobbled along beside Lila while she looked for dog food, which they found at the back of the store. Piled high against the wall were kibble bags with mysterious labels for "maintenance," "foundation," and "premium." Lila could relate only to the bags' rainbow of saturated colors.

Pet Stop's owner, Albert Wu, walked over and introduced himself. Dust from the bags of kitty litter he'd been stacking streaked his Hawaiian shirt and toupee, which looked like a malnourished beaver lounging on his head. When Albert smiled, his whole face crinkled and his eyes narrowed to slits. He bent down and stroked Grace's chest.

"Can I help you with anything?" he asked.

"I need kibble for her," Lila said as Grace gave Albert a goofy, high-on-dope look.

"What's she been eating?"

"Some gravel-looking stuff my friend bought for her."

"That doesn't give me a lot to go on." Albert's face crinkled again, and the beaver on his head seemed to rustle.

He explained the difference between "maintenance" and "premium." He pointed a sallow finger at the cerulean blue bag. "This one's for your average all-around dog. It flies out of here." The index finger tapped cadmium red. "I'd go with this. It's got a higher fat content. Looks like your dog could use the extra calories."

That was the one Lila chose. At Albert's urging, she also picked out a nylon forest-green leash with a matching collar that would dazzle against Grace's complementary reddish-gold fur, and Lila looked at the ID-tag selection, stapled to a cardboard square. Grace could have plastic or metal, shaped like a mouse, dog bone, fire hydrant, circle, or heart. Lila ordered the heart to come by mail in red metal and the smallest size, like a gnome's valentine. Printed on it in block letters would be Grace's name and Lila's phone number. Once Grace's neck healed more, she could wear the collar and tag – and the world would know she belonged to Lila.

As Grace turned her attention to the messages left by other dogs on the quarry-tile floor, Albert rang up the purchases and handed Lila a receipt for more than she'd bargained for. She wrote a check that took a hefty chomp from her account. She didn't mind, though, because she wanted to do right by Grace. Adam Spencer would have to admit that Lila was being responsible.

Adam called, as he did now every couple of days, when Grace and Lila were having dinner.

First thing, he asked, "How's Grace doing?"

In other words, is Grace still *there*? You haven't given her to someone? Or taken her back to the Humane Society? You're not being a negligent flake?

"She's fine," Lila said.

"Is she eating?"

"She's gaining more weight."

"You're not feeding her table scraps, are you?"

"No."

"Dogs can't eat chocolate. It's poison to them."

I didn't know. "I know."

"Did you walk her today?"

"I do every day."

"Just checking."

As usual, Lila felt like an amoeba on his microscope slide.

She never told Adam that she wouldn't give Grace back to him. Lila wanted to avoid another fight. He'd find out soon enough that Grace was hers. There was no point borrowing trouble.

With hopes of a reenactment of someone going postal, Lila was watching *True Crime* on TV with Grace. But the story for the night was of a rotten-toothed survivalist who had kidnapped a teenage girl. Police were combing the mountains with bloodhounds. Behind a forest of microphones, the girl's ashenfaced parents were begging people to come forward with clues.

Everyone was hoping she was alive, but "rape" hung in the manhunt's air, a lurid suggestion of what they'd find. David Carpenter had plundered a woman like that when he started down the road to become the Trailside Killer. Would Yuri Makov have raped anyone? Lila imagined him sneaking up behind her after work and gagging her with duct tape. As she kicked and clawed, he would tape her wrists together, shove her into his Nissan's trunk, and slam it closed. As he hauled her away, exhaust fumes would engulf her . . .

But Lila couldn't finish picturing this gruesome story. Yuri seemed too refined to rape anyone or get semen on his always well-pressed slacks. Shooting was surely as close as he'd wanted to get to his victims. What did that say about him?

Probably that he was standoffish and he wasn't after power over women or picking them off one by one, alone. He wanted more violence. More impact. More drama. A bigger sweep of evil to make a bigger public statement. But what had Yuri been saying when he shot everyone?

As Lila leaned back into the sofa and pondered that question, she could almost hear him scream, "I hate you. I'm better than you are. I'm going to kill myself, and you're coming with me."

But whom did he hate? Why?

The questions unsettled her. For comfort, she reached down and patted Grace, who was lying at her feet. Before, touching Grace had taken concentrated effort. Now Lila hardly knew she was doing it.

In the three weeks since Lila had brought Grace back from the Humane Society, she always seemed to lean against Lila or rest her chin on her foot. Those were Grace's two favorite positions. If she couldn't touch Lila, she stayed as close as she could get. While Lila bathed, Grace curled up on the bathroom rug. When Lila slept, Grace plastered her body against the bed skirt. She seemed to have figured out that Lila was officially hers, and she'd never let her out of sight. If Lila left the house without bringing Grace along, she waited for her at the front door with a gift—a kitchen towel, a throw pillow, one of Lila's pink slippers, her sock.

Because Grace was constantly around, Lila had gotten to know more about her, such as how her fur could have been a useful teaching aid for Clairol. The fur on her face was Champagne Blonde. In the middle of her forehead was a Strawberry Blonde widow's peak, and above her ears were feathery Copper Blonde tufts. Her shoulders and chest were delicately streaked, as if highlighted with Platinum Blonde. Her tail, which looked like a geyser spewing fur, was Light Auburn, but the tip returned to Strawberry. If someone painted Grace, the subtle shades of her fur would be hard to capture.

Lila also got to know Grace's dietary preferences, which emerged as she polished off her cadmium-red bag of kibble and transformed herself into a glutton. Whenever Lila went to the kitchen, Grace cornered her and fixed her with desperate eyes that insisted she was faint and needed food. Wanting her to gain more weight, Lila obliged, and Grace became a connoisseur of snacks. Besides dog biscuits, she devoured—after barely chewing—cheese, cantaloupes, bananas, snow peas, carrots, and zucchini. She acted like she'd sell herself into slavery for toast with peanut butter.

At first Lila gave Grace the treats strictly in her bowl, but then Lila handed them to her, and she gently took the bits and slices without a tooth touching a finger. When Lila finished her yogurt, she held out the container for Grace to lick, and she was also careful not to brush Lila's skin with her tongue.

Lila admitted she'd been wrong to call Grace a savage. She could be polite. Even to bugs. She loved beetles and studied them on the deck by resting her chin on the wood so close to the beetles that her eyes crossed. Insects were her favorite hobby, next to the dreaded tennis ball.

The first week that Grace was Lila's, they had rows about the ball. Repeatedly, Grace brought it into the house, and Lila shouted a stern "*No!*" She picked up the ball with paper towels and threw it outside until, finally, Grace brought it back inside so often that Lila broke down and let her chew it in the living room.

That must not have been a large enough concession from Lila, as Grace made clear by dropping the ball at her feet in the kitchen and den. After going through rolls of paper towels, to save trees Lila caved and touched the slimy, filthy fuzz with her fingers. From there, throwing the ball to Grace was just another small step.

She caught the ball with a Venus-flytrap snap and seemed so joyful about it that Lila obliged and threw it again. The retriever in Grace shone. She was at her very best when she picked up the ball and brought it back to Lila. If you'd ever told Lila that she wouldn't recoil from dog saliva, she'd never have believed you.

21

Lila helped Grace out of the Volvo, and, with ebullience, she hobbled on the sidewalk. Her nostrils flared as she skimmed her nose over an empty Coke can, chewing gum, and ancient spit. She'd surely never been on a city street, and she seemed thrilled. *Woweeee! Ecstasy!* exclaimed her quivering nose.

Yikes, said Lila's quivering stomach. They were on Spring Street, which was narrow and deserted. The afternoon fog grayed the shabby buildings, which felt like they were closing in on the sidewalk. Without Grace, Lila might never have made the trip to this depressing part of San Francisco. She'd come to find Yuri Makov's flat, though she didn't know exactly where it was.

On TV she'd seen the building it was in—a two-story stucco box the dull taupe of cheap nylon stockings. Three black doors led to separate entrances. On the front wall, three dented mailboxes hung above a row of water meters, and rolled-up, yellowing newspapers littered the stairs to the porch.

Alberto Hernandez, the TV reporter, had avoided tripping as he made his way to the middle door, to Unit 2. Ignoring the drizzle that matted his pompadour and darkened his khaki bomber jacket, he rapped on the door. "Was this Yuri Makov's apartment?" he asked as the door swung open.

"*Da,*" said a man who Lila assumed was Yuri's roommate.

A brontosaurus of a man, he loomed over Alberto. His hair was slicked back from his thick forehead in a European style, and his jowls looked like hams. His huge hands could have strangled Russian bears.

"I'm from KROS-TV. Can I ask you a few questions?"

Yuri's roommate glared at the TV camera. "I have not time."

If Alberto had been made of weaker stuff, he'd have turned and fled, but he'd stiffened his wiry legs and pressed, "How long did you live with Makov?"

"I not speak."

"Was he upset when he left for work yesterday?"

"I tell you I not speak."

"Did you have any idea what he planned to do?"

The roommate curled his beefy lip and muttered surly, Slavic-sounding grunts. He stepped back and slammed the door.

Alberto had turned to face the camera. "Unfortunately, Makov's roommate couldn't provide any information for us. This is Alberto Hernandez signing off at Makov's flat on Spring Street."

At "Spring Street," Lila's breath caught in her throat. Dozens of times, on her way to work, she'd taken a shortcut down that street's three blocks to avoid early morning traffic on Van Ness Avenue. Maybe Yuri had looked out his window and seen her pedal by on her bike. If he'd wanted, he could have shot her then. But, clearly, he'd had bigger plans. Killing one person wasn't going to be enough for him.

Lila hurried Grace to the end of the block and crossed the intersection. Ahead was a dreary brown building with three entrances. But there were no water meters, and the doors were chartreuse. Wind blew a ripped manila envelope against the tire of a rusty Ford parked out in front. Beside it, garbage over-flowed a bin.

Grace and Lila crossed another intersection, but Yuri's building was nowhere in sight. Perhaps she'd heard Alberto Hernandez wrong, and he'd said Spruce or Ming Street. Discouragement seeped into her as she and Grace stepped up on the curb of Spring Street's last block. But halfway down the other side of the street was a building that looked like Yuri's. They jaywalked toward three black doors and three dented mailboxes.

As Grace and Lila approached, she hesitated. Yuri's roommate could slam the door in her face, as he had in Alberto's, or even attack her. Beastly men, like those breaking down the door in Lila's recurring nightmare, could be hiding in Yuri's flat, and she'd told no one she was going there. She grabbed a clump of Grace's reassuring curls. Though Lila had never seen Grace bark at anyone but Agnes Spitzmeier, Lila was glad Grace was there.

Dodging newspapers on the stairs, they climbed to the middle door, and Lila knocked. No answer. She was about to knock again when a deadbolt turned and links of a guard chain clacked on wood. As the door opened, at her nearly six-foot height, she had to bend back her head to look into the flushed face of Yuri's roommate. He might have snacked on growth hormones. He could have been a giant in a Diane Arbus photograph.

He wore a gray velour running suit, the jacket of which was unzipped to his waist and exposed a chest like a granite slab. Below his neck, a gold chain ran through what looked like a woolly mammoth's fur. There was something oppressive about him; to show off at parties, he might rip phone books in half. He looked like he'd been born to intimidate people.

When Lila introduced herself, his nod acknowledged she existed. But he frowned at Grace as if she were a cockroach and he was about to stamp his foot and make her skitter out of sight. Grace flashed him her most misanthropic glower, and the fur along her spine rose like a Mohawk haircut. She pressed back her ears and let him know that protecting Lila mattered more to her than oxygen.

"May I talk with you for a minute?" Lila asked.

She took his nod as begrudging permission, but his glance at his watch as a sign she'd better keep her talk short. She was glad he did not invite her in because, even with Grace, Lila would not have wanted to be with him behind a closed door.

"I'm one of the people Yuri Makov shot. I was hoping you could help me."

"I know nothing." The man's voice was nasal and unpleasant.

"Can't you tell me about him?"

Two mountainous shoulders shrugged.

"What was he like?"

"Smart man. Moscow University study."

"Did he try to work as an architect here?"

"Nobody want. Must janitor."

"Did that bother him?"

Another shrug.

"I heard he got fired," Lila said.

"He tell nothing."

"Was he mad about anything?"

The man's hand went to the doorknob.

"Please," Lila begged. "I'm trying to find out why Yuri was upset. Don't you have any idea why he shot everybody? What was he angry about?"

"You people. Ask, ask, ask. Is too much." He waved his hand with impatience, like he wanted to flick Lila off the porch.

"I need to know. It's really important."

"He speak nothing. Police I tell. His mother I tell. Everybody . . ."

"His *mother*?" Lila's heart took a running leap against her ribs. "How can I find her? Do you know?"

"*Nyet.*" He crossed his arms over his chest and shoved his hands under his armpits.

"You don't know where she lives?"

"Here she telephone."

"I need to talk with his family. Please, can't you help?"

His yawn exposed a giant uvula and silver teeth. "Cousin. Near Monterey. Yuri she sponsor."

"Do you know his cousin's name?"

"*Nyet.*"

"Is his mother near Monterey too?"

"I know nothing."

"What about Yuri's friends?"

"I am not friend."

"But he lived with you."

"Room rent."

"Did anybody visit him?"

"Enough. Enough. Ask, ask, ask. Okay, good-bye." Scowling at Lila, he stepped back into his entry hall.

As he was closing the door, Lila asked, "How did Yuri get to the U.S.?"

"Lottery green card. Moscow." A deadbolt turned with a scraping sound.

A couple walked by jabbering in Spanish. Grace must have sensed Lila's disappointment because she pressed herself against Lila's leg.

"That jerk has the compassion of a turnip," she grumbled as she and Grace made their way around the rolled-up newspapers back to the sidewalk.

Lila glared at a wooden Russian doll on the windowsill of Yuri's landlord. A kerchief and apron were painted on the squat, peasant body. Red circles represented rosy cheeks. She was a matryoshka doll that opened again and again to keep revealing a smaller doll inside. It seemed like the dolls would go on forever and there would never be an end. Maybe she was a sign from the universe.

On the way home in the car, Grace leaned against Lila's shoulder extra-hard, as if she were trying to cheer her.

"I bet Yuri expected the streets here to be paved with gold, and he'd be the Frank Lloyd Wright of California. I bet he was really mad he had to work as a janitor," Lila told her. "But that couldn't make him shoot a bunch of people, Grace. It just couldn't."

Grace studied a fly buzzing against the windshield's corner, trying to find a way out.

"Why did he do it?" *Why? Why? Why?*

His oaf of a landlord's "ask, ask, ask" came to Lila's mind. She shuddered.

"Yuri must have had a reason."

Grace eyed the fly, which had landed on the visor.

"I have to talk with his family." Lila drove onto the ramp that would curve around to the Golden Gate Bridge. "I've got to find his mother."

22

Tired from the trip to Yuri's flat, Lila ate dinner and climbed into bed. As usual, Grace curled up on the rug, as close to Lila as she could get. Moonlight silvered the floor and windowsill. As Lila closed her eyes, wind churned the redwoods, and their cones clattered on the deck outside the French door.

Just as Lila's conscious thoughts were about to turn over the key to her mind to her subconscious murk, something creaked outside. Unnerved, she snapped her eyes open, bolted up in bed, and turned toward the window. She cocked her ears in the dark. The side gate's hinge or a foot on the deck floor could have caused the sound. She could not tell from how far away or from what direction it had come.

Another creak. Her shoulders tensed. Straining to figure out what had made the creak was like straining to understand what had exploded in Weatherby's lobby. God only knew what threat was out there.

"Grace?" Lila whispered as prickles of fear crept through her.

Grace got to her feet and leaned against the mattress. Lila rested her hand on Grace's shoulder and reminded herself she wasn't alone. She craned her eardrums, listened. Something thunked on metal. Or on wood? Lila thought of the thugs in her nightmares and the psychopaths loose in the world. Just as she'd frozen in fear in her Weatherby cubicle, she stiffened against the headboard.

When something crashed on the deck, Grace managed to lunge at the French door despite her injured leg. She barked like a person screaming, red faced, through a bullhorn. She rose on her hind legs and snarled as if a rabid tiger had sprung over the railing. As Lila pressed her pillow against her chest, Grace limped to the window and looked outside. Whatever she saw upset her more, because she yowled like she might break the glass and dive into the backyard.

A scream lodged in Lila's throat. No one would hear her. She couldn't fight off anyone with her injured arm. If someone wanted to kill her, she was defenseless. Though Grace's leg hadn't healed, she was Lila's only protection.

Grace seemed determined to make any killer run for his life. As she hobbled back and forth in front of the French door, her barking boomed to a crescendo. Her barks ended with raging exclamation points.

Slowly, though, her punctuation changed to angry periods, and she panted between barks. Then, in a diminuendo, her protests quieted to growls and whines, which seemed like parting shots. Grace must have felt her foe had retreated, because her ferocity cooled and she silently shuffled back and forth at the door. When she finally calmed, the room also seemed to calm, as if the walls and floor had been roped into the brawl and were settling down, victorious.

Lila slid back under the covers and tried to slow her breaths. As she searched her mind for what might have caused the creaks and thunks, her adrenaline took its sweet time fading from her bloodstream. Her anxiety lingered.

Grace looked out the window. She slowly padded over to

the bed and rested her chin on the mattress next to Lila's pillow. In the moonlight, Grace's eyebrows bristled as they did when she was worried, and Lila knew the worry was for her.

Grace's eyebrows clearly stated that the responsibility between her and Lila went both ways. *I'll always protect you. I love you! You can count on me.*

Lila pulled her arm from under the covers and stroked Grace's widow's peak and shaggy ears. "What a good girl you are. The very best."

Grace sat on her haunches and put the paw of her good front leg on the mattress. She plainly asked, *Do I have to lie on the floor in my usual spot? Would you let me get on the bed?*

Lila threw back the covers and struggled to help Grace climb up. When Lila got into bed again, Grace lay down behind her back. Very gently, Grace placed her paw on Lila's healing arm and rested her chin on Lila's shoulder.

As she listened to Grace's soft, calming breaths, Lila had no doubt Grace was watching over her. Feeling safer than she'd felt since getting shot, she closed her eyes and slowly breathed in sync with Grace. In her hug, Lila fell asleep.

The next morning the mattress was sagging behind Lila, and something was weighing down her shoulder. All night Grace had kept vigil and not moved an inch. Though it was daylight, she was still guarding Lila. Grace's breath warmed Lila's neck.

She reached back, took Grace's paw in her hand, and ran her fingers over the rough gray pad and rounded nails. Warmth was emanating from Grace's flesh. Kindness seemed to be embedded in her very cells.

"Oh, thank you, Grace. Thank you."

The morning was sunny, and the blue sky seemed ostentatiously generous, as if it were putting on a charity ball. In the pure, still air, the crows were belting out squawks like jazz violinists. No one would have believed that the night before had served up fear.

Lila checked outside to see what might have made the thunk and crash, and she found a raccoon's tracks across the deck and, below it, a broken terra cotta pot. *Perhaps the raccoon had been looking for slugs and knocked the pot off the deck*, she thought, relieved she had nothing to worry about.

Grace pranced into the kitchen the best she could on her gimp leg. As always, her plumed tail was high in the air with eager expectation for the day ahead. Lila made the usual breakfast of high-fat kibble and canned chicken morsels, but this morning she also poured in gratitude and love.

She made herself a cup of pomegranate tea and went to the table. Grace sat in front of her and tapped her knee with her paw: *Here I am! Pay attention! Notice me!*

"I see you, Grace." Lila ruffled the fur on Grace's forehead and took a sip of tea.

The eager paw landed on Lila's arm. Tea spilled on the floor, just where Grace had chewed the brush.

No point fretting over spilled tea. Lila got a paper towel and mopped it up. "Oh, well."

Grace's dog tag arrived in the mail. After Lila fed her a celebratory hot dog, she worked the tiny heart's metal loop onto Grace's collar and gently buckled it around her neck, which had healed so new fur almost completely covered the scars. Grace must have liked the tag because she panted and smiled. As she shifted her weight, the heart made a pleasant clink against her collar's buckle.

From then on, the clink reminded Lila of her and Grace's connection to each other. Adam or Marshall couldn't think of claiming Grace if Lila's name was on the tag. It formally announced that she and Grace were a family, and no one could change that. Their commitment to each other was official in the Book of Life.

23

At the computer Lila looked up the white pages and typed in "Makov" and "Monterey, California." When a window appeared on the screen with "zero results," she felt like a steamroller had squashed her heart. "Dammit," she told Grace. "Yuri's cousin must have a different last name, or his mother isn't listed. Maybe she doesn't have a phone."

Grace was lying on her stomach, her chin resting on the floor. Her eyes were riveted on ants parading single file across a baseboard. To her, they were like a movie so compelling you forget your popcorn and sit on the edge of your seat. Grace seemed like she'd give those ants an Academy Award. She could have been an entomologist.

Losing hope in her search for Yuri's mother, Lila went back to the white pages and typed "Makov" in "California" without mentioning a specific city. When six Makovs appeared on the screen, she yelped. Two of the Makovs were in Los Angeles, but four were in the Bay Area, not far from Monterey or her. She jotted down their names, phone numbers, and addresses in San Francisco, Vallejo, Carmel, and Daly City. She grabbed the phone and called Vladimir Makov on Pine Street in Carmel, which was closest to Monterey.

When a woman answered, Lila stammered; she'd called on impulse without thinking what to say. She considered hanging up, figuring out the best approach, and calling back. But she was so excited at the prospect for answers that she blurted out, "Are you related to Yuri Makov?"

"Excuse me?" The woman had no Russian accent. She seemed American, born and bred.

"I'm looking for Yuri Makov's relatives. I was hoping you were one of them."

"I'm not."

"Did you know him?"

"No. Maybe my husband does."

"Did," Lila corrected. "Yuri Makov died a few months ago."

"Are you settling his estate or something?"

"No. It's hard to explain." Lila wished she'd hung up when the woman answered. She regretted becoming as spontaneous as Grace. "Would you ask your husband if he knew Yuri?"

"He's not here," she said. "Are you from some collection agency? We're not responsible for anybody's bills."

"Yuri Makov shot me."

"Oh, my." The woman sounded like a toe meeting a piranha.

"He went postal in my office."

"We don't know anything about that, hon. Good luck."

Click.

"Dammit, Grace! Dammit!"

Grace took her eyes off the ants, glanced at Lila, and went back to watching their parade. Bugs were all that could have kept Grace from coming to Lila when she'd spoken with distress. But ants were Grace's favorite insects after beetles.

Lila pressed her lips together in frustration. *Think, Lila, think. Use your brain.* Eager to call the other Makovs, she plotted her strategy: Right up front, she'd throw herself at their mercy and say she was one of the people Yuri had shot; surely they'd learned in the newspaper or on TV about his going postal, Lila would add. She'd recount how hard it had been and how far she had to go to heal. "I'm trying to find out about Yuri. Understanding what happened will help me recover," she'd say. Then they'd shower her with information.

Lila called Janet Makov in Daly City, then R. S. Makov in San Francisco. Neither answered, and Lila didn't leave a message. She tried Boris Makov in Vallejo. His "hello" sounded barrel-chested, as if he had Luciano Pavarotti's lungs. She poured out her story quickly to get to the heart of her call.

Boris interrupted, "So what do you want from me?"

"I'm trying to find Yuri Makov's relatives. I want to talk with them about him."

"Never heard of him."

"Do you have family who might know him?"

"I don't have any family. It's just me."

"Do you know any other Makovs?"

"No."

"Oh, well, uh . . . thanks."

Lila set down the phone and told Grace, "This isn't going very well."

Lila's heart practically dragged behind her as she went to the kitchen, where from a *National Geographic* photo she'd been painting an African granary door. Carved into the wood was the face of an apoplectic desperado with fat scarlet lips and bulging ochre eyes. He could have scared the most courageous grain-thieving rat, and he looked annoyed enough to spit. Lila knew how he felt. She sat at the table and picked up her paintbrush.

When someone knocked on the front door, Grace got up from her place at Lila's feet and, yowling, limped into the entry. But suddenly her yowls changed to joyful whimpers. Besides

Lila, Adam was the only person who could draw such a welcome from her. With trepidation, Lila went to the door.

Through the windows, Adam was grinning at Grace. His light-brown hair, slightly shaggy at the neck, suggested he'd been too busy for a haircut; his confident posture said he didn't worry about such incidentals. When he clapped his hands together, Grace whined with shining eyes. "Hey, girl! I've missed you!" he called through the glass.

Lila, the "damned flake," opened the door.

"Hello, Lila," he said, polite and formal.

At least he hadn't said her name as if a rare tropical disease were running loose in it. "Hello, Adam," she said, polite and formal back.

Grace reared up on her hind legs and rested her front paws on his chest like she was trying to hug him. As he rubbed her ears, she licked his face and cried so everyone on the entire mountain must have known she was thrilled about something. Pressing her hands together, Lila felt left out and jealous.

"If you've come to make sure I haven't given Grace away, you can see she's here," Lila said.

"I didn't come for that. I came to get her. I told you I would in a month."

A threatened sparrow fluttered in Lila's chest. Though she'd been waiting for Adam to demand Grace back, she was no more prepared for him than she'd been for Vladimir Makov's wife. Again, Lila quickly searched her brain for how to handle an unexpected situation. "You came to get her?" she stalled, as bland as rice.

"I've finished my fence. I've bought organic dog food and a great new bed for her." Adam helped Grace land on all four paws from her hugging position, and she leaned against his legs. "You're going to love it with me, girl. I've got great sunny spots in the grass for you. You can watch people through the gate and hang out with the squirrels."

Lila hooded her eyes and bristled her porcupine quills. Pushing her Pleaser off the porch, she said flatly and with all the control she had, "It's amazing. When I wanted you to take Grace, you wouldn't do it. Now that I'd never give her to you in a million years, you show up for her."

"What are you talking about . . . never give her to me?"

"She's mine."

Adam looked at Lila like she needed a muzzle. "You told me you didn't want Grace. You said you didn't like dogs. God knows you tried to give her to everybody you met . . ."

"I'm sorry. I've changed my mind."

He rolled his eyes toward the porch's ceiling. "I haven't changed *my* mind. Because of you, I just rushed around to build a fence. I haven't unpacked my boxes yet. It wasn't easy hurrying like that. I did it because of you."

"I didn't mean to cause you trouble."

"You have."

"I'm sorry." Lila gathered her defenses, which she needed to stand up to him. "You could get another dog."

"So could you." He said it like he was entitled to Grace; he was the lord of her manor, and Lila was her peon.

"Grace is happy with me. I've taken good care of her." To prove it, Lila lifted Grace's collar and pushed back a patch of fur so Adam could see that the Vitamin E cream had calmed her scars. Lila pointed out that Grace had gained weight on her special premium kibble and she wasn't slouching anymore. Lila showed him that the formerly crusty spots on Grace's back were healing.

"That's all well and good, but Grace needs a bath." Adam worked a loose curl from her haunch and held it out to Lila. "You're not brushing her, either. You don't know how to care for a dog."

"Grooming's not everything. Love counts for a lot." Lila flipped up the tiny metal heart on Grace's collar so he could see.

"Her ID tag has my phone number on it, and possession's ninety-nine percent of the law."

The outside edges of Adam's eyes slanted down, hard and intense, so they looked compelling and stubborn at the same time. "I care about Grace."

"So do I."

Exhaling a loud and hostile breath, he shoved his hands into his jeans pockets and looked toward the forest as if he were deciding how to handle Lila. When he shook his head, he let her know that he wished he could throw her in an alligator's path. On the street, the mailman shut the box with an aggressive scrape of metal. In the Gravenstein apple tree, a crow cawed as if some insignificant peanut of a finch had stolen the seed he'd planned to eat for lunch, and he was mad.

"Look, Grace is what matters," Lila said.

"I agree."

So at least we agree about something. "I've tried to do everything right for her. She's happy here. Surely you see that."

"Except you haven't bathed or groomed her."

"She's not going around like a waif."

"She needs a bath. You have to keep her clean so her skin will finish healing," he said.

"So I'll bathe her, okay?"

"What about your arm?"

"I'll take her to a groomer." *Even though I can't afford it.*

By shaking his head, Adam let Lila know he didn't believe her. "I'll be back in a few days. If she's not clean, she's coming home with me. Do you understand?"

"You don't have to talk like I'm a three-year-old," Lila snapped, gathering her power.

Her Pleaser pressed the back of her hand against her forehead and swooned in a vapor.

* * *

As Betsy was working her magic on Lila's arm, she told her about Adam.

"It's not doing you any good to get agitated," Betsy said.

"I can't help it. I'm scared he'll steal her. That's how he got her in the first place."

"You'll know where to go to get her back." Betsy pulled Lila's arm straighter than it had been since Yuri shot her.

Before Betsy covered her with the Navajo blanket and left her to meditate, as usual, she stepped out of her black suede clogs and sat, cross-legged, on the floor beside Grace. Betsy's silky, purple-paisley skirt circled her like a mandala. As she patted Grace's head, tiny gold whales bobbed at Betsy's earlobes.

At the end of Lila's last appointments, Betsy had worked on Grace's leg to get her walking like a normal dog. Now Betsy gently kneaded it again, and Grace rested her head in Betsy's lap and surrendered to the pleasure of massage. Grace's look of ecstasy announced that she'd added Betsy to her personal pantheon. Grace had become a hedonist.

"I get mad every time I think of that horrible man hurting Grace," Lila said. "There's evil everywhere. The world is an awful place."

"That's not true!" Betsy's forehead furrowed in ridges, like tiny ocean waves where her earrings' whales could swim. "Sure, there's evil, but the world isn't awful. It's sacred."

"The tree Grace was chained to wasn't sacred. Neither was the office I got shot in." To round out her picture of how awful life could be, Lila returned to Adam's threat to take Grace back to his unsacred house.

"Lila." Betsy often said her name before making a pronouncement. "You know better than anybody that life isn't fair. We all take turns at injustice. You can't control that. But everything evolves to good in the end, and the Great Spirit stands by us as we go through tough things."

"I'm not sure everything evolves to good," Lila said, stubborn.

Betsy's fingers played softly on Grace's leg as if it were an angel's flute. "They do if you wait long enough. I'll bet good comes to you from being shot."

"Not a chance," Lila said. "I can't deny what my brain tells me."

Betsy smiled and exposed the gap between her front teeth. As she stretched Grace's injured leg, Betsy's whales sparkled. "Lila, your brain can only get you so far. It's not the only place to look for answers. You've got to let loose and think with your heart."

After Betsy left the treatment room, Grace and Lila lay in the quiet for a while until Grace got up and bowed and stretched. She came to Lila and nuzzled her hand to ask for a pet, and Lila obliged. Then Grace waved her plumed tail like she was flagging down a limo to take her to pick up her twenty-million-dollar Lotto prize.

As she pranced around, smiling, her limp seemed less severe than before, and her leg was hardly wobbling. If she'd had an audience, she'd have been kicking her cancan skirt and winking at men in the front row. *Wahooo!* proclaimed each swish of her tail.

Grace's prancing announced that all she wanted in the world, besides Adam and Lila, was to shed her afflictions. And since Betsy's treatment must have brought new relief from stiffness and pain, Grace now seemed sure that robust health was just over the next hill, and the Great Spirit would never let her down.

Standing on her hind legs, she rested her front paws on the treatment table and encouraged Lila out from under the blanket into the glorious afternoon. The world champion of thinking with her heart, Grace acted like being bereft was ancient history, and she zoomed toward exuberance.

Lila guessed Grace wanted her to be exuberant too. She said, "Okay, I'm getting up."

Lila snapped Grace's leash on her collar and led her out of Betsy's office. On the street, Lila looked around for armed maniacs and for the brute she imagined Marshall was. Ahead of her and Grace, an elderly couple held hands and licked ice cream cones, and a Japanese tourist aimed his camera at a woman who was sitting on a curb, studying a map. Outside the Bus Depot Café, a street fiddler sawed away beside his violin case, open for coins. His bluegrass drifted across the town square.

Lila hurried Grace across the street and headed down a narrow road, where she doubted Marshall would go. Four boys were building a cardboard fort on the creek bank while a cocker spaniel splashed around them. Grace paused to watch, then to sniff a path; she whimpered like she expected Bambi to bound out of the woods. Lila slowly led her up a flight of stairs through the trees. Since Grace had run off the raccoon on the deck two weeks before, Lila felt safe. Grace was her fierce protector.

Halfway up the stairs, they came to an iron gate flanked by two stone ducks embedded in concrete and wearing bandanas, floppy hats, and tacky rhinestone-studded sunglasses. Lila laughed at the whimsy. "Look, Grace!"

The warm afternoon must have brought out her itches. She seemed interested only in nibbling her paw.

"I'm going to do a painting of this gate."

Focused only on scratching, Grace raked her hind paw's nails through her fur as if she intended to claw off her side. The miserable expression on her face shouted that she wished she could wriggle out of her skin and rush to Pet Stop for flea shampoo and a back scratcher.

Lila could not deny Grace a bath for another minute. No matter how leery Lila was of Adam Spencer, she had to iron out the wrinkles between them and ask for his help. She had to act on her love for Grace and think with her heart.

Lila bent down, hugged Grace, and lightly ran her hand along Grace's side to show that a gentle scratch could be as good as a fierce one. Lila promised her, "We'll get you right."

24

"Ready for your morning ablutions, girl?" Adam asked.

Grace wagged her tail with an ecstatic swish that could have blasted off the floor the imaginary sultan she fanned with her plume.

"Hello to you, too," Adam said to Lila. He stepped into the entry in jeans and a navy sweatshirt. Slung over his shoulder was an olive-green duffel bag.

He looked at the doorways leading to other parts of the house. "So where do you want to bathe Grace?"

"The master bath," Lila said.

"Fine." He took long strides into the kitchen, then stopped in front of Lila's last four paintings, lined up against the wainscoting. "Cristina told me you were a painter."

"I'm doing a series of gates and doors."

He bent down and studied Lila's painting of a garden gate with a decoupage print of Our Lady of Guadalupe tacked to the wood. Then he quickly passed by the apoplectic-desperado granary door and the door with the dolphin knocker, and stopped to examine a door Lila had just finished. It had a curved wrought-iron handle, as graceful as a swan's neck, below a brass handprint, palm forward like a policeman telling you to stop.

"The hand's supposed to keep away evil spirits," Lila said.

"If you opened the door and showed what's inside, the painting would be more interesting."

Adam's criticism smarted.

He stooped down for a closer look at the three other paintings. "Same goes for these. People want to know what's going on behind the door."

Who asked your opinion? "I want the barrier, not the opening."

"That's a shame."

Lila led Adam down the hall to the master bath, which had a shining marble floor. A camel could have hosed down in Greg's giant shower, and hamsters could have nested in Cristina's monogrammed towels' thick pile.

Adam opened the glass door, removed the showerhead from its hook, and extended the flexible hose. "This'll do," he said.

He set down his bag as if it were a briefcase and he and Lila were about to discuss a business plan. But as Grace sniffed his loafers, he unbuttoned his jeans and unzipped his fly.

Lila blanched, then froze. Adam must have noticed, but he ignored her. He kicked off his shoes, pulled off his brown socks, and with one quick motion, slid out of his jeans. Black Watch plaid swimming trunks flapped against his thighs.

Lila felt like someone trying to keep eye contact in a nudist camp. As she leaned against the sink, her Horny Guttersnipe, the cousin of her Pleaser and Crazy Aunt, could not help but notice Adam's manly, naked legs. When he took off his sweatshirt and tossed it on the wicker table next to Lila, her Horny Guttersnipe also couldn't help but note the strength of his arms and the patch of brown hair on his beautiful chest. She cried, *Tee-hee! We're talking "hunk" here!*

Lila forced her eyes to Adam's face. She told herself that, after Yuri and Reed, she might not trust men, but she had not gone blind, and she could not expect herself to clump through life without finding a man like Adam attractive. Nevertheless, she promised herself that being physically drawn to him did not mean she was vulnerable, and, after all, he was there only to help Grace—and at most he and Lila would be casual acquaintances. She repeated these things to herself as Adam opened his duffel bag and pulled out a hair dryer, a bottle of dog shampoo, a brush with steel bristles, and, finally, four towels, each of which was neatly folded into thirds.

"Did Martha Stewart do your laundry?" Lila asked.

He gave her an odd look. "What?"

"Your towels. How a person folds towels says a lot about him."

"Oh, that." He bent forward and turned on the shower's faucet. "My dad taught me to fold them that way. He learned it from his grandmother."

"I thought maybe you'd grown up in a five-star hotel."

"Nope. A Pennsylvania fruit farm. No stars, just apples."

Hauling crates must have built up his muscles! Lila's Horny Guttersnipe winked at Lila and chortled.

Adam ran water over his hand to test the temperature. "Are you always sarcastic like that? Towels, hotels?"

"Are you always judgmental?"

"Not always." Smiling, Adam rested his fists, akimbo, at his waist. He glanced around the bathroom and said, "We can't wash a dog who isn't here."

Only then did Lila notice that Grace had sneaked away.

As Adam adjusted the water, Lila went to retrieve her from her hiding spot under the bed, where she never went anymore. When Lila lifted the bed skirt, Grace peered out at her with a wary expression, which informed her that whatever she and

Adam had planned, Grace wanted none of it. At the same time, though, she thumped her tail on the floor.

"Come on, Grace. You may as well give in without a fight."

She averted her eyes as if she did not understand what Lila was asking, and, further, she believed Lila was addressing some other dog under the bed.

Lila did not want to tug Grace's collar even though her neck had healed. So Lila wheedled and hinted of a future chicken-skin reward until Grace finally wriggled out and allowed herself to be led to the bathroom. As Lila unbuckled Grace's collar and set it on the counter, Lila's Horny Guttersnipe again noted Adam's bare chest.

"Let's do it." Flinch. "Um, let's give Grace a bath," Lila said.

"You ready, girl?" Adam asked Grace as she panted and looked wary again.

When he bent down and nudged her into the shower, her toenails clicked on the tile. He stepped in with her, and Lila rolled up her jeans to her knees and stepped in too. She and Adam crowded together.

As he ran the showerhead over Grace's chest, Lila patted Grace's light auburn haunch. Once her front half was soaked, Adam and Lila changed places. He wetted down her back end while Lila comforted her from the shoulders up. He poured shampoo into his hand and gently worked it into her fur, and Lila lathered her up the best she could with her good hand. When Grace looked like a vanilla-frosted cake, Adam rinsed her; dingy gray foam gurgled down the drain. So he and Lila soaped and rinsed again—and Grace stood there, law abiding, but anyone could see from her face that she wasn't thrilled.

While Adam and Lila worked together, they were quiet. At first the silence seemed slightly hostile, but then it grew companionable, as if they'd long bathed dogs together. Lila didn't mind sloshing around with him. After they finished hosing down Grace for the second time, Lila liked how solicitous he was, gently helping Grace out of the shower.

Immediately, she shook the water from her fur and splattered the cabinets and walls. "Way to go, Grace," Adam joked and threw a towel over her back so she looked like a small jousting pony.

He handed Lila another towel, and, together, they rubbed Grace down. Then, side by side, he dried her with his hair dryer, and Lila swiped at her fur with his grooming brush. When they finished, the Argonauts would have turned their ship around to collect Grace's fleece. She practically sparkled.

"Thanks for coming over," Lila said. *You're not as bad as I expected.*

Adam smiled as he put the cap back on the shampoo. "I appreciate your help. I hadn't counted on it."

After his kindness toward Grace that morning, something needed to be said about his fence. Lila told him, "I was wrong not to let you know sooner I was keeping Grace. I'm sorry. I know I put you out."

"You did," he said without giving Lila an inch of slack, and tossed the shampoo into his duffel bag. "But I was going to build a fence eventually."

While Lila swabbed water off the walls and cabinets and picked fur out of the shower drain, Adam dried himself off with his last clean towel, pulled his jeans up over his bathing suit, and shrugged into his sweatshirt.

"If your arm hasn't healed in a couple of weeks, we need to bathe Grace again," he said.

"I'll be strong enough to do it myself."

He leaned against the sink and put on his socks and shoes. "You don't like to be alone in the house with me, do you?"

"Oh . . ." Gulp. "I don't know . . ."

"Are you afraid of me or something?"

"Some."

"I'm not Charles Manson."

"You're a man. Men shoot people."

"So do women. If I wanted, I could be scared of you."

"I'd never hurt anybody."

"Neither would I," Adam said. "You afraid of getting shot again?"

"Wouldn't you be if someone had tried to kill you?"

"Maybe." Adam stuffed his dog-grooming tools and soggy towels into his bag. "You know your chances of two unrelated men trying to kill you in one lifetime?"

"No." Lila shook her head.

"Okay. Take nine left-handed Peruvian nuns. They're rustling hippos across Siberia. You with me?"

"Uh-huh."

"Your chances of another man shooting you again are less than those nuns running you down in your living room at 9:07 tomorrow night."

Lila pictured nuns in wimples and habits, prodding hippos whose hooves were sinking into snow. She laughed. Hard. Something in her chest cracked open to the sun. Adam laughed too. Grace, who was sitting at Lila's feet, looked up, startled.

"I don't think Grace has ever seen me laugh before," Lila said.

"It's time she did." Adam hoisted his bag onto his shoulder.

When Lila and Adam headed toward the kitchen, Grace followed close on his heels and made clear she didn't want him to go. At the end of the hall he turned around. "If you come with me, I'll show you the dog park."

Lila cleared her throat. Adam as hunk-at-a-distance was one thing; Adam as trustworthy man was another. "I don't take Grace downtown," she lied.

Adam frowned. "You have to take her to the park. She needs exercise."

"We could run into Marshall."

"He hates dogs. He'd never be at the park. Besides, he works Saturdays. Today he's miles from Mill Valley."

"I don't want to risk it."

The outside edges of Adam's eyes scrunched down. Obviously, he suspected Grace's safety wasn't what he and Lila were talking about. "We could leave her here and go by ourselves."

"I've got work to do."

"And she's got a leg to strengthen."

"I'll strengthen it."

Adam patted Grace good-bye and opened the front door. "You can't stay scared forever."

Lila rewarded Grace for her cooperation in the bath by feeding her cheddar cheese and chicken skin on a slice of wheat bread. She downed it in two bites and looked up at Lila with moist eyes to beg for more.

"Maybe later." Lila ran her fingers through Grace's fluffy gold fur.

Lila made herself a cup of lemon-ginger tea, sat down to paint, decided she didn't really want to paint, went to the refrigerator for an apple, changed her mind, took the apple back to the refrigerator, returned to the table. She rested her chin in her hands and stared out the window at an airplane crossing the sky like a trout who'd lost her stream. Lila got up and turned on NPR but concluded that she didn't want to think about rising interest rates, so she clicked off the radio.

"I can't let some man stir me up like this, Grace."

Twenty minutes later Adam was back at the front door. He had changed into dry jeans and an oxford shirt, which was open at the top—and any woman in her right mind would have rejoiced at his alabaster-pillar neck. He was holding a brown grocery bag, which Grace gave a thorough sniffing.

"I've solved your problem with Grace," he said, stepping into the entry before Lila invited him in. "Turn around and close your eyes."

She couldn't do that. Not for a man who stole dogs, and Grace was by the front door. "Why should I turn around?"

"I have a surprise. Trust me. You'll like it."

I don't trust you. That's the point. But Lila was curious enough to go ahead and turn around. She could always grab Grace if she heard Adam lead her outside.

Adam's grocery bag rustled, and Grace squeaked. More crinkles of paper. Shuffles of paws.

The wait started to feel like Lila was standing in line for the last hot fudge sundae to be served in America. "What are you doing?"

"Something great. You'll see."

Lila sighed an impatient sigh.

Finally, Adam said, "Okay, now you can look."

When Lila turned around, Grace was wearing shaggy black-and-white-splotched fabric, anchored to her back by elastic around her belly and neck. Stuffed white-felt horns, attached with a chinstrap, stuck out above her ears. Hanging down her front legs were white strips of material with black hooves printed on the bottom, held in place by strings tied above her paws.

Grace did not know that she was now a Holstein, but she must have sensed Lila's delight at the outfit. She straightened to her very best posture and tossed back her head, like a model on the cover of *Vogue*.

"Grace can go downtown now. Marshall won't recognize her," Adam said.

"Yes, he would. Even if you covered her up with a sheet, he'd be suspicious of any dog you were with."

"Maybe, but I told you he's nowhere near Mill Valley today."

"Then why the cow disguise?"

"To humor you."

Lila smiled. "Where'd you get it?"

"At a thrift store. I bought it for my niece's dog for Halloween."

"You go to thrift stores?"

"All the time."

25

Surrounded by a chain-link fence, the dog park was a grass field, large enough for soccer games, with dead, trampled patches. A bed of scraggly day lilies grew behind a spigot and concrete drinking trough. Beside it, a woman was reading a newspaper on a weathered wooden bench and ignoring what must have been her black Lab, who galloped across the grass to Grace.

Hey! You're a delicious babe! he panted. He whined and pushed his face toward her. His black-spotted tongue swung from the side of his mouth; you could tell he was about to lick her somewhere. Grace might have snapped at him, but she only flattened back her ears.

When he rudely sniffed her bottom, she whirled around and gave him a look that said, *Oh, pul-eeze!* She sat down and leaned against Lila's leg.

She waved her arms at him. "Shoo! Shoo!"

Unwilling to give up, the Lab practically inhaled Grace's armpits.

"Don't get worked up. He's trying to meet her," Adam said. "She needs to make friends."

"Not with a pushy, insensitive dog. He's coming at her too fast."

As if he intended to come at her faster, the Lab drooled on Grace's Holstein spots. *Oooooo! What a luscious cow!*

Grace gazed across the field as if she'd left her body and would stay away till the thug was gone.

Adam looked on with an indulgent smile. "Grace isn't scared. She's shy. This is new to her. You're being overprotective."

"After all Grace has been through, she needs protection. Can't you see she doesn't like him?"

"She will if you'll let her get used to him."

"I don't think she likes the park."

Ignoring Lila's concerns, Adam took off Grace's cow costume and unlatched her leash. "Come on, girl!" He started running across the grass.

As the Lab chased him, Grace trotted after them and slowly caught up. She limped, but nothing like before Betsy had worked on her leg—and the more Grace ran, the stronger she looked. Right before Lila's eyes, Grace seemed to get more limber.

Soon she was circling the park with Adam and the Lab. The sun sparkled on her golden head and swishing tail, and she was glowing with energy and health. She looked more beautiful than Lila had ever seen her.

And Grace was smiling. *Whoopeee! Look at me! I've never been free to run before!*

Adam shouted, "What'd I tell you? She loves it here. You should have brought her here every day."

"I know." With regret at having been so wrong, Lila stuck a fork into her steaming slice of humble pie. She gladly took a bite and swallowed.

* * *

Thankful to Adam for introducing Grace and her to the park, Lila agreed to have lunch with him without stopping to consider what it might mean. Only when they got to the La Luna Café did it hit her that she was practically on a date with a man she hardly knew. *Oh, my. Well . . .*

Tired from running, Grace curled up under the outdoor metal table. As people bustled by with shopping bags, a waiter in a stiff white jacket that pulled too tightly across his chest came to take Adam and Lila's order.

"Smoked turkey on wheat. Mayo, mustard. Whatever you've got, put it on. And a bottle of water. Everything to go," Adam said.

The waiter scribbled in his pad and turned to Lila. "And?"

"I'll have the camembert on wheat with avocado and sprouts. No, wait. That's too much fat."

"Live it up. It's Saturday," Adam said.

"Is the tuna salad organic?"

"I'll have to ask." The waiter gave her a look that said asking was an imposition.

"Never mind. I'll have the sliced chicken. Whatever."

"Drink?" the waiter asked.

"Do you have bottled tea? Oh, forget that. I'll have water like his."

The waiter disappeared before she could change her mind again.

"You obviously have trouble making decisions," Adam said.

Only when I'm nervous. "There's a lot to choose from."

Adam tossed his menu on the table and tilted back his chair on two legs. "Let's get this getting-to-know-you thing over with fast, all right?"

"Are you type A?"

"I don't like wasting time on small talk. Okay if I ask you questions?"

"Depends on what you ask."

Adam shooed away a yellow jacket that landed on his wrist. "So where'd you grow up?"

"Santa Fe."

"Siblings?"

"I wish."

"Was it hard being an only child?"

"Not too bad. My parents threw fantastic birthday parties. One year my father built a teepee for my slumber party."

"So you were spoiled?"

"Hardly. And you just sounded critical again."

Adam chuckled. "Sorry."

Lila smiled. With her thumb and index finger, she twirled the teaspoon on her paper place mat. "Any siblings on your Pennsylvania fruit farm?"

"Two brothers. Thank God there were three of us because my mother made us take care of her garden. She grew enough veggies to feed Bach's twenty kids."

"Imagine folding their towels."

"I don't even want to think about it."

"Are you a musician?"

"Nope. I teach astronomy at Sonoma State." As a busboy clattered dishes in a metal bin, Adam crossed his arms over his chest. "The first time I looked through a telescope, I had to keep refocusing because Mars was traveling across the sky so fast. I couldn't get over the motion and silence up there in the dark. Blew me away."

So there went the uptight engineer with mechanical pencils lined up in his shirt pocket. "I've never looked through a really powerful telescope," Lila said.

"I can show you sometime."

An image of her and Adam—squinting through a lens, close together in the dark—flashed through Lila's mind, and her

Horny Guttersnipe leapt up on the table and tangoed. Her spike heels clicked around the place mats and her feather boa floated in the air. Lila urged her, *Get yourself under control.* Breasts jiggling, her Horny Guttersnipe threw back her head and chuckled with abandon.

"You dating anybody?" Adam asked.

"No." As Lila rested her arms on the table, she decided to go ahead and lay her relationship with Reed facedown in the street to writhe around in all its blood and gore: "I lived with a man for a long time. We split up six months ago."

"What happened?"

Squirm. "I found out he had another girlfriend."

"Sounds like a winner."

"I'd been thinking about breaking up for a long time. She just forced the issue," Lila said. "But I hate to tell you—most men are jerks. If they don't cheat on you, they shoot you."

"Whoa! Does 'sweeping generalization' mean anything to you?" Adam asked.

"I'm right, though."

"I'll bet on some distant island in the middle of nowhere you could find *one* decent man."

"Maybe."

"Women aren't always perfect, either. I lived with a compulsive shopper for five years. I broke up with her because I didn't want to be in debt for the rest of my life."

"Very wise of you."

"That's what I thought."

"Something must have drawn you to her, though."

"She was pretty, fun, smart. She was always interviewing interesting people. If she hadn't been so irresponsible, she'd have been great."

Lila wondered how Adam would compare the girlfriend to her. At least they'd gotten their dismal pasts out of the way.

The waiter set their lunches on the table in a paper bag, which was a clean and honest white.

Adam picked it up. "Let's go."

At the Pet Stop, Albert Wu was washing his front window with a squeegee like you find at gas stations, a sponge on one side and a rubber blade on the other. He dunked the squeegee into a bucket of soapy gray water and smeared it around on the glass. Outside in the sunlight, his beaver toupee looked exhausted, like it had built one dam too many. Albert wiped sweat off his forehead with the back of his shirtsleeve.

"We're looking for a treat for Grace," Adam said.

Albert smiled so his face crinkled. "Check out the bin by the counter. We've got rawhides, all kinds of biscuits, anything a dog could want." Albert wiped his squeegee's sponge across the glass again.

Inside, Adam held a desiccated pig's ear out toward Grace. She sniffed it with ebullience.

Lila screwed up her face. "You can't give her that."

"Why not?"

"I feel sorry for the pig."

"You can see Grace loves it. You need to give dogs what they like."

Normally, Lila would have argued with Adam, but he'd been so right about the dog park that she gave in with a wince.

Magnolia, Albert's cockatiel, let out a piercing screech.

Adam went to her perch and stroked her chest. She cocked her head and peered at him sideways. "Bad day, bird?"

Lila smiled.

"You're prettier when you do that," Adam told her.

"Do what?"

"When you smile. You seem more approachable."

"Thanks." Lila wasn't sure how approachable she wanted to

be. If her heart had been a piece of paper, it would have had something fluttery, like "eeeeek," written on it.

The Unitarian Universalist Church looked like a giant rowboat turned upside down. Around its stern was a brick wall; Adam said he'd looked over it by chance and discovered the garden, whose entrance was a gate of iron swoops and curlicues that would have made an interesting painting.

He led Lila and Grace down a gravel path to a wooden bench under an apple tree. The garden was like Eden minus the snake. Fig and pear trees were starting to bear fruit next to the walls, and lavender and roses grew in beds. In one corner was a sundial on a stone pedestal; in another, an Ionic-column fountain, dripping water from its capital into a mossy pool. Inside the church, someone was practicing "The Star-Spangled Banner," and "the land of the free" traveled, forte, through the air.

Lila unhooked Grace's leash, and she plopped down on the gravel. Adam handed her the pig's ear, which she took with an ecstatic chomp. He sat on the bench, and they unwrapped their sandwiches in the same companionable quiet as when they'd bathed Grace.

"Why don't you have a dog?" Lila asked.

"Used to. A blond Lab kind of like the dog at the park. Named Hubble. He died a few years ago."

"Why haven't you gotten another dog?"

"I wanted Grace, remember?"

"Are you ever going to forgive me?"

"The jury's still out."

"I said I was sorry."

"I want to see you grovel." Adam smiled.

Lila smiled too, even if it did make her look approachable.

*　*　*

When they finished their sandwiches, they wadded up the paper wrappers and put them and the empty water bottles into the bag.

Adam threw it into a garbage can behind a camellia bush. "Know how this sundial works?"

"Not really."

"Okay, when the earth turns on its axis, the sun seems like it's moving across the sky."

"Right."

"So the sun casts a shadow from this iron stick. The shadow points at the time." Adam rested his finger between Roman numerals I and II, etched in the stone around the dial's base. "For the time to be accurate, you have to set the sundial right for your latitude and aim it directly north. But that's not hard to do. I made one of these in Boy Scouts."

"You were a Boy Scout?"

"On my honor." Adam sat back down and rested his elbows on his knees. "When I lecture about sundials, I hand out a page of maxims."

"Like what?"

"Time and tide wait for no man."

"I've heard that before."

"Okay, try 'Time is a dressmaker specializing in alterations.'"

Lila leaned down and patted Grace's golden haunch. "Time can change things; that's for sure."

Lila and Adam walked home slowly because Grace was worn out. Panting and looking wilted, she plodded along, dragged her paws, and occasionally scraped her toenails on the asphalt. Though she no longer wore her cow costume, Adam gently encouraged her, "Git along, little dogie," and he told her that she and Taurus, the bull in the sky, could get together and produce golden stars. He told Lila about the Hyades, which form Taurus's face, and the Pleiades, which shine from his shoulder.

At the front door, patches of sunlight on the porch looked like Holstein markings. As Lila turned the key in the lock, she said, "I can wash Grace's cow costume before I give it back."

"Don't bother. It's just a little rumpled. Keep it in case we need to disguise her again."

He had a future in mind, Lila thought with a tingle. A car drove by with its radio's bass too loud, so the music had a heartbeat thump.

"I enjoyed our lunch," she said.

"I did too," Adam said. "I asked you out today, so now it's your turn. Call me if you want to get together."

Errrch. Call you?! *Stick out my neck that far?* Calling him would be so different from accepting his invitation.

For the rest of the afternoon Grace sat at the front door, staring through the glass like she wanted Adam to come back. Lila didn't know what she wanted anymore.

26

At the kitchen table after breakfast, Lila turned the pages of *Columbine: The Story of a Rampage*. Grace, on her early morning patrol, was rustling through ferns and lecturing blue jays behind the house. Ever since Adam had taken her to the dog park, she wanted to roam the yard and explore the blackberry patches, the creek bed, and anything that cast a shadow or snapped a twig. Adam would have been pleased at her new confidence and spirit of adventure.

In the past month, he'd often come to Lila's mind. She'd remembered the Peruvian nuns, Grace's cow costume, and his gentleness helping her from the shower. But those pluses had not been enough to cancel the threatening minus of calling him and suggesting they get together. Whenever she considered it, self-preservation won over risk, and she snapped her clamshell shut.

There were better things to do than brood about making the next move toward Adam when she wasn't sure she was up to a relationship with any man. Lately, she'd painted a dentist's office door with a fleur-de-lis-shaped peephole, a Victorian house's door with a lace curtain over the oval window, and a Safeway door with posters for lost dogs taped to the glass. Each week she and Grace had gone to see Betsy, and nearly every day Lila had taken Grace to the dog park, where she retrieved her tennis ball and strengthened her leg.

In the past few weeks, Lila had also finished calling the Bay Area Makovs, and then she contacted all the California ones listed on whitepages.com. Finding no one who knew Yuri, she Googled "Makov" and pored through thousands of citations. Makov was a common name, and the Makovs were a varied lot. Louis Makov had written books on the police, of all things. Jonni Makov was a punk drummer in a Czech rock band, and Pavel Makov was president of a Peoria bank. Lubov Makov, an engineer, had published *The Microwave Anisotropy Probe Control System*. Arthur Makov was a quarterback for the Texas Aggies. Sergei Makov was a Russian bishop, and on Facebook, Helge Makov's spaghetti straps slid off her teenage shoulders, exposing tops of breasts that looked like ski jumps.

None of those Makovs got Lila closer to Yuri, however, and her frustration drove her to the library, where she checked out the Columbine book. She wondered if the same malicious urge that drove Eric Harris and Dylan Klebold to shoot up a school might have driven Yuri Makov to go postal. But now as she finished the book's first chapter, she had more questions than answers.

In a year Harris and Klebold had built a hundred bombs, which they intended to detonate at Columbine High School; then they would shoot surviving students as they ran for their lives. Lila wondered if Yuri had carefully planned what he was going to do, or if one morning he'd tossed off his covers, climbed out of bed, and in a flash of evil decided to kill people. Or maybe in all those months as he'd quietly vacuumed and dusted Weatherby offices, he'd been suppressing a volcano and waiting for the right morning to let the lava flow. Lila wished she could climb into his brain and discern: spontaneity or premeditation?

Harris and Klebold had shot themselves, just as Yuri had. Lila tried to put herself in his place as he lifted the gun to his temple and curled his finger around the trigger. Was he sweating? Icy? Hesitant? Remorseful? Afraid? Relieved that he was free to move on? Did he just shoot himself in a crazed reflex without thought or feeling?

Lila wanted Yuri to have begged God for forgiveness at the end, but, more likely, suicide had been a way to shield himself from facing consequences, a cowardly act to avoid his victims' and their families' hate. He may have thought dying by his own hand was better than an executioner strapping him to a table and injecting him with a lethal drug, and he might have wanted his death over with sooner rather than later, and on his own terms. Or he could have seen it like stepping off a cliff into an abyss. How could Lila know?

She wasn't much closer to knowing Yuri's motive, either. The chapter made clear that Harris and Klebold had sought revenge against other students' slights and snubs. "I hate you people for leaving me out of so many fun things," Harris, described as a cold-blooded psychopath, had written in his journal. Depression and anxiety were said to have driven Klebold, who had once referred to himself as a "god of sadness."

A study in the book concluded that most school shooters had feelings like Harris's and Klebold's. The students were depressed or coping with losses and failures, and seventy-one percent felt bullied, persecuted, or shunned. To fight back, the students killed out of rage, just as Dr. Leibowitz had claimed on TV that people going postal did. So Lila was back full circle to anger—and its relative, depression, which was said to be anger turned inward.

She stared out the window at Grace, thrashing through a patch of vinca, and at an English laurel, which deer had eaten back to naked stems. But Lila hardly saw Grace or the bush because she was mentally standing up to Yuri and trying to get back her power. *What were you doing?* she demanded of him. Without averting her eyes, she stared him down.

Imagining his face, she couldn't see anger. Not in his dark eyes or set jaw. Not in his look of concentration as he brushed a feather duster over bookshelves and computers. Not even in his aloofness, which may have been a defense against being looked down on as an immigrant and janitor. Maybe he'd dressed better than other Weatherby employees to tell them he was better than they were.

Had he used indifference to hide feeling hurt or alone? Who in the office might have snubbed him as students had snubbed Harris and Klebold?

Suddenly, Lila pictured who. Yuri might have thought she had. Her stomach felt like it had been thrown from a skyscraper window.

One evening Yuri had been grooming a schefflera in the lobby near the desk of Emily, whom he later killed. She'd left for the day, as had nearly everyone in the office. Lila had stayed because Cristina was going to drive her home after working late.

Lila walked by Yuri, who, as usual, might have just stepped out of a Macy's catalogue on his way to a casual dinner, in corduroy slacks, a V-necked sweater, and a shirt with a button-down collar. Though he seemed absorbed in his snipping, he looked up as Lila passed, and he beamed. He seemed like he'd purposely waited for her—a benign spider hoping for a friendly fly.

"Hello!" he said.

"Hi." Lila pressed the elevator button.

In the longest second in recorded history, silence crawled between them with an arm and leg tied behind its back.

Wanting no one to feel awkward, Lila's Pleaser jumped in. "You're doing a good job with that plant."

Yuri held out a schefflera branch as if he were about to lead it to a dance floor. "Grow . . . good."

"Yes. You're helping it." Anyone could tell he was sensitive to greenery. "Uh, you enjoy working with plants?"

"Enjoy?" He cocked his head the way Grace did when she was trying to understand.

"You know, you like."

"You."

Surely he couldn't have been saying he liked Lila. Oh, God. She chose to think he meant "you" to be a question—as in "Do *you* like working with plants?"

"Well, I do like plants a lot. I grew tomatoes every summer when I was a little girl," she said.

Where's the elevator?

Yuri's lips turned up in a smile that was too eager and needy, and it felt oppressive. He seemed to want more from Lila than even her Pleaser might be willing to give.

Still, her Pleaser wanted all exchanges to go smoothly, so she smiled back, though the smile was wan.

"I . . . happy. You here." He pointed at the floor.

He probably wanted Lila to say, *Well, golly, I'm really glad you're here too. What a nice way to finish the afternoon.* She managed only, "Uh, well . . ."

Just then the elevator arrived with an off-pitch bong, and, thank goodness, she could leave.

"Good-bye," she said.

"Good-bye," he said, but now his smile looked rained on.

Lila practically hurled her body into the elevator to escape the awkwardness. Before the doors closed, she wouldn't let her Pleaser turn around and wave an insincere good-bye. Perhaps in Yuri's mind Lila had snubbed him—and maybe she unintentionally had. But, oh, how she wished she'd handled that uncomfortable situation better. What are you supposed to do when someone is being nice but you get a creepy feeling about it?

Last week Lila had told Betsy that the only way she'd get over being shot was to know why it had happened. The only way out of trouble was through it, she'd said, and you got through it by understanding it and going on from there.

"Do you have to understand? Does it really matter?" Betsy asked.

"It does to me. I've been doing everything I can think of to find out."

"That keeps you tied to the man who shot you," Betsy said.

Lila hadn't liked the sound of that. She pushed its camel's nose out from under her mental tent back into the sandstorm. But the camel pushed his nose back.

Grace shuffled up the steps outside the kitchen and yipped to let Lila know she wanted in. Grace's usual energetic climb had seemed slow, and through the French door's glass, her face looked troubled.

Lila set *Columbine* aside, got up, and opened the door. "Whatsamatter, Grace?"

When Grace looked up, the whites below her pupils formed the beseeching crescent moons she'd presented in her early, ultraneedy days. The fur on her right front paw was dark and wet.

"Been jumping up to drink out of the birdbath again?" Lila asked as Grace limped inside.

Lila turned to close the door behind her. Fuzzy-edged red smears marked the stairs from the yard. As Grace walked across the kitchen floor, she left bloody paw prints like the muddy ones she'd left when Lila had first known her. Lila's knees started knocking together.

27

Lila grabbed her purse and Grace's leash and hurried to the door. For Grace's sake, Lila tried to act like all was well and blood was no worry. But her stomach was tied in a hitch knot. She was trembling when she told Grace to come. As she hobbled a couple of steps, pain showed in her eyes. To spare her, Lila would have gladly taken the pain, quadrupled.

Even if Lila's arm had not been injured, she could not have carried Grace. So Lila slowly coaxed her through the kitchen to the garage. Each time Grace put weight on her right paw, she flinched. Still, she kept going because Lila asked her to. "You're such a good, brave dog," Lila said.

When they got to the Volvo, Lila covered the front passenger seat with blankets. She urged Grace to put her front paws on the seat so Lila could push her from behind. But lifting her hurt paw must have asked too much. Grace stood there, staring ahead with glazed eyes. Lila gently nudged her to make sure she understood what she should do, but she whimpered and did not move.

Lila's left arm was too weak to lift even part of Grace. Lila

had to get help. Slowly she and Grace made their way back into
the house.

"Adam? It's Lila." She gripped the telephone receiver.

"It's been a while."

"I'm sorry. I really am."

He paused, like he was letting that sink in. "What's up?"

"Grace cut her paw. She needs to go to the vet. I can't lift her
into the car."

"I'll be right there."

Tears came to Lila's eyes. "Oh, thank you. Thank you so
much."

Adam brought a royal blue hand towel, which he gently
wrapped around Grace's paw. He picked her up from her
kitchen bed as if she were made of Baccarat crystal, and he carried her outside. Lila followed them up the path to his silver
Honda and opened the door to the backseat. He set Grace
down and closed the door behind her.

When Lila slid in the back on the other side, Adam said,
"Hold the towel around her paw and press on the wound."

Lila pressed, and she kissed Grace's widow's peak. As Adam
sped down the hill, Grace whined and licked Lila's hand like
she was trying to comfort *her*. Lila blinked back tears.

Adam glanced at her in his rearview mirror. "We'll be there
in a few minutes."

"Nobody ever told me how terrible it would be to see Grace
suffer," Lila said, her voice cracking.

Dr. Armand Hightower was not so high as his name would
have led you to expect. He was short, pudgy, round, and bald—
a croquet ball of a veterinarian, whom Alice in Wonderland's
Queen of Hearts might have whacked through hoops. But behind his aviator glasses, there was compassion in his eyes.

Stooped over Grace's paw, he pushed apart her bloody fur and probed, then dabbed the spot with gauze. "She's got a nasty cut."

Lila wrapped her arms around herself to keep her heart from pounding through her chest and bounding off like a wounded deer. "I don't know what happened. I let Grace out like I always do," Lila said. "I thought the yard was safe. I wish I'd checked for something that could cut her."

Under the fluorescent lights, everything in the room seemed jittery, including the doorknobs and stainless steel towel dispenser. The leopard in a photo on the wall was frowning.

When Adam wrapped his arm around Lila's shoulder, she avoided looking up into his eyes because she expected to see judgment toward her for failing to keep Grace safe. But, to Lila's surprise, he smoothed her tee shirt with his hand and showed no sign of blaming her. Grateful, she leaned against him like she was a horse outside in a blizzard, and he was a warm barn wall.

When Dr. Hightower was about to carry Grace to surgery, Lila asked, "Will she be all right?"

"Once we clean the cut and stitch her up, she should be fine," he said.

"You'll be good to her?" Lila asked.

"Don't worry." Dr. Hightower glanced at Adam and smiled.

"You're sure?" Lila asked. "She's had a terrible life."

"Come on, Lila. Let's go sit in the waiting room," Adam said.

She kissed Grace's widow's peak again and hugged her. "We'll be right here, Grace. I promise."

You could tell that Dr. Hightower wanted his waiting room to be a happy place where everybody's needs were met. On a table in one corner were children's games, building blocks, and Dr. Seuss books; in another corner, a tin of shortbread cookies, a jar of dog biscuits, and a pot of coffee. On the walls were posters of robust dogs and cats who gave clients hope that their own pets could be healthy. Sitting in chairs were teddy bears to clutch, as needed. Lila grabbed a fuzzy white one.

"Want some coffee?" Adam asked.

"No, thanks."

"A cookie?"

"No."

"How about a dog biscuit? You should eat something to keep up your strength."

Despite her worry, Lila smiled at him.

Lila and Adam sat side by side in molded plastic chairs. He stretched out his legs in front of him and crossed his ankles. When he reached over and took her hand, she was glad instead of wary, as she'd have expected. Reassurance seemed to be residing in his epidermis. Though strong from hauling apple crates, his hand was gentle.

"So tell me. Did your phone line snap in two or something?" he asked.

"No."

"So why the month's silence?"

"I don't know. I didn't feel right calling you."

He chuckled. "You wanted to be pursued?"

"No."

"Then what? Something to do with your ex-boyfriend?"

"Probably. At least partly," Lila said. "It's been a crazy time."

"You need to get over it."

"Easier said than done."

"How about trying?"

Adam rubbed his thumb over the top of Lila's hand. "There's this lady who seemed to blame herself about a dog's cut paw. She wished she'd gotten on her hands and knees and combed every inch of half an acre before letting her dog out this morning."

"I wish she had," Lila said.

"Seems a little excessive to me. Too much to expect of herself, don't you think?"

"She feels guilty."

"Guilt's a waste of time." Adam twirled a button on his shirt. "Feeling like something's your fault is a way to fool yourself into thinking you're in control. Problem is we're not in control of much in this world. Most of what happens is beyond us."

"I wish that were true."

"It is," Adam said.

"I'm not so sure."

"Is letting loose of things a problem for you?"

"You could say that."

As the waiting dragged on, Adam got up, poured himself a cup of coffee, and shuffled through magazines by the receptionist's desk. When he came back to the sofa, he handed Lila a *People*; on the cover famous couples were gazing with longing at each other.

"Here's something to distract you," he said.

"Thanks." Lila set the magazine in her lap.

After he studied the table of contents of a *Sports Illustrated*, he looked at her unopened *People*. "You're not reading."

"I can't. I'm too worried."

"I can't, either. I was just pretending." He closed his magazine.

"Thanks for caring," Lila said.

"Couldn't help but."

"I appreciate it. Really."

* * *

Adam checked his watch and put his wrist in front of Lila so she could also see the time. Though they'd been there less than an hour, it felt like three days. As he got up and paced the room, his loafers' heels tapped the tile floor. He stopped and studied a poster of a black Lab with a chartreuse tennis ball in its mouth like the one Grace carried around. But the Lab's was new, and Grace would have nothing to do with any ball except hers, which housed more germs than a New Delhi gutter.

When Adam came back, Lila whispered, "You should get another dog."

"I will eventually."

"The right time will come."

"It does. For everything." Adam settled back down beside her.

Another fifteen minutes inched by like a slug on Thorazine. Lila counted how many times Adam checked his watch: eleven. He may have counted how many times she rubbed her forehead—until the number needed commas. But rubbing her forehead didn't stop the worry.

A woman in tennis togs came into the clinic with her basset hound. A man chewing an unlit cigar dragged in his German shepherd mutt. When an elderly couple struggled from the parking lot with three cat carriers, Adam got up and opened the door for them. They whispered apologies to no one in particular as the waiting room filled with hostile squawks and yowls.

Lila barely heard them because she was picturing Grace conked out on an operating table with an anesthesia mask over her muzzle, or lying, woozy, in a recovery cage. Grace's fur would be matted with blood, and her paw would be throbbing. If she were conscious, she could be worrying that Lila and Adam had left her at the clinic forever. Lila ached to get her home.

Finally, Dr. Hightower walked Grace into the waiting room, and Adam and Lila rushed to her.

Her right paw and lower leg were wrapped in elastic white tape, and her eyes were glassy. Still, she swished her tail and emphatically said, *Thank God you're here! Please, please, take me home!*

Lila got on her knees and wrapped her arms around Grace, careful not to jostle her. Lila squeezed her as tightly as she dared as Grace squeaked and licked Lila's face.

"Good girl," she said.

I love you, said Grace's whimpers.

As Adam stroked her head, she pressed it against his hand. *Home! Home!* begged her nuzzles.

Lila thanked Dr. Hightower. Three times. He gave Adam antibiotics, pain medication, a printout of care instructions, and the bill. Dr. Hightower asked that Adam and Lila bring Grace back for a checkup on Monday. When Dr. Hightower returned to an exam room, Adam went to the receptionist and handed her a credit card

"Hey, wait a minute." Lila leapt up and tore across the room.

"I can pay," Adam said.

"You can not."

"The bill is bigger than you think. You don't have a job."

"I don't care how much the bill is for. Grace is mine."

"Is this going to put you into debt?"

"No. And I'm not your ex-girlfriend."

"I was just trying to help."

"I don't need it."

Adam's lips turned up slightly, the beginning of a smile.

Lila and Adam settled Grace in her pumpkin position on the kitchen pillow. Her face looked droopy, and her bandaged paw stuck out like a short white cane. But she seemed as if she'd soon get back to her old self. As Lila broiled her a chicken breast, relief welled up inside her and made her giddy.

Adam seemed relieved too. He changed Grace's water and set the bowl next to her so she could drink without getting up. When her chicken was done, he cut it into pieces and showed Lila how to sneak in pills so Grace would swallow them and never know the difference.

As he walked to the front door, he said, "I don't want to distress you again by suggesting you call me. But if Grace needs anything, you know where I am."

"I do."

"No broken phone lines."

"None," Lila said. "And thanks. You've been our saving grace."

Adam put his hand on the doorknob, as if he were about to leave. Then he turned around and brushed Lila's lips with a quick kiss. It told her that whatever was between them was not going to be platonic, and she'd just washed up on the beach of a relationship.

As he walked up the path to the street, Lila's Horny Guttersnipe tap-danced around the entry and hummed, "Happy Days Are Here Again."

"I don't care what you want," Lila told her. "I'm not getting involved with any man. He's just a friend."

Lila's Horny Guttersnipe winked. *Tee-hee!*

While Grace was sleeping off her anesthetic, Lila tiptoed out of the house to walk downtown for more chicken. When she came to the stone ducks at the gate's entrance, they still wore sunglasses, but now they also sported ratty wigs like you'd buy at a party store. Delighting in the absurdity of tangled, brunette locks on ducks, Lila rummaged through her purse and found a wadded pink ribbon from a floral arrangement someone had sent her in the hospital. She tied the ribbon around the neck of one of the ducks and stood back to admire her contribution.

They seemed free and happy, as if they'd given up being on guard at the gate all the time and had taken up lolling around and enjoying the sun. With the ribbon, they weren't identical twins anymore, either. Now they looked like a duck and a drake. If you looked at them just right, you could almost call them a couple.

28

Adam lived half a mile from Lila in a white Victorian farm-house whose peeling paint and missing shingles made you think of a senior citizen in need of a hug. Once you walked along the stone path that curved around his vegetable garden, though, all you thought about was green thumbs. Hanging off vines were emerald green snow peas, lettuce grew like a carpet, and the zucchini looked like they were going to need birth control. On the front porch a wisteria climbed the railing, and two wicker rocking chairs invited Lila and Adam to sit. They didn't because he wanted to print photos he'd just taken for her.

He left Lila in the living room and went into his study. Grace was home watching Animal Planet after Dr. Hightower had just proclaimed her cut "improving" and covered her stitches with a hot-pink elastic sock. She'd lain on his exam table as if she were the Queen of Sheba and acted like she'd have been shocked if Lila and Adam hadn't fallen all over themselves to light the myrrh in her incense burner. At home, they'd fed her chicken. After Adam had settled her on the bed in front of the TV, they'd left so he could show Lila gates she might want to paint.

While his computer printer hummed, she snooped around the living room. A wingback chair and brass floor lamp sat on an oriental rug in front of the fireplace. Above the mantel was a watercolor of an orchard, perhaps where he'd picked apples growing up, and a Betsy Ross flag hung above the stairs. Floor-to-ceiling shelves crammed with books covered one wall. Next to a Morris chair by a window in the corner, a brass telescope was aimed at the sky.

Lila bent down and studied a photo of a little girl who must have been Adam's niece, a little older than Rosie—blonde braids, a missing front tooth, and eyes that slanted at the outside edges like his did when he concentrated. An Irish setter, for whom Adam must have bought the cow costume, was sleeping at her feet. She was holding a calico cat on a porch swing, painted the same violet as a picket gate that Adam and Lila had just seen.

"Some ancient languages supposedly didn't have a word for 'violet,' " he'd said. "The theory is that people hadn't physically evolved enough yet to see violet's end of the color spectrum."

"Imagine the colors we can't see," Lila said.

Adam focused his camera on the gate and clicked. "There must be lots of pleasures waiting for us to evolve to them."

He seemed like he was addressing Lila's color-loving artist, but her Horny Guttersnipe shimmied.

Lila ordered her, *Sit down and fold your hands in your lap!* She sulked. *Phooey!*

Adam handed Lila three photos printed on computer paper. Thrilled, she shuffled through them.

The first was the violet picket gate under a trellis and flowering passion vine. The second was Chinese red, as tall as three people, with a green-ceramic roof and hinges as black as ravens' wings. The last, made of iron bars, was flanked by brick columns that served as pedestals for two stone Buddhas. High above them seven strings of prayer flags extended from a redwood's trunk like ribbons from a maypole.

"Look at the interesting things behind those gates," Adam said.

Here we go again. The art critic. "Uh-huh," Lila said.

He noted two mossy griffins holding up a stone bench in the English garden behind the violet pickets, and miniature stone pagodas tucked among ferns behind the Chinese gate. "See the monk raking leaves under the prayer flags? He'd make a great painting. Especially his yellow robe."

"The color's saffron," Lila said.

"You paint people, don't you?"

"Sometimes."

"So why not him?"

"Okay, okay."

"There's a whole world behind those gates. That's what I want you to see." To help her examine the photos, Adam turned on a lamp with a brass bugle for a base. "I know what I'm talking about. I'm right."

"And not the least bit pushy or judgmental." Lila smiled.

"Exactly." Adam's grin had triumph in it. "I'm just looking out for your best interests."

Just as companionably as they'd bathed Grace, Lila and Adam made a salad with lettuce and carrots from his garden, a stir-fry with chicken and his snow peas, and brown rice, which Lila spooned into his favorite thrift-store bowl. Glazed in the bottom was the face of a lion like Rosie's Gerald, but Adam's lion looked perplexed, as if he couldn't figure out where the mound of mint jelly beside his wildebeest carcass had come from. Lila and Adam served themselves on attractive but mismatched china thrift-store plates.

As steam from their food glowed in a blue candle's light at the kitchen table, they discussed the Second Time Around Shop, where Adam had bought the plates.

"I've found a better place to get great things," he said. "Goodwill has an ongoing auction on the Internet."

"Never heard about it," Lila said.

"You'd be amazed what you can find there. That bugle lamp in the living room cost five dollars, and all it needed was a little polish. I got a dollhouse for my niece. It was practically new."

"Sounds better than eBay."

"A lot less expensive. You have to check every few days because auction items change, but that's no big deal. You can find the site if you Google 'Goodwill.' "

Lila took a bite of chicken; its delicious smell would have driven Grace wild. "Lately Google hasn't helped me much. I've been disappointed."

"Google's practically a miracle," Adam argued. "What were you looking for?"

"Oh, just a woman I was trying to find around Monterey."

"You can find anybody on the Web."

"Not her."

"Who is she?"

Lila stopped the fork on its way to her mouth and considered how to explain. Adam, like Cristina, could judge her as crazy for trying to track down Yuri's family, and yet maybe Adam could help. Lila dove in and risked, "I'm trying to find the mother of the man who shot me. I know she lives near Monterey. I've tried everything I can think of on Google, but nothing's worked."

"Why would you want to talk with her?"

"I want to know why her son shot everybody."

"Forget him. You should be glad he didn't kill you."

That word "should." Judgment, as Lila had feared. She almost backed off, but then Adam looked at her with his eyes slanted at the edges, like his niece's, intent and sincere. Lila said, "It's easy for you to say 'forget him.' He didn't shoot you."

Adam took a hurried bite of rice and washed it down with a gulp of wine. "Okay, what's so important about finding answers? What's the point?"

"If I don't understand him, I'll never get over what he did. I won't be able to put him behind me. At least psychologically, I won't ever heal."

"I don't mean to be blunt, but that doesn't make sense."

"Not to you, maybe, but it does to me. And, please, will you not be so critical?"

"I didn't mean it that way," Adam said. "But I don't think you need to understand the motive of some maniac. All you have to know is he was crazy."

"That's what Cristina says, but I'm sure there's more to it."

"Such as?"

Why did I start this conversation? Lila wished they could go back to Goodwill. "I've tried hard to find out what happened. The dead ends have made me wonder if *I* might be responsible for what Yuri did. Yuri Makov was his name. From Russia."

"There's no way you could be responsible." Adam's face didn't look judgmental now. He seemed genuinely concerned.

"He liked me. He sent me a valentine. Sometimes he tried to talk with me at work."

"That's no big deal."

"It may have been a big deal when he asked me out one night," Lila said.

Remembering the "aahs" and "uuhs" that had peppered Yuri's sentences on the phone nearly canceled her pleasure in Adam's supper. Soon after she'd seen Yuri in the lobby, he'd called her at home and said, "You want go me . . . uuh . . . ballet . . . aah . . . night Saturday? Beautiful fun . . ."

She pictured him, beads of self-conscious sweat on his forehead as he forced himself on. He sounded like he was reading something he'd written to impress her, but, still, his English slogged along. And the ballet, of all things? Was that meant to impress her too? Her Pleaser wanted to spring forth and sprinkle daisy petals on Yuri to make him feel better, but Lila's mind was racing to answer a more important question: *How did he get my unlisted number?*

Finally, she managed, "I'm sorry. I'd really like to go with you, but I have a boyfriend. I don't go out with other men." *A lie, but what are you going to do?*

"Yes . . . aah . . ." Clearly, Yuri was trying to translate what she'd said, but from her tone of voice, he must have known she'd turned him down. Maybe he'd not planned how to handle rejection, but only how to say he'd pick her up at seven and he knew where she lived.

The very thought of that was cringe inducing. After breaking up with Reed, Lila had not listed her new phone number and address specifically to prevent men she didn't want to know from finding her.

Adam wiped his napkin across his mouth. "So what if Yuri asked you out? You didn't go, did you?"

"Of course I didn't. But it was creepy. The only way he could have found my unlisted number was by sneaking through my personnel file."

"You think he did that?"

"I'm sure he did."

"You reported him to HR," Adam said, like any sensible person would have done it.

"No. I didn't want to make a fuss."

"He was practically stalking you, for God's sake. A fuss would have been appropriate. He was wrong."

Maybe I was too. Lila studied her salad as if she hoped for redemption in lettuce and tomatoes. "I didn't want to go to HR because I was worried I might have led him on. He seemed so shy. I felt sorry for him, so I was nice to him. Maybe nicer than I should have been."

"How do you mean? You baked him brownies or something?"

"I talked with him once in a while. I encouraged him to go back to school. I complimented him on his work so he'd feel like a worthy person."

"So what?"

"So he could have thought I cared more about him than I did. When I wouldn't go out with him, I might have made him mad."

"Men get turned down for dates all the time without getting angry. Even if you did make him mad, it couldn't have led to such a disaster."

"Yes, it could." *The butterfly effect.* "He was sensitive."

"Anyone who could shoot so many people was not sensitive," Adam insisted.

"No, I could have hurt him so he took his anger at me out on everybody."

"Surely he wasn't mad at *you*."

"When I've looked back the last couple of months, I'm afraid he could have been."

Adam set down his fork. Neither he nor Lila was eating, though worry was chomping her stomach.

"You're blaming yourself so you can feel like what some lunatic did was rational, but it wasn't. Life isn't predictable. Sometimes bad things happen to good people no matter what they've said or done. You can't explain it. There's no point trying."

"I still think it might be my fault."

"You weren't in control of what happened." Adam puffed out his cheeks and slowly blew out air, like releasing steam. "Whatever upset him, it's got to be some problem you know nothing about."

"I've done everything I can think of to find out what it

was." As Lila explained her months of looking for an answer, Adam listened so attentively that his whole body could have been covered with ears. "I try to tell myself I'm not to blame, but that doesn't help. I have to find out the truth to know for sure I'm not responsible," Lila said. "Mrs. Makov knows more about Yuri than anybody. If she can't explain why he shot us, nobody can. I have to talk with her, or I'll spend the rest of my life wondering. Mrs. Makov is my last hope."

"Did you ask the police how to reach her? They must know."

"They accused me of having a relationship with Yuri. I don't want to talk with them about any of this."

"Okay, let me try to find her." Seeming to forget that he and Lila were in the middle of dinner, Adam wadded up his napkin and set it by his plate. "You spell it *M-a-k-o-v*? She's around Monterey?"

"Right."

Adam took long, hurried strides into his study.

The computer screen saver's photo of a meteor shower flickered silver light on Adam's face. Lila rested her hands on the back of his chair and watched him type "people search" on Google. It felt good that he was trying to help; truly, sharing a burden reduced its weight. For the first time in months, Lila didn't feel alone. There was hope.

Then the first of nearly fifty million citations for "people search" appeared on Adam's screen. He exhaled a long breath and said, "We might be here all night."

He went to Yahoo, even though Lila said she'd tried it. He typed in "Makov" with no first name, then "Monterey," and he scrolled down and clicked on "California." In a blink, a message popped up on the screen that let him know no Makovs were listed.

"See, that's what kept happening. I tried several sites," Lila said.

"Several's not enough."

Adam moved on to Lycos and got the same response. As he tried AnyWho and USA People, his mouse clicks seemed to pick up determination; but Mrs. Makov was elusive, and Lila began to feel like she was watching failure unfold before her eyes. She went to the kitchen and washed Adam's wok and rice pot so he wouldn't sense her disappointment. When she returned to his study, he was looking at GenieSearch.

"Victory! Got her," he said.

Lila broke out in chill bumps.

Adam moved the cursor down a list of names and stopped. "Here she is. Meet Olga Makov."

Lila and Adam reheated their dinners in the microwave without taking the salad off their plates. Who cared about soggy, wilted lettuce when Olga Makov lived at 176 Ashton Avenue, Monterey, California, and they had her phone number?

Finding her felt like someone had chased away the dark. Everything in Adam's house looked brighter, the brass candlestick between them gleamed, and the candle flame sparkled. Though Adam disagreed that Lila was to blame for what Yuri had done, he'd cared enough to find Mrs. Makov for her—and that made all the difference. Instead of leaving her to search on her own, he was walking beside her. Cristina had been right that Adam and Lila could be good friends.

After dinner, on their way up Tamalpais Avenue to Cristina's, where Adam had left his car, he enveloped Lila's hand in a delicious clutch, and warmth traveled through her. You might think holding hands is a ho-hum act; but when Adam held Lila's, her Horny Guttersnipe swooned. *Forget the "good friend" business*, she sighed. *We're talking ecstasy here.*

A taxi came around a curve, and the driver dimmed his

headlights. Adam and Lila stepped off the narrow road to get out of his way as he passed by too fast. When they were alone again, Adam wrapped his arms around Lila and gave her a long, slow kiss that made her tinglers whoop and her toes involuntarily curl. Then without a word, he took her hand again. As something four-footed rustled in the brush, they continued up the road.

The night was dark, and stars were twinkling their hearts out. To Lila, just extravagantly kissed, the Big Dipper seemed like it was scooping up Truffle-in-Paradise ice cream.

Though she told herself she shouldn't get swept away, she'd become like Grace, who was so good at letting loose in life and going with the flow. Now going with the flow with Adam felt exactly right.

29

As Lila crossed the Golden Gate Bridge, fog darkened the horizon and threatened to roll in with a chill. Though she'd forgotten her sweater, she didn't care because she was thinking so hard with her heart about Grace. Lila had left her lying in her sphinx position as the morning sun streamed through Adam's kitchen window and brightened her golden fur. "You have to stay here. You're not well enough for a long drive to Monterey," Lila had told her. "You'd have to sit in the car for hours, and you'd get stiff and bored."

Grace's sad eyes insisted, *Oh, please! Please! Don't leave me! I want to be with you!*

"Adam'll take good care of you. He loves you," Lila said.

But Grace did not touch the pig's ear he gave her, and the only thing that could have stopped her from demolishing it was worry.

When Lila walked to the car, her own worry followed her. She and Grace had never been separated for more than a couple of hours. As if to reassure Lila before she drove away, Adam reminded her of their plan: When he set out at four o'clock to teach his class, he'd leave Grace on his porch, and Lila would pick her up by five. Grace would be alone for no more than an hour.

Still, Lila was concerned because Grace had seemed distressed. Weaving through San Francisco traffic, Lila imagined Grace's sweet face looking mournfully down from billboards, along buses' sides, and out of cars' rear windows—and the sumo wrestlers who'd rolled on Lila's heart at the Humane Society started a rematch. If she hadn't been so hungry for answers about Yuri Makov, she would have turned back.

She also worried about meeting Yuri's mother, who'd seemed confused on the phone. "Hallooo? Hallooo?" she'd barked into the receiver. As Lila had introduced herself and explained that she wanted to see her, Mrs. Makov kept repeating "Sorry?" Finally, though sounding reluctant, she agreed to talk with Lila. Mrs. Makov might have resented the intrusion, or she might not have wanted to reveal her thoughts to a stranger.

As Lila approached the outskirts of Monterey, sprinklers tossed water in giant circles on artichoke fields. Seagulls soared above sand dunes between the ocean and farms. Near the freeway exit to Mrs. Makov's house, mobile-home parks replaced the artichokes, and strings of faded plastic triangles flapped in the wind above truck stops named Alice's and Eat.

Lila drove down Ashton Avenue, a lonely gravel road through empty fields. She checked her watch to make sure it was after one o'clock, when Mrs. Makov had said she'd be home from her school cafeteria job. Lila prepared herself not to like Mrs. Makov because she'd reared a murderer; she would have a sullen face, as purple as borscht, and her bad teeth would be a complementary yellow. If Lila let her imagination loose, she saw Mrs. Makov as a mother version of Goya's *Saturn Devouring His Son*. A monster with bulging, crazed eyes, she would gnaw Yuri's arm.

Though that picture was extreme, Lila didn't know what

Mrs. Makov might turn out to be. With misgiving, Lila asked herself, *What are you getting into?* Yet if she ever hoped to heal and have a normal life, she had to keep going.

Olga Makov lived in a grievously depressing house with gray aluminum walls. It looked like a mobile home that had lost its way to a trailer court and ended up alone on the edge of a spinach field. Above the front picture window was a frayed, oxblood-red awning, not for shade, because little sunshine burned through fog here. Hummingbirds must have long ago stopped visiting the empty feeder in a leggy rhododendron. Red sugar-water had splashed on the sidewalk and dried to a crust.

At the door Mrs. Makov looked up at Lila with sad, dark eyes. Her body was as short and squat as Gertrude Stein's, and in her black carpet slippers, her flat feet looked like small rafts. Brown support hose restrained her thick legs; a dirty apron was tied around her plump stomach. She wore a blue uniform, and a black hairnet flattened her cheaply dyed, carrot-blonde curls.

"I'm Lila. I called on Monday."

Mrs. Makov shrank back with obvious discomfort, but she moved aside and allowed Lila into the living room, as dark and damp as a cave. Mrs. Makov led her past a doily-covered table in the kitchen that smelled of sour cream, then through a doorway next to the refrigerator.

"I live cousin here. My room," Mrs. Makov said. As she sat on her narrow bed, she gestured for Lila to take the only chair, the metal folding kind used for bingo games in nursing homes. "Yuri good boy." From a TV table beside the bed, Mrs. Makov picked up a photo of him and handed it to Lila.

Like in the one she'd seen on the TV news, Yuri grinned at the camera as if he were your favorite kid brother, about to tell a silly joke.

"Knock-knock," he'd start.

"Who's there?" you'd ask.

"Boo."

"Boo who?"

"I didn't mean to make you cry!" He'd rear back his head with a peal of laughter that would make you laugh too.

Lila handed the photograph back to Mrs. Makov. "Yuri changed so much from the boy in this picture. Why was he unhappy in this country?"

She gave Lila a blank look.

Lila nodded toward the picture. "Yuri was happy in the photo." She smiled and pointed at her mouth to convey "happy." She said, "He was not happy here." Frowning to look miserable, she pointed at the floor, as if it represented the United States.

"Here hard. No easy. He work, work."

"Did he hate his job?"

"No like. No good."

"Why didn't he learn English better and go back to architecture school? He could have been an architect here." Lila was speaking too loudly, but turning up the volume didn't seem to help Mrs. Makov's comprehension, because she shrugged and said nothing. So Lila moved on. "Did Yuri have brothers and sisters?"

"Brother. Kiev."

"Is his father here in the U.S.?"

"Father dead."

Mrs. Makov looked uncomfortable about that, too, so Lila dropped the topic of Yuri's family and got down to her overarching question. "Mrs. Makov, was Yuri angry about anything? Do you know?"

"Hard work. No easy. Want important."

"To do important work? To be important?"

"America people important."

"Is that what he was angry about? That he wasn't an American?"

"No angry. Good boy. He here come. He help. He give." As she rubbed her thumb over her fingertips to convey that he'd given her money, tears slid through the wrinkles on her downy cheeks. She dabbed at them with a wadded paper towel from her apron pocket.

Lila didn't want to press Mrs. Makov when she was upset, but today might be the only chance for answers. "Do you know why Yuri shot everybody?" Lila asked. To make sure Mrs. Makov understood "shot," Lila raised her thumb and pointed her index finger like a pistol barrel.

Mrs. Makov's face looked even sadder, and she seemed to cringe. "I cry, cry. Go away never. Everybody cry." She blew her nose.

"But what made him do it?" Lila tried again.

"Yuri good boy."

Except when he shot people.

Up against rock-hard denial, Lila wrapped one hand around the other and searched her brain for what to say. Even if Mrs. Makov was the mother of a man who'd tried to kill her, Lila felt sorry for her, caught between her love for Yuri and her knowledge of his horrible crime.

Though Lila didn't want to hurt her, she needed an explanation badly enough to press again: "You don't know why? There has to be a reason." Her voice sounded harsh, threatened.

Looking miserable, Mrs. Makov stared at the floor. "I sorry. Sorry. Go away never." She spoke as if she were talking to herself as much as to Lila.

Mrs. Makov got up and shuffled over to her chest of drawers, the veneer of which was peeling to expose raw, unfinished wood. She pulled the top drawer open and lifted out a small package wrapped in crumpled, yellowing tissue paper. With tenderness, she unwrapped a scarf knitted from maroon and orange acrylic that had started to pill.

She handed it to Lila. "Yuri. Moscow."

"This was his?"

She nodded. "I make for him. As boy."

Lila felt like she was holding a leper's shroud. She quickly gave it back to Mrs. Makov.

She set it in her lap and gazed at it with loving eyes. Without a word, she let Lila know that no one could chip through her defense, and Lila would find no insight in this house.

She had come to a final dead end, and it tore into her heart. As she sat there, frozen, the metal chair's slat dug into her spine. Finally, Lila got to her feet, said good-bye, and walked out of the room. Mrs. Makov was weeping on her bed.

Outside, fog cooled Lila's face. Her temples throbbed. Her body ached from having been so tense. More than simply crushed with disappointment, she felt stunned. How do you respond when you reach the end of the line and there's no hope? And when acceptance seems too much to ask of yourself? Grief pressed down on Lila's chest and made it hard for her to breathe. The possibility of guilt made it harder.

It's over. Give up. You've failed. The thoughts felt like hammer blows.

She was rummaging through her purse for the car keys when a battered green Volkswagen stopped in front of the house. A galumphing Great Dane of a woman, wearing the same black hairnet and blue uniform as Mrs. Makov, climbed out of the car and walked toward Lila.

"Are you Lila?"

"Yes."

"I'm Olga's cousin Marina. She said you were coming. I wanted to see you, but I couldn't get off work till now." Her smile was friendly, but the stress lines in her face suggested that meeting Lila was not easy for her. Marina's accent only vaguely hinted of Russian and suggested she'd lived a long time in the U.S.

She shifted a heavy canvas bag from one shoulder to the other. "If it helps you any, we're really sorry. That's all we can say. It's been awful for everyone."

"I know," Lila said. And after meeting Mrs. Makov, she knew more than ever how awful. "I came here to find out why Yuri shot us. Mrs. Makov wouldn't tell me."

"She couldn't. She has no idea. Nobody really knows," Marina said. "Yuri was having a hard time. Harder than he expected when he came here. I think he was overwhelmed."

"From being in a new culture? Learning English?"

"That and a million other things," Marina said. "You may not believe me, but he was sensitive. Once I saw him cry over a Shostakovich CD because the music was beautiful. He wanted a son to name Ilya after the painter Repin. Yuri was gentle."

"But violent."

"Well, yes, that, too . . ." Marina looked off into the distance like she was still trying to reconcile the opposites, yet knew she never would. "Olga's never going to get over it. Tanya comes over here every day and cries."

"Tanya?"

"She and Yuri knew each other since they were kids. A year ago she got a visa to join him here. They were saving money to get married."

30

As Lila started back along the artichoke fields and traveled up the coast, wind blasted the car and whipped the ocean into whitecaps. She was seething. She kept repeating: Number one, Yuri Makov had been a fraud. Number two, she'd been a fool. Number three, if he hadn't shot himself, she'd want to kill him for her months of questioning whether she'd made him mad enough to shoot people.

Narrowing her eyes in anger, she pictured him and Reed out in the whitecapped ocean, in the same disloyal boat. Testosterone dripped from their sails' halyards, and their bow was pointed—the better to penetrate the waves. Written on the stern was the boat's name: *Cheater*. In the cabin, beds were ready for trysts. After admiring their reflections in the water, the men adjusted the mainsheet and sailed on to satisfy themselves.

Joe Arruzzi had been right that shit happened. All the time. With maniacs like David Carpenter or Eric Harris, you could almost understand how the shit evolved from cruel parents or insensitive students. You could even see how someone as disturbed as Patrick Sherrill could build up rage from what he saw as persecution at his job. But Yuri was different. He had a mother who adored him and a girlfriend who was eager to marry him. He was educated and interested in the arts. He would have had a successful future in the U.S. if he'd worked for it. In time, he could have had a good life, like his forum name on NICOclub.com.

So why had he chosen violence? If Lila tracked down every person he'd ever met, she'd surely get a different reason from each one. He'd be like the elephant that the blind men touched in different places and concluded it was a flapping ear or a spindly tail. Lila had thought she might have hurt or angered Yuri. Agnes Spitzmeier thought he was mad she'd fired him. His landlord might have felt Yuri was working too hard at a job he didn't like, and his cousin Marina might say he felt overwhelmed in the U.S. and he resented not earning enough to get married.

Maybe all the irritations added up, and Yuri was miserable and mad. So what? Plenty of people had irritations like his, but they didn't go out and shoot people. Somehow they coped. He should have.

Cristina's voice came to Lila's mind: "Yuri was nuts!"

In her head, she heard Adam say, "You're trying to make what some lunatic did seem rational."

They'd understood Yuri better than she had. They'd seen he was a psychopath—and certainly not the spurned, gentle soul her Pleaser might have inadvertently led on. You peel off a layer of an onion, and you've got an onion underneath—and from Yuri's surface to his core, he'd been an unfaithful sneak, a predator.

Lila would never know what had made him that way. His shooting people would never make sense. She saw it plainly now while she slowed in the traffic and crept along the freeway south of Santa Cruz.

When the traffic thinned, she was free to pick up speed. She continued north and put more distance between Olga and Marina Makov and herself, and the miles calmed her anger. By San Jose it had turned from fire engine red to tangerine. By Millbrae, it was salmon pink; by San Francisco, a sickly, urine yellow. By the time Lila crossed the Golden Gate Bridge, relief elbowed the anger out of the way, and she felt like she'd opened up her chest and let extra-black buzzards fly out.

It was pointless to think about Yuri anymore, not with her mind or her heart. Adam had been right that sometimes bad things happened to good people—and to good dogs, like Grace. Sometimes bad things happened for no discernible reason and through no fault of your own. You didn't ask for them, and you couldn't control them. Betsy would say you had to accept them, but accepting wasn't the same as forgetting they'd happened.

Last week after discussing Yuri, Betsy had covered Lila with the Navajo blanket and said, "There's plenty we can never forget, but we can forgive who's hurt us."

Lila had said, "Even if I understood why Yuri shot everybody, I can never forgive him."

"Oh, yes, you can," Betsy had said. "You're thinking of forgiveness as kissing and making up like you learn in Sunday school, but I'm talking about something different." She'd adjusted the blinds so the room got shadowy. "My kind of forgiving means looking for freedom."

"How am I supposed to do that?"

"Well, you don't have to do a whole lot. You just set down your grievance and let go the best you can. Then you wait for the Great Spirit to send you the grace of healing."

Though Lila still didn't see how she could forgive Yuri even in Betsy's way, she guessed she was willing at least to ask the Great Spirit to heal her. Since her search for answers had prolonged the pain and gained nothing, she could at least try to set down the misery and anger Yuri had caused her.

Okay, Lila told herself. *I know I'll never forget what he did. But hereby, as of this minute, on Freeway 101, I will do my best to let it go.* Mount Tamalpais was a witness, as were the clouds and sun and egrets wading through the tidelands in the distance. Maybe nothing would change; maybe Lila would keep carrying her grudge till the day she died. But she was open to whatever the Great Spirit wanted. She would try to forgive and move on.

Grace, who would be waiting on Adam's porch, was the model of Betsy's forgiveness, Lila believed. Grace might never have forgotten Marshall's cruelty, but she'd put it down somewhere and walked away. She accepted whatever happened as if she knew far better than Lila did that you can't always explain abuse and dwelling on it is a waste of time. Here Lila had thought that to heal, she'd have to figure out why Yuri shot her, but Grace was what had been healing her all along.

Lila parked in Adam's driveway and hurried through his gate, past the flourishing tomato plants and the zucchini, which would soon be hiding huge broods under their leaf skirts. As she made her way along the brick path that curved around to the back of the house, all she could think of was how much she wanted to hug Grace.

Soon she would be dancing around Lila's feet and wagging her whole back end the way she always welcomed Lila, who could hardly wait to bury her face in Grace's golden fur. Lila would tell Grace how much she'd missed her. Lila would thank her for seeing her through the most troubled time she'd ever had, and for showing her what was important and how she should live.

At the back steps to Adam's porch, Lila stopped as if someone had turned a switch and paralyzed her legs. The screen door's lower half was ripped; a giant plus sign had been cut through it. Though Adam's foot could have torn it, Lila knew better. She also knew that if Grace had been in the yard, she'd have run to her.

Lila didn't want to get to the top of the steps and learn the truth. She wanted Grace to be waiting on the porch more than she'd ever wanted anything in her life. But when she reached the top step and looked, Grace was gone. Lila couldn't breathe. Her hands began to tremble. She knew how a house felt when a flood washed away its foundation.

31

Lila opened the screen door. The only sign of Grace was the dent in the pillow, where she'd been curled up waiting for Lila. Next to it was a white ceramic water bowl and Grace's pig's ear, as good as new. She had never touched her favorite treat; all day she had worried.

Adrenaline propelled Lila to Adam's kitchen window to see whether he'd left Grace in the house. But if she'd been inside, she'd have whined to get out to Lila. Grace wasn't in the kitchen. The house was silent.

Lila hurried to the yard and searched around each tree and bush, even though she knew Grace would have come if she'd been outside. Then Lila ran to Adam's only other gate, next to the compost heap at the bottom of his property. The gate was clawed—and open. Even in her pink sock, Grace had gouged the wood and fought to disengage the latch.

Shouting "Grace! Grace!" Lila tore through the gate to the forest behind Adam's house. She ran in zigzags to check every fern, bush, and log. When she didn't find Grace, Lila hurried, panting, to the street, where the mailman was driving by. She waved and yelled, "Stop! Stop!"

He pulled over to the curb. Resting his palm on a knobby knee extending from his Bermuda shorts, he looked down at Lila from his truck's high seat, and his expression said that he'd like to offer her a Valium.

"What's wrong?" he asked.

"I've lost my dog. A golden."

"Haven't seen him."

"Her," Lila corrected. "Grace. She has a pink bandage on her paw. And an ID tag with my phone number."

"I'll keep a lookout," he promised. "You sure you're all right?"

His concern distressed Lila more. She felt as if her frenzy were spilling out of her all over the street. How could Adam have let this happen? How could she have trusted him with Grace? After he'd accused Lila of being irresponsible, he'd turned out to be the world's greatest deadbeat in the responsibility department. He'd not protected what was most precious to her.

Lila could never forgive him or the Great Spirit for allowing Grace to get lost. Lila had been right: No matter what Betsy said, the world was awful. Lila clenched her fists in fury, but anger wasn't going to help her find Grace.

Still, as Lila called and called, anger at Adam almost choked her. She walked up and down every road near his house and yelled for Grace till her throat was raspy. Lila sneaked into yards, pushed back bushes, and checked behind garbage-can enclosures and under cars. She knocked on doors and stopped strangers on the street to ask if they'd seen Grace.

Sometimes they asked if Lila needed a glass of water. Or they took her phone number and promised to call if Grace showed up. Each time someone said, "I haven't seen her," Lila grew more frantic.

In case Grace had managed to hobble up the hill on her hurt paw, Lila went home to look for her. As Lila parked in front of the house, she mentally got on her knees and begged Grace to be waiting for her at the door. If Grace were able, Lila knew she'd be sitting on the doormat.

As Lila walked down the path to the house, she willed Grace to greet her with welcoming squeaks and with tail swishes exuberant enough to revive the imaginary sultan from a dead faint on the floor. Lila willed Grace to gobble down her supper and settle on her pillow for a production of *The Napping Dog*.

But all the willing in the world couldn't change the silence that was waiting on the porch. Lila could not force Grace's presence. As Lila got out her key to unlock the door, she thought the house looked as bleak as a person who'd lost her best friend. Just as Lila had.

Lila checked the voice mail, but no one had called to report finding Grace. Unable to think of supper, Lila stared out the kitchen window and pictured a silver cord connecting her heart to Grace's. One yank from her, and Lila would fly to her; a tug from Lila would bring Grace home. Lila went to the porch and looked out on the street just in case her tug had worked. But Grace wasn't there, and Lila's frenzy slowly quieted to desolation.

As afternoon faded to dusk, she went around the neighborhood and called Grace again, then walked down the hill toward the creek. Evening shadows darkened the forest, and fog crept over Mount Tamalpais and ushered in cold. She imagined Grace shivering and looking for a warm place to spend the night, or nosing through a garbage can for food to stop her stomach's growling. Then Lila's mental pictures grew more disturbing. She saw Grace, hit by a car and dying beside a road in dusty, sharp-edged gravel. Or captured by Marshall and beaten and starved and rechained to her tree. Or trapped in a dog dealer's van, about to be turned over to a medical research lab, where Grace would be locked in a small cage before experiments that Lila pressed her hands against her temples to keep from imagining.

By ten o'clock, Lila walked back to Adam's house. Though she was still angry and would never trust him again, he was the only person she could turn to. For Grace's sake, Lila had to seek his help and try her best to be civil.

Just back from giving a Milky Way lecture, he was eating a tuna sandwich at his kitchen table and listening to a CD of Dvořák's *New World Symphony*. Clearly, he'd assumed that Grace was home safe with Lila and their plan had worked without a hitch.

"She's lost. I can't find her," Lila said. "I love her more than anything on earth, and you didn't keep her safe."

Adam blanched and hurried to the back porch to see the ripped screen for himself. He grabbed a flashlight, and he and Lila rushed down to the gate by the compost heap.

As he shone the light on Grace's claw scratches in the wood, he said, "I can't believe it. She was Houdini." He opened and closed the gate to check the latch, which was as high as his shoulder and seemed impossible for even a large dog like Grace to reach. The latch worked fine.

Shaking his head with dismay, he said, "I sure underestimated how desperate Grace would be to find you."

"Yes, you did. I never should have left her here."

Adam lowered the light to the ground.

He might have chosen not to respond in order to defuse Lila's distress and avoid a fight. But she was still upset. At least he'd not been too proud to admit he'd been wrong. Still, thinking of Grace searching for her while she searched for Grace hurt all the way to Lila's bone marrow.

Lila kept a cool distance from Adam as they designed a poster on his computer: Across the top was LOST DOG in bold, black letters. Below, REWARD in red. Adam and Lila gave their names and phone numbers, and his address for the last place Grace had been seen. A description included her pink sock and her green collar with its red ID heart.

To get a photo, Lila called Cristina from the kitchen and asked if she could e-mail the picture from her poster to find Grace a home.

"I'll do it right this minute," Cristina said. "Oh, my God. That poor beastie."

Cristina sounded sleepy. Lila was sorry to have wakened her, but Grace was too important.

"Adam shouldn't have suggested we leave her on the porch," Lila said. What did she care if he heard her? He knew how she felt.

"Don't be mad at him. It's not his fault," Cristina said. "These things happen."

Right. Just like good people get shot.

After Lila had finally let go of some buzzards of anger, a new flock had flapped into her heart. Along with guilt. Though she blamed Adam, she also blamed herself for trusting him. The buck stopped with her. Once again, something terrible could be her fault.

"You have to call me the second you know anything, good or bad, okay?" Cristina asked.

Please, don't let it be bad. "I will," Lila said.

"Leave food in front of the house. Grace might come back when you're not there."

"All right."

"Check with the Humane Society. Oh, this just breaks my heart. Of all the animals . . ."

After Cristina e-mailed the photo, Grace's sweet forehead frowned from Adam's computer screen. Except when Lila had left her that morning, for months Grace had not looked so troubled as she did in that picture. She'd become happy as her life had grown secure and she and Lila had learned to love each other. And now . . . just looking at Grace made Lila feel like she was being sucked into a black hole.

As the posters rolled out of Adam's printer, he pulled up a chair next to Lila at the computer and sat down. She stiffened.

He got up and leaned against the window frame across the room. "We've got lots to do," he said, more formally than he'd spoken since they'd first met.

"I know."

"Looking for a lost dog can be agony. You're not in control of anything. You have to be up for it."

"I'll be up for it."

He took the posters off his printer.

When Adam and Lila left his house, their flashlights' beams were fuzzy in the fog, which dripped from bay leaves and redwood fronds. The cold wind made the trees shudder and rain down more drops, so the ground was sodden just when Grace needed a warm, dry bed.

"Why can't the weather cooperate? It doesn't have to be so cold and damp," Lila grumbled.

"Try not to think about it," Adam said.

"I can't help thinking about it."

"Be glad we're not looking for Grace on Triton. It's the coldest place in our solar system. Close to minus four hundred Fahrenheit."

"That doesn't help," Lila said. "And what if Marshall sees our posters? He'll recognize Grace."

"Let's hope he doesn't find her before we do."

"If he did, what would we do?"

"I don't know."

When they put up poster number thirty-seven, Adam and Lila had covered the roads near their houses, so after two a.m., they moved on to Blithedale Avenue, a major thoroughfare to town. Except for occasional shafts of light from the edges of drawn curtains, all the houses were dark. They made it seem like Lila and Adam were the last of the living.

As he attached a poster to a grape-stake fence, tires hissed on wet pavement up the hill. Headlights rounded a bend, and a police car pulled up. As the drizzle-streaked window opened, a face with apple cheeks emerged, along with static from a short-wave radio.

The policeman smiled, exposing a chipped front tooth. "You guys out for a walk this late?"

"We've lost a dog." Adam handed him a poster.

"Bummer." The policeman turned on his car's interior light and studied Grace's photo. "You know, I might have seen her."

"Where?" Lila asked.

"Down in Cascade Canyon. Behind the library. Early this evening. She was wandering around the creek. She must have been looking for water."

Now in September, the creek was dry except for rare, slimy puddles. Lila's throat felt parched.

"Alarm." The man on the short-wave sounded like his throat was parched too. "It's going off at 38 Summit."

Lila wanted to run to Cascade Canyon, but Adam insisted they go back for his car so they could drive Grace home if they found her. Twenty minutes later, they were squinting into shadows by the library, which was surrounded by redwoods, salal, and ferns. Adam turned at a stop sign and drove along a different creek from the one Lila had always walked with Grace. The unfamiliarity made the woods seem extra-dark and lonely. From here, Grace wouldn't know her way home.

When Adam had driven the road's full length without a glimpse of Grace, he suggested they park and search on foot. It was too late at night to shout without waking people. But as Adam and Lila walked back toward the library, she cupped her hands around her mouth and whispered "Grace!" with hopes the wind would carry her voice into the woods.

Adam shone his flashlight into bushes, hollow tree trunks, and spaces between boulders—anyplace Grace might have sought shelter from the cold. When his light hit two bright eyes near a madrona tree's exposed root, for one glorious second Lila thought they might be Grace's. Then Lila saw rings around them.

With crushing disappointment, she asked, "Could a raccoon hurt Grace?"

"Yep."

To Lila's recently imagined thirst, she added the pain of skin shredded by claws. "I guess I shouldn't think about raccoons, either?"

"Push them out of your mind."

"I can't bear it."

"I know."

Lila and Adam did not find Grace in Cascade Canyon, so they went downtown and pinned posters on kiosks and bulletin boards. Around four a.m., as the sky was beginning to turn pink, Adam brought Lila home. Tired and dejected, they walked to the door.

"I want you to know I'm sorry," he said. "Grace is such a

gentle dog. I never dreamed she'd break out of the porch or run away."

"I made a big mistake to leave her with you."

"Maybe so, but we didn't know it was a mistake. We meant well. Things didn't work out the way we planned."

"I didn't lose Grace off *my* porch."

"Okay, I miscalculated. It was an honest mistake. I'm not perfect. That's all I can say. I'm sorry."

Adam looked sincere, and he'd tried hard all night to find Grace. Lila couldn't continue being mad. In her heart she heard Betsy say, *The only person your anger hurts is you. Let it go. Accept. Move on.*

"I'm sorry, too," Lila said, not sure exactly to whom she was apologizing—Adam? Grace? Herself? "We just have to find her."

"All we can do is try." Adam wrapped his arms around Lila. She melted against him.

For a long time, they stood there—with her a needy chrysalis who had found a cocoon. Unlike your average hug, though, their holding became a serious cling, as in what two people might do in a leaking boat in the middle of the Atlantic while shark fins circled them. By holding each other, Adam and Lila admitted they were miserable, and they'd have given anything to have Grace back. But even more, they said they were in this mess together—and they were there for each other. A hug can say a lot of things.

Even though Lila didn't expect anyone to have called about Grace in the night, she tried her voice mail again. No word of Grace. As Cristina had suggested, Lila set kibble in front of the house. In case Grace should come home in the next hour, Lila left on the floodlights, which turned the forest an inviting silver.

Exhausted but wired from stress, she climbed between her cold sheets and pulled up her blanket. As she strained to listen through the wind for Grace's whine at the door, Lila could not still her thoughts enough to sleep. Worry had set her spinning inside, like a roulette wheel before the dice named winners and losers. This was the first time she'd gone to bed without Grace in the house—and for the past two months Grace had slept on the bed next to her.

Lila ached to hear Grace's reassuring snores; her sighs, like air squeaking out of a bicycle tire; and the shuffle of her paws when she dreamed. On nights when Lila had gone to bed feeling lonely or anxious, Grace had always picked up the mood and rested her chin on Lila's arm to let her know she was safe. Now she also ached for the warmth of Grace's breath on her wrist. Any sign of Grace's presence would have brought Lila the comfort she and Adam had just tried to hug into each other. But now there was nothing. In every way, there was a loss of grace.

Finally, Lila fell into a fitful sleep. As the room filled with pale morning light, she turned over. As usual when shifting positions, she took care not to roll onto Grace. Then Lila woke enough to remember Grace was gone—and Lila's whole body felt like a gaping wound.

She opened her eyes to a day she didn't welcome. She threw back her blanket and checked the doors to see if Grace had come home. When she saw that she had not, Lila got back into bed, fidgeted, and waited till the hour was late enough for her to get up and continue the search. More worry and anxiety bored into her.

But Lila mentally shook herself to attention. In clipped words, she informed herself that no matter how many mountains she had to move—even with a demitasse spoon for a shovel and a coat hanger hook for a pick—she would move them to find Grace. Lila couldn't control the outcome, but she could do her best to search for Grace. Whatever it took, Lila would do it to bring Grace home.

32

Side by side on the Humane Society's metal stools, Adam and Lila flipped through pages of the lost-and-found notebook. Fortunately, Tony was off duty and could not glower at her, and Adam did not bring up the horrible day when she'd surrendered Grace there. He insisted that they read every listing for found dogs *and* cats. Shelters could make mistakes, he said, and animals got mixed up or misfiled.

Lila and Adam pored over each description. When they found no golden retriever, he said Grace might have gotten so dirty on the streets that she'd been registered in the book as a black Lab; checking the kennel was essential.

As soon as Lila and Adam walked through the kennel door, the smells of bleach and damp fur hit them. A cacophony of barks, which boiled down to cries of *"Help!"* made her want to put her hands over her ears. The dogs' stress seemed to bounce off the concrete walls. The air was filled with desperation.

And injustice. Behind bars on each side of a cement aisle were inmates who'd never committed a crime and were wrongfully imprisoned—like Grace when she'd been chained to a tree. Two miniature dachshunds shoved their noses through the bars of their shared kennel and yapped at Lila and Adam. A collie mix rested his front paws on his kennel door and begged with moist eyes for a home. A small biscuit-colored dog saw Lila and Adam and wagged his tail like a windshield wiper but let it droop when they did not stop. A cocker spaniel mutt chased her tail, and a lumbering yellow-eyed dog threw himself at his kennel door to reach them.

At the end of the concrete aisle was a strawberry blonde dog the size of a retriever. Though her face was turned away, her tail and haunches looked like Grace's. As Lila's heart speeded up, she grabbed Adam's hand and pulled him toward the dog.

"Grace!" Lila shouted.

The dog turned her head. Her muzzle was rectangular, like an Airedale's, and her ears pointed up instead of flapping down.

"This is so terrible," Lila said.

"Needle in a haystack," Adam said.

"I can't stand it."

"You have to."

Before they left, he filled out a lost-dog form. As Lila watched over his shoulder, she tried to blot out the memory of those kenneled dogs—and Adam's warning on their way back to the reception room:

"We have to check here every day," he'd said. "Sometimes dogs get put down before their days of grace are over and their people have a chance to find them."

When Lila and Adam got back to his Honda, he called her voice mail—but no one had tried to reach her—and then he tried his own.

"I've got a message," he said.

As Lila leaned over to share his phone's receiver, the freeway roar a block away made it hard to listen in.

A woman with a New York accent said, "I've just seen your

dog. She was pawing around a Dumpster at the Wayfarer's Market. She looked so hungry . . ."

Adam pulled back from Lila and leaned against his door to hear the rest.

When he turned off his cell phone, she asked, "Why'd you move away?"

"To protect you."

"Was the message that awful?!"

"Nope. But it would have made you sad."

"Sadder," she corrected.

The Dumpster behind the market was as big as those you see overflowing with plywood and insulation scraps at construction sites. It was parked under a grove of redwoods beside a dry creek bed. Littering the ground were cardboard boxes, plastic bags, wadded paper towels, empty yogurt containers, and squashed aluminum cans. All a dog might have found to eat were a few rotten bananas peppered with fruit flies.

"My poor, poor Grace," Lila moaned.

"I know you feel like we're grinding along without getting anywhere," Adam said.

"That's exactly how I feel."

"We'll find Grace. Don't worry."

But Adam's face looked worried. If he'd been Grace, he would not have touched his pig's ear.

Across from each other at his pine kitchen table, Adam and Lila ate a gloomy, dismal lunch. The iced tea had lost its zip. Adam's homegrown alfalfa sprouts didn't crunch. The sandwich bread seemed tired, as if it had never heard of yeast.

Adam occasionally reached over and squeezed Lila's hand to buck her up, and she tried to give him a confident smile. But in their hearts they were not doing much better than their sandwich bread—until the phone rang and dangled a carrot of hope.

Adam got up and answered. "Yes, she's still missing," he said.

He crossed his feet and rested his shoulder against the wall, and Lila got up and pressed herself against him to listen in on the conversation.

A man, who had a pleasant, neutral voice like you hear in TV ads, said he'd seen Grace dodging traffic on Miller Avenue, a main road into town. "A truck almost hit her. She looked like she didn't know to get out of the way."

"She's not street-smart," Adam said.

"I could tell. I tried to catch her, but she ran off."

"What time?"

"About an hour ago."

"What part of Miller?"

"The four-way stop sign by Maggie's Deli. A little toward Tam Market."

"Ask about her sock," Lila whispered to Adam.

"Was her paw wrapped in pink?" he asked.

"Not that I saw. Jesus, I hope she lasts till you can get her. She looked so scared. It was pathetic."

The kitchen wall blocked Adam from pulling away and keeping Lila from hearing that.

Miller Avenue seemed like a NASCAR track whose crazed drivers breakfasted on tenpenny nails and stomped accelerators to the floor with aggressive size-sixteen feet. As tires zoomed by, Grace wouldn't have had a chance unless she'd been rumbling along in a panzer.

Adam drove up and down Miller Avenue three times, then along each side street. He parked near Maggie's Deli, and he and Lila walked for blocks and hollered for Grace. Finally, there was nothing to do but give up on that lead.

Adam asked, "What do we do now?"

"We have to keep trying."

"Any suggestions?"

"Grace, Grace, where are you?" Lila was thinking as hard as she could with her heart.

She and Adam went to the dog park, but no golden retriever was romping on the grass. They dropped in at Pet Stop, but Albert Wu had not seen Grace. As Lila's outlook was fading from determined to glum—and Adam went to check the Dumpster again—she walked to Betsy's office in case Grace had shown up for her weekly massage.

Betsy was bent over her desk, filling out insurance forms. She got up and gave Lila a grandmotherly hug. Betsy knew her too well to miss the anguish on her face. "What's wrong?"

"I've lost Grace."

The curve of Betsy's smiling lips straightened, and the silver dolphins hanging from her ears got as still as stone. "Don't worry. You'll find her."

"I've looked everywhere. I'm afraid I'll never see her again." Lila's lungs felt like they were filling up with mold.

"Oh, Lila, won't you ever learn? Your negative thoughts can create a negative reality." Betsy reached over to her desk for a Kleenex box and handed it to Lila.

As an angel eyed her from the wall, Lila took a tissue, mopped her tears, and blew her nose. "I've never felt so helpless. I'm scared Grace is dead beside a road somewhere."

"You can't give up your search," Betsy said.

Lila wadded up the tissue and tossed it into the wastebasket. "Why do these awful things keep happening?"

"That's not the right question. Ask, 'What's the meaning in this crisis? What's it trying to teach?' " Betsy said. "Hard times can be gifts. They can force us to change and get us where we're meant to be." At that, Betsy's silver dolphins starting going at it, diving through the air around her salt-and-pepper curls.

If idealism were measured on the Richter scale, Betsy's

could have fissured Hoover Dam, Lila thought. She didn't mention that she was also feeling huffy at the Great Spirit for what was happening.

Betsy opened her desk's top drawer and shuffled through papers, then told Lila to open her hand and close her eyes. Trusting Betsy not to drop a parrot gizzard onto her palm, Lila did what she asked, and something small and hard clunked against her skin. When she opened her eyes, she was holding a dime-size, rose-quartz heart.

"You keep that close. It'll remind you that love is what's most important," Betsy said. "The minute you find Grace, we'll set up an appointment to work on her leg again."

As Lila reminded Betsy that Grace wore a red metal heart about the same size as the pink quartz one, Lila squeezed it till it made ridges in her palm. She wanted the quartz heart to be a sign that she would find Grace. Lila tugged at the silver cord that bound their hearts together.

Adam got back to the car before Lila did. He was thrumming his fingers on the steering wheel, but he seemed to be thrumming to a dirge played by a hospitalized tuba. As Lila slid onto the seat beside him, he said, "Grace wasn't at the Dumpster."

"Betsy hasn't seen her, either."

"I'm not surprised. We got another call. Someone just saw Grace on the frontage road to 101. She was limping south along the chain-link fence."

Where cars swarmed like hornets. Lila groaned. "How could she have gotten *there*?"

"I don't know."

"Why didn't somebody catch her?"

"She found an opening in the fence and ran onto the freeway."

Lila groaned. "It couldn't be any worse."

"Yes, it could. Somebody could call and say a car has hit her." Adam started his Honda and backed out of the parking spot.

Lila closed her eyes and gripped the rose-quartz heart. In her own heart, she promised the Great Spirit not to be huffy anymore. She said she'd do anything if only she and Adam did not find Grace dead. Lila would track down every negative thought in her mind and shoot it. Without complaint, she'd learn whatever the Great Spirit wanted to teach. She'd go with the flow and never try to control anything, and she'd never again say a mean word about anyone, including Yuri and Reed.

She would stop being mad at the universe and believe in its goodness, as Betsy did. Lila would forgive anybody anything. She'd throw resentment from her train and travel with only kindness in her suitcase. As a gesture of good faith, if the Great Spirit wanted, she would put red roses on Yuri Makov's grave. If Reed got married, she'd dance at his wedding. She promised.

As Adam sped toward the freeway, Lila thought that anger was an anemic toad's breath, and forgiveness was a cool strong breeze. Forgiving was easy compared to losing Grace forever.

33

Lila and Adam did not find Grace dead on the freeway. By the time they got there, she'd disappeared. They did not know if she'd run away or if someone had picked her up and driven off with her—and if that someone had been Marshall or another dog abuser.

True to Lila's word to the Great Spirit, however, she fought being negative and picturing the worst. Still, her promise could not stop her from being realistic. As she lay in bed early on her second morning without Grace, the reality was that she'd been gone for more than forty hours, her trail had grown cold, and the chances of finding her were dwindling to zero.

When the phone rang, Lila reached out from under the covers to answer, then hesitated. At best, Adam would be calling to plan another day of searching. At worst, Animal Control would be letting her know that a car had hit Grace in the night and she'd been killed. Hating to face another day without her, Lila braced herself and picked up the receiver.

"Lila!" Adam's shout was a pile driver to her early morning ears. "They've got our girl!"

Lila bolted up in bed. "*Who?*"

"The sergeant we met on the road. He put up our poster at the station. Last night one of his men lured Grace to his car with a roast beef sandwich."

"Is she okay?"

"Supposedly filthy and hungry. She's at the station."

"What if they made a mistake?"

"The sergeant thinks they've got her."

"Are you *sure* it's Grace?"

"Only one way to find out. How soon can you be ready?"

"In two minutes." Lila threw back the covers and leapt out of bed.

She grabbed her jeans, which were draped over the love seat, and stepped into them as she went to the closet. She pulled out a tee shirt without seeing what color it was and put on clogs without bothering with socks. From the dresser, she picked up Betsy's rose-quartz heart and slipped it in her pocket.

As hard as Lila had begged Yuri Makov not to shoot her, she begged the Great Spirit, "Please, please. Oh, *please.*"

The police station's walls were green plaster, and the floor was speckled gray linoleum. In a central room were rows of metal desks, and down a hall, doors led to private offices. Recessed floodlights in the ceiling washed the olive cast from the skin of Officer Sanchez, who was resting his palms on the black Formica counter. With his fingers spread out, his hands looked like giant asterisks for footnotes you were eager to read.

"I'll get Sergeant Lewellyn," he said and started down the hall toward the office where Lila assumed the lost dog was being held.

She would have vaulted over the counter and run after him if Adam hadn't put his hand on her shoulder. "Easy, easy," he said, like he was trying to coax the man-eating glimmer from the eye of a tiger.

Adam's cheeks were covered with light-brown stubble, and his eyelids drooped in a sleepy, sexy way. Lila's Horny Gutter-snipe had little inclination to contemplate that delicious look, however, because the rest of Lila was wild with anticipation. She interlocked her fingers, squeezed till her knuckles turned white, and begged Grace to be there. Lila kept her eyes riveted on Officer Sanchez's back and willed him to sprint down the hall.

"I'm so scared the dog won't be Grace," Lila said.

"Don't worry. She'll burst through that door and tear over here."

"She can't run on her hurt paw."

"Wanna bet, lady?" Adam asked as Officer Sanchez opened the door and Grace shot out.

She must have heard Lila's and Adam's voices and known they were there. She raced toward them wailing deep-throated cries that said, *Where have you* been*?! I've been desperate to find you! Why didn't you find me sooner?!*

When Adam opened the counter's half door and let Grace through, she hurled herself at Lila's legs so hard she almost knocked her over. Lila sank to her knees, grabbed Grace, and hugged her like a lifeline.

"Oh, Grace! Grace!" Lila said again and again as her lips brushed Grace's fur.

She squirmed and licked Lila's face. *Oh, Lila! Lila!* Anyone could tell that was what Grace's squeals were saying.

"Good girl," Adam said. Grace leapt up and rested her paws on his shoulders like she was trying to hug him. She licked his face too.

Then, squeaking and howling, she bucked and circled him and Lila like an ebullient conga dancer. Grace rolled on her back and kicked her paws in the air. She got to her feet and ran around them again. And again. Her fur was flying. Her ears were flopping. Her plumed tail was swishing, pure joy.

Grace's pink sock was gone; she'd lost her collar. Dirt had turned her golden fur a liverish brown, and hunger had brought out her ribs like a corrugated roof again. But two days on the streets had not dimmed the light in her eyes. The confidence she'd gained in her and Lila's months together still shone out of her.

Lila grabbed her again and kissed her. As she wriggled in Lila's arms, two brown shoes and khaki pant legs appeared beside her. Sergeant Lewellyn said, "We sure don't get to see happy reunions like this every day."

Lila jumped to her feet and hugged him, too. "If we hadn't met you on the road, we wouldn't have Grace."

Thrilled, she almost blurted out that for months she'd been nursing a grudge against two policemen—and Sergeant Lewellyn's kindness had made it fade away. But what was the point of letting the sorry past with Joe Arruzzi and Rich Mason—and Yuri Makov—spoil the exuberant present with Grace? With gratitude, Lila took her in her arms again. That was where Grace belonged. They belonged together.

34

Grace's stitches had not ripped out, but they were loose. Adam wanted Dr. Hightower to check them. As Adam drove out of Mill Valley toward the clinic, Grace stared out his Honda's back window, on the lookout for squirrels who might need to be taught a thing or two. Though dirty and hungry, she was smiling, smudging the window with her nose, and acting like Adam and Lila were taking her to a dog-biscuit factory. You'd never know she'd left them for a minute, much less for two harrowing days. She was doing just what Betsy said: Letting go. Moving on.

"Do you think Grace has forgiven us for leaving her on the porch?" Lila asked Adam.

"I'm sure she has."

"You'd think she'd hold a grudge."

"Dogs don't do that."

"People need to be more like dogs."

"That's what I've told you all along." Adam reached over and squeezed Lila's hand.

She, now the dog person she swore she'd never be, squeezed back.

In Dr. Hightower's reception room Adam and Lila gave Grace handfuls of biscuits, which she crunched to bits and gobbled down. A vet tech in a coat with dog and cat faces printed on it led them to an exam room, where Dr. Hightower lifted Grace onto the table. She smiled and panted as if she were glad to see him and she knew he was trying to help.

"So let's have a look," he said to her.

She presented her paw, like the pope allowing you to kiss his signet ring.

Dr. Hightower bent down and studied the stitches. "We need to clean her up and redo a few of these," he said.

"Will it hurt? She's been through too much," Lila said.

"Has to be done," Adam said.

Dr. Hightower patted Grace's head. "We'll fix her up. It'll just take a few minutes." He looked at her paw again.

Seeing him examine Grace made Lila think of her first visit to Dr. Lovell after she left the hospital. He'd breezed into the room and smiled at her below his wispy blond mustache. But he must have quickly sensed her anger and distress, because his smile faded. "You haven't gone for counseling, have you?" he'd asked.

"No. I don't plan to," Lila had said. In other words, *The world is the pits. Counseling can't change that. Door closed.*

"It's your decision," Dr. Lovell had said and proceeded to examine her arm.

She'd sounded irritable because she'd not yet seen through the fog of what had happened to her or understood that above the fog the sun shines. And she hadn't yet adopted Grace, who became her counselor by setting an example. Lila hadn't seen the importance of laying down grudges and walking on.

On Dr. Hightower's table, Grace acted as if her injury were

just a part of life, and without resentment she would tolerate whatever happened till the sun shone through her fog of trouble and warmed her again. It occurred to Lila that there was lots to be said sometimes for staying on the surface the way Grace did, instead of diving down to the murk. And the right way to get through life might be to accept what *is*, not obsess over why it happened.

In the meat department of the Wayfarer's Market, the refrigerated air chilled Lila's and Adam's faces and turned them pink. After examining sausages, chicken breasts, and hamburger, Lila and Adam decided to get a rotisserie-cooked chicken so Grace wouldn't have to wait for them to make her something to eat.

In the deli section, a man with a gold stud in his tongue put a chicken in a plastic container for them. Lila could hardly wait to feed Grace lunch. Nothing would be too good for her. After all she'd been through, she deserved anything she wanted.

Maybe with luck after a crisis, Lila thought, you rose like a phoenix from an ash heap, and your misery earned you a reward. She was ready to climb on a phoenix's back and let him take her flying. Lila was ready for her ash heap to recede so far behind her that she wouldn't see it anymore.

Adam removed Grace's new pink sock and helped her into his tub as if she were a Murano glass dog he'd just hocked his life to buy on eBay. He and Lila lathered and rinsed her three times, till brown-gray water stopped streaming from her fur. Though Grace had not been fond of baths, she did not resist the scrubbing. Once out of the tub, she did not shake water all over the bathroom as she had before. Impeccably cooperative, she sat at Lila and Adam's feet without complaining. She didn't even shiver.

"You think dogs feel gratitude?" Lila asked Adam.

"No doubt about it."

He handed her a blue-striped bath towel—folded neatly into thirds—and he shook out its mate so they could dry Grace together.

While Adam was putting away Grace's shampoo and telling her what a beautiful girl she was, Lila went to the kitchen. The sun was shining through the windows like it was personally asking her to notice how good life could be. She opened the back door and let in the morning's warmth and the raucous caws of crows in Adam's pear tree. She called Betsy from his phone.

After her voice mail wished Lila a "really great day"—like the one she was having—she told Betsy that her rose-quartz heart had helped find Grace, and Lila intended to carry it in her pocket forever. She promised to call Betsy in a couple of days to make Grace and her a therapy appointment. Then she phoned Cristina and whooped, "Grace is home!"

"Thank God," Cristina boomed as loud as Agnes Spitzmeier. "I was so worried about that precious!"

"No need to worry now."

"Sauté her some hamburger."

"We just gave her half a chicken."

"That's not enough. Give her liver snaps. Beef jerky. Rawhide sticks. Anything that precious wants, you promise?"

Lila promised.

"I'm glad Adam was there to help you find Grace. He's a good man," Cristina said.

"I'm at his house now. We just bathed Grace."

"I knew you'd get to be friends."

"Yes, well . . ." Lila would tell her more another time.

"I need to ask you something," Cristina said. "We're thinking about staying here longer than we planned."

"I thought you wanted to come home."

"Rosie loves her school, and telecommuting is easy for me.

In the fall we want to see the autumn leaves in Vermont," Cristina said. "Would you keep house-sitting?"

"Sure."

Cristina's house was half a mile from Adam's. He and Lila could wear a path through the woods on visits to each other.

The eggs Adam and Lila scrambled seemed like they'd been laid by a jubilant chicken, and the strawberry jam sat like a magic carpet on their toast. The kitchen had a golden glow because of their relief at finding Grace—and because they were glad to be together.

"Too bad Grace can't tell us where she went. I bet she had some interesting adventures," Adam said.

"I don't want to think about them."

"Maybe she fought off werewolves. She could have met a few trolls."

"All I care about is she's home."

On a pillow in the corner, Grace was lounging on her back with her legs flopped out, the Duchess of Supine. She was snoring her loudest rendition of "Adenoids in Trouble." No one would ever have known she'd just been lost or her neck fur hid a ring of scars. In a little while, she would wake, ready to accept whatever life sent her.

35

No man had as appealing a chest as Adam Spencer did. He was digging a hole for a Japanese maple, whose beautiful scarlet leaves should have commanded Lila's attention. But she forgot the tree because sweat was glistening on Adam's skin and sunlight was glinting on his light-brown chest hair. As he stomped a shovel into the earth, she took joyful note of his quads and glutes.

Lila's Horny Guttersnipe was resting under the pear tree, watching Adam with a contented smile on her face. She never sulked as she had before. Lila had set her free, and Adam had worn her out with pleasure. Now smug with well-being, she knew her days of deprivation had passed. She acted like a Roman at the end of a banquet, too tired to ask a slave to peel her a final grape. At first Lila had been shy about her scarred breast, but Adam said she was beautiful. Her Horny Guttersnipe liked that.

Grace was lying beside Lila, studying a grasshopper she'd trapped between her front paws. Her eyes were crossed, and she had on what Adam and Lila called her "goofy face." In the painting of her that Lila had just finished, however, she'd made Grace look as alert and smart as she usually was.

From Adam's photo, Lila had painted the violet-picket gate with the passion vine and trellis, and, just for him, she left the gate ajar so he could see the garden. For hours she'd labored over the hollyhock and foxglove blossoms and the gray-green catmint leaves. She painted the two griffins holding up the bench, too, and on a whim she sat Grace on the mossy thyme in front of it. Lila made Grace's widow's peak strawberry blonde and the feathery tufts of fur above her ears the right coppery color. Lila curled her light auburn tail around her haunch and took care that the tip matched the widow's peak strawberry.

In a month Lila intended to give Adam the painting for his birthday. For now, the maple he was planting was meant partly as a gift for her. He wanted it as a focal point outside his kitchen window—and as a place for Lila to come if she needed soothing. Adam also suggested that the tree could be a memorial for the people Yuri had killed.

As he finished digging, he said, "Maybe we should include Makov in the memorial too."

"Why?"

Adam shrugged. "Just a thought. He'd want to be part of it. He'd feel like you forgave him."

Not once had it occurred to Lila what Yuri might have wanted. She'd been so mad at him she hadn't cared. Now that Adam had mentioned Yuri, though, perhaps, wherever he was, he needed the peace of knowing she didn't hate him anymore. In her mind, she told him that she'd let go of her grudge and moved on.

Still, Lila couldn't bring herself to go whole hog, dress him in an Armani suit, and put him in an opera box, where he could hear Maria Callas sing eternal arias. So Lila imagined him in a meadow ringed with white-capped mountains, and she let the von Trapps yodel for him once in a while. She arranged for his dead father to bring him pierogi, and she invited the people Yuri had shot to visit him if they wanted to.

Adam and Lila lifted the maple out of its black plastic pot and set it in the hole. They rotated the tree so its most leafy side was turned toward the kitchen window. Lila steadied the trunk while Adam spread out the roots and shoveled in planting mix and freshly dug soil. As he watered the maple, the wet earth smelled fresh and promising. In time, the tree would grow to Adam's roof and shade the porch.

When Adam, Grace, and Lila arrived at Pet Stop, Albert Wu was setting Magnolia, his cockatiel, outside the front door on her perch.

"So here's the wandering dog," Albert said. As he smiled at her, his malnourished beaver toupee seemed to fluff up with extra vigor, and his cheeks crinkled and hid his eyes.

When Lila and Adam had been searching for Grace, they'd told Albert that she'd broken through the screen door. So he urged them to buy a special metal grille that was guaranteed to hem her in.

"I don't need it," Adam said. "I'll never leave her on the porch alone again." He sounded humble. He'd learned a hard lesson.

He and Lila left Albert stacking dog beds in his front window, and made their way to the collar-and-leash department. Since Grace's paw had now healed enough for walks, they tried scarlet and navy collars on her. Neither dazzled against her fur the way the forest green one had so they got her another green one—along with a bag of peanut butter biscuits and a pig's ear.

At the cash register, Adam asked, "What do you want to do about Grace's ID tag?"

"Get her another one."

"Which one?"

"I haven't thought about it."

Adam picked up the cardboard that the sample tags were stapled to. "What about this fire hydrant?"

"Grace is too dignified for that. She's an elegant dog." Lila ran her finger over the gnome's valentine. "I still like the heart best."

"It's too small."

"It worked fine before."

"There's not enough room for my phone number on it."

For a second Lila thought Adam was saying he wanted Grace back and he was bumping Lila off the tag. Then it dawned on her that he wanted to share Grace and to be engraved on the tag *with* Lila.

The week before, they'd been looking through the New to You Shop, and on a top shelf in the kitchenware department had been a shiny copper soup pot without a nick or scratch. Just as Lila was about to pick it up, Adam reached over her head and grabbed it.

"Perfect condition," he said.

"*I* want it." She was feeling that rush of excitement when you find a treasure in a thrift shop—like a lion feels when a gazelle with sumptuous flanks limps by.

"I saw the pot first." Adam was grinning.

"You just picked it up faster than I did."

"Want to flip a coin?"

"I guess, but I was first."

"Why don't we share it?" Adam asked.

Sharing a soup pot was simple, but sharing Grace was serious. If Adam were on her ID heart with Lila, they were talking about being there for Grace through thick and thin, together. They were talking about working as a team. They were talking about responsibility and commitment, long term.

"If we get the largest heart, we can both be on it," Lila said.

"Good. It's settled."

Lila guessed it was.

As he filled out the order for the large heart they would share, she got the shivery feeling that what was going on was bigger than they were.

Epilogue

On a chilly, autumn evening, Adam, Grace, and Lila gathered around a campfire outside Sedona, Arizona. The setting sun was turning the sky a glory of pastels, and the rocky red mountains a soft, earth-tone purple. Wind rustled in the pine trees, puffed up the blue-dome tent, and billowed the fire's smoke toward Santa Fe, where Adam and Lila had visited two of her high school friends and left in a gallery five of her paintings—of flung-open gates and doors.

Adam set up his telescope and arranged the tripod's legs in the soft, red earth. Grace, who'd hiked with him and Lila all day, was napping on the pillow they hauled everywhere for her. The fire was crackling, spitting sparks, and warming her golden haunches.

As the sun fell behind the mountains and the evening turned cool, an owl hooted from somewhere among the red rocks. Lila wrapped her bedroll around her shoulders and threw another log on the fire. Leaning back in her camp chair, she locked her fingers behind her head and watched the two thousand stars Adam said you could see with your naked eye.

"What are stars made of?" Lila asked.

"Hydrogen and helium."

"How many in the universe?"

"Well . . ." Adam took off his lens cap and peered through his eyepiece. "We have about a hundred billion galaxies, and each one averages a hundred billion stars. That makes the total about the number of grains of sand on every beach on earth."

That seemed too vast to comprehend so Lila went back to watching the measly number of stars her naked eye could see. They seemed like they were twinkling themselves into hissy fits of beauty, and the Great Spirit was shining straight through them into her.

If she looked deeper, she saw the spirit pulsing through the spots on Grace's Holstein costume, *The Diary of Anne Frank*, and the silver whales dangling from Betsy's ears. The spirit was flowing through Agnes Spitzmeier's horse teeth, the malnourished-beaver toupee on Albert Wu's head, and hearts, whether they were made of flesh, red metal, or rose quartz. If Lila looked in just the right way, she could see the spirit in her proud flesh and the buzzards who'd flown out of her chest on the way home from Monterey. The spirit had been in her Pleaser, Crazy Aunt, and Horny Guttersnipe—and even in Yuri and Reed. It had been hiding in the paintbrush Grace had chewed, and it had shimmered in her widow's peak and the imaginary sultan whom she fanned on the floor with her geyser tail.

"Want to see the Great Bear?" Adam asked.

Lila got up and looked through the eyepiece. "I can't find any grizzly."

"Look for the Big Dipper. It's a part of the Great Bear."

Lila smiled to herself when she found her former scooper of Truffle-in-Paradise ice cream.

"Mizar's part of the Great Bear too," Adam said.

"I've never heard of Mizar."

"It's the first binary star ever discovered."

"I've never heard of a binary star, either."

"It's two stars held together by each other's gravity," Adam said. "The attraction makes them whirl around each other."

"Like us."

"Right."

Lila could feel Adam smiling in the dark. "Any such thing as a trinary star?" she asked.

"Yep."

"That's like you and me and Grace."

Adam must have liked the analogies, because he put his arms around Lila from behind and rested his cheek against her ear. As Lila continued looking through the telescope, Grace stirred on her pillow. Her ID heart clinked against her collar buckle, as if she were putting in her two cents' worth and letting them know she liked sharing the trinary star.

What Lila liked was that out of the infinite possible combinations of beings, the gravity of life had drawn Grace, Adam, and her together. And now, connected, they would never break apart. They would whirl on like Mizar.

Acknowledgments

Behind this book are kind, encouraging people, to whom I owe huge gratitude.

I would never have written a word without my agent, Cullen Stanley, who was with me when Grace was just a concept. Through the long creative process, Cullen stood by me and offered invaluable suggestions. She was a beacon in the fog.

Michaela Hamilton, my editor, has guided me through the publication process with intelligence and warmth. Her love of animals has bonded us and made my work for her a pleasure. Steven Zacharius, my publisher, appreciated Grace because of his love for Brinkley, his golden retriever. Kristine Mills Noble designed the beautiful cover for the book, Adeola Saul deftly oversaw its promotion, and Rebecca Cremonese managed its production with kindness and good humor.

Kathy Renner, Elsa Watson, and Anjali Banerjee were astute readers of early drafts. Caitlin Alexander, equally astute, read the last version. Dr. Frank Walker explained what happens when a bullet goes through a person's chest. And Wendy Hubbert, my friend and the editor of my last nonfiction books, rescued me when I was in a muddle and got me going down the right path.

Other friends propped me up and nurtured me as I wrote: Gisele Fitch and Jane Allan boosted my spirit on walks. Suzanne Kerr and Marielle Snyder were always interested in my book's progress. Darryl Beckmann believed in Grace when she was barely an idea, and Linda Anthony was determined to see her in print. David Sackeroff gave me sturdy, needed pep talks. Patty Johns provided kindness, and Alexandra Kovats saw to the health of my soul.

Logan, my German shepherd, and Phoebe, my beagle, reminded me daily of my love of dogs and my vocation as an animal writer. And, as always, John, my beloved husband, was the wind in my sail. Without him, I'd never have become a writer. His presence in my life is the greatest gift of all.

AN UNEXPECTED GRACE

Kristin von Kreisler

ABOUT THIS GUIDE

The following questions are intended to
enhance your group's reading of
AN UNEXPECTED GRACE.

To invite Kristin von Kreisler to meet with your group
by Skype, or in person if you're in the Seattle area,
contact her at www.kristinvonkreisler.com.

DISCUSSION QUESTIONS

1. Though *An Unexpected Grace* is about Grace, a golden retriever, it is also about the idea of grace, which is the undeserved, unsought good that comes to us. How is Grace a grace to Lila? In what other ways does grace come unexpectedly to her? How does it work in the story?

2. In the beginning, control is very important to Lila when she tries to take control of awkward situations with Yuri Makov and she tells Betsy that all she wants is to get her life under control. How else does control come up in the story? Does Lila's attitude about it evolve?

3. When Lila is painting during her first days with Grace, she alters her breath so it's not in sync with Grace's. But after Grace chases away the raccoon, Lila purposely breathes in sync with her. What does this say about the change in Lila's feelings for Grace? How does the relationship evolve?

4. Why does Betsy want Lila not to see herself as a victim? What difference does it make? How are women who have been truly victimized supposed to view what happened to them?

5. What's the significance of Betsy covering Lila with a Navajo blanket that has stripes of trees, eagles, and lightning that represent growth, independence, and power? How do these symbols relate to Lila's journey in the story?

6. Why does Lila paint only closed doors and gates in the beginning? Why might Adam urge her to paint them

open? At the end when Lila paints the garden behind the violet gate, does that indicate a change in her?

7. Is Lila justified to think she might inadvertently have caused Yuri to go postal? Is it truly important for her to understand his motive? What's driving her? Did her quest help her, or was it a meaningless waste?

8. How do Lila's Pleaser, Crazy Aunt, and Horny Guttersnipe cause her stress or conflict? Does she have other qualities that might make colorful characters too? Does everyone have secret parts that take over sometimes and need to be controlled?

9. When Lila dated Reed, her ex-boyfriend, she painted a series called *Odd Juxtapositions.* How might that title reflect Lila and Reed as a couple? How is Lila's relationship with Adam different from hers with Reed?

10. What does Betsy mean when she tells Lila to think with her heart? Is there a difference between thinking with your heart and with your mind? And what's the difference between Sunday school forgiveness and Betsy's forgiveness as freedom?

11. Adam tells Lila," Life isn't predictable. Sometimes bad things happen to good people no matter what they've said or done." Is that always true, or is there always a cause, like the butterfly effect? Was Lila at fault in her treatment of Yuri? *Could* she have contributed to his going postal?

12. Adam tells Lila that she and Grace are similar because they both suffered from a random act of fate. Do you

agree? How important is fate in the story? In what other ways might Lila and Grace be similar?

13. What is the significance of Lila putting the ribbon around the stone duck's neck? Does it reflect anything going on inside her?

14. How is Lila's visit with Olga and Marina Makov a turning point in the story? What does Lila discover about Yuri? And about herself?

15. Betsy tells Lila that "hard times can be gifts" and getting shot might be the best thing that ever happened to her. Do you agree with Betsy? Do Lila's hard times change her? What does she learn from them?

16. At the end of the story when Adam's name goes on Grace's ID tag, Lila has the shivery feeling that what's happening is bigger than they are. What does she mean? And what does she mean when she says that she liked how the gravity of life brought her, Grace, and Adam together?